Miranda Sherry grew up in Johannesburg in a house filled with books, and began writing stories when she was seven. She has done numerous strange jobs, including puppeteer, bartender and musician. Miranda currently lives in Johannesburg with her sort-of husband and two weird cats.

BLACK DOG SUMMER

Yesterday, Sally was living in an idyllic South African farmstead with her teenage daughter Gigi. Now Sally is dead — murdered — and Gigi is alone in the world. But Sally cannot die. She lingers unseen in her daughter's shadow. When Gigi moves in with her aunt's family, Sally comes too. When Gigi's trauma stirs up long-buried secrets, Sally watches helplessly as the family begins to unravel. Then Gigi's young cousin develops an obsession with African black magic, and events take a darker turn. Now Sally must find a way to stop her daughter from making a mistake that will destroy the lives of all who are left behind . . .

MIRANDA SHERRY

---◆---

BLACK DOG SUMMER

Complete and Unabridged

CHARNWOOD
Leicester

First published in Great Britain in 2014 by
Head of Zeus Ltd.
London

First Charnwood Edition
published 2015
by arrangement with
Head of Zeus Ltd.
London

A catalogue record for this book is available
from the British Library.

ISBN 978–1–4448–2459–9

Published by
F. A. Thorpe (Publishing)
Anstey, Leicestershire

Set by Words & Graphics Ltd.
Anstey, Leicestershire
Printed and bound in Great Britain by
T. J. International Ltd., Padstow, Cornwall

This book is printed on acid-free paper

For Grant

BEFORE

I had just put the coffee on the stove when they came.

I remember washing out the mugs at the sink. I paused when I caught the whiff of something strange slice through the coffee-scented warmth of the kitchen. The smell was bitter, a waft of pungent onion mixed in with alcohol. I stood for a moment with the washing-up gloves still on my hands and tried to place it.

'Morning, Monkey,' Seb said, drawn from his bed by the friendly morning bubble of our old Italian-style coffee pot. He scratched his stubble and yawned widely.

'Morning. You sleep OK?'

'Not too bad. I'm getting better at being alone in that bed, but not much.'

'Simone will be back in a week, Seb.'

'I know,' he said and grinned. 'I'm pathetic, aren't I?'

'Please, I bet she's waking up in her icy bed in Scotland right now and missing you just as much.'

I turned back to the sink just in time to catch a dark spot of movement in the yard outside the window. 'That's strange, this must be the first Sunday in living memory that Phineas and Lettie didn't set off to church at dawn.'

'No, they left,' Seb said through another yawn. 'I heard them take the bakkie out early this

1

r. I think the world would have to end
 ettie would permit them to miss a
 y service.'

'Then who was — '

'Jesus!' Seb yelled and I spun around to see a strange man hurtle through the open doorway. For a second, my eyes locked on the intruder's. They were very wide open in his dark, sweat-streaked face, the whites yellowed like the sweat patches in the underarms of an old T-shirt. His gaze flicked from mine to the thick splintered plank of wood that he held in one hand and before I could even draw breath to scream, the yellow-eyed man had slammed the wood into the side of Seb's head and sent him sprawling across the kitchen floor.

And then two more men came through the door.

And then I screamed.

1

When I was alive, I had hair that was white in summer and the colour of dead grass in winter and long, too-skinny fingers that, early on, earned me the nickname 'Monkey'. Now, I no longer have fingers of any kind, or nails to break when helping Johan and Phineas fix the wire fencing around the perimeter of the farm, or any fences to fix, for that matter.

But something seems to have gone wrong with my dying.

I always thought that when the moment came, I'd follow the light or join the stars or whatever it is that's supposed to happen, but I have been dead for three sunrises, and I am still *here*.

I try going as high up away from the ground as possible to see if I can pass a point where things will suddenly snap into place and a tunnel will open and there will be a big glossy sign saying 'Afterlife. Exit ahead'. From way up here, Southern Africa looks like a creature that's rolled over to expose the vast curve of a mottled brown belly with a grey tracery of veins. Far off in one direction, I can see the white frill of surf that borders the dark turquoise of the Indian Ocean.

But there's no sign, no snap, no tunnel. Nothing.

I go higher; high enough to see where the layer of blue above me turns into black, but the only thing that changes is the noise. It gets worse.

The noise. It has taken me a while to work out what the whispering, humming, singing, screaming awfulness comes from, but now, on my third day of not being Sally any more, I think I have it figured out. The noise comes from Africa's stories being told. Millions upon millions them; some told in descending liquid notes like the call of the Burchell's coucal before the rain, and some like the dull roar of Johannesburg traffic. Some of these stories are ancient and wear fossilized coats of red dust and others are so fresh that they gleam with umbilical wetness, and it would seem that, like me, they're all bound here, even the stories that are full of violence and blood and fury, and there are many of those.

At first, I couldn't distinguish one story thread from another within the solid roaring wall of sound, but now one of them seems to have separated itself from the rest. It is a pale, slender thread with an escalating alarmed tone, like the call of a hornbill looking for love. This small story has my living blood still in it: I can sense it pulsing through the body of my sister (who now sits weeping at her dressing table) and fluttering alongside the tranquillizers in the veins of my daughter as she lies between the white and blue sheets of a hospital bed.

It's just one story amongst millions, and yet it has become so loud now that it drowns out the others. It is howling at me, raging, demanding my attention. I look closer to find that this small, bright thread of story weaves out from the moment of my passing and seems to tether me to this place. Perhaps this is why I have not left yet.

4

Perhaps I have no choice but to follow the story to its end.

Yes, it screams, *follow me. Listen to me.*

It does not stop screaming.

And so I look for an opening, a beginning to grab on to . . . I try Gigi first, but my daughter is lost and floating on a chemical sea and is not, it would seem, present in the story herself right now. In the hope that she'll be back soon, I stay and watch her chest rise and fall beneath the ugly hospital gown they have given to her to wear.

But Gigi remains absent, and the story howls at me again, even louder. It is unbearable. I have to move on.

I try my sister, Adele, but regret, like a too-thick synthetic blanket on a sweltering day, is wrapped tight around her. It reminds me of the ones that the women waiting for taxis by the side of the road in Musina would use to tie their babies on to their backs. It is olive green with blotches of brown and the occasional sharp starburst of ugly red, and it prevents me from getting close.

Liam?

I find him sitting in the exquisite moulded leather interior of his latest Mercedes. The car sits stationary inside the closed-up garage and its solid white doors are locked. The keys are not in the ignition, they have fallen to the carpet beneath Liam's feet and rest beside the clutch pedal like silver puzzle pieces waiting to be solved. Liam's head, with its ever so slightly thinning spot on top, is pressed into the steering

5

wheel and his whole body shudders as if it is trying to climb out of itself. He is weeping. His grief is a sharp, raw shock and I recoil. Fast.

Not Liam.

Just then, Liam and Adele's daughter, Bryony, steps out of her bedroom and on to the sunny upstairs landing. My niece is barely recognizable. The last time I saw her she was a tubby two-year-old with shiny cheeks. She is eleven now, and her skinny legs poke out from beneath the skirt of her freshly ironed school uniform.

Bryony is so filled up with the urgent desire to be part of a story that I can feel it like heat radiating off her skin. I am startled to find that I can feel right inside her too: I can touch the raw ends of all those tender-vicious young-girl thoughts. For a second I pause, uncertain, but Bryony is my way in, and the story is demanding that I follow.

I do.

2

Bryony stops. Normally she would go downstairs to the kitchen to get some breakfast, but after a moment's considering, she walks in the other direction, heading for her parents' bedroom doorway at the end of the passage.

The morning sun beats through the muslin blinds of the bedroom window, making the room look as if it's been pumped full of golden gas. But there's a small, dark spot right in the centre of it: Adele. To Bryony, her mother looks older than she ever has before, her skin almost greenish against the black fabric of her top. She looks just like Granny in that photo hanging on the wall on the landing.

Adele sits at her dressing table and looks at her greenish self in the mirror before lifting a tissue to wipe at her lower eyelids: first one eye, and then the other. The skin beneath her eyes is already pink and stretched-looking as if it has been scalded, which it very well might be, considering how corrosive salt is and how many tears she's squeezed out. There have been so many tears since THE phone call on Monday that Bryony is sick to death of them.

Aunt Sally wasn't sick to death; she was murdered.

Bryony wants to say 'murdered' out loud, just to see how it feels, but that would only set her mother off again and Adele probably doesn't

7

have enough moisture left to get her through the funeral as it is. Bryony leans her spine hard into the corner of the doorframe and concentrates on the feeling of her toes sinking into the soft cream carpet.

Golden morning light. Wipe, wipe, wipe under the lower lashes. Pink, burnt skin.

'You shouldn't wear mascara today, Mom. If you're so worried about it. You know you're going to cry some more, so just don't wear it.'

'Don't be daft, darling.' Adele's voice sounds thick and clotted from the crying still waiting behind it. 'None of the women in our family can go a minute without mascara; we look like a collection of albino lab rats. You'll understand when you're older.'

Bryony looks down at her bare toes. There's a small scratch on the left big one that looks like a smile, especially with the two small freckles above it. She wiggles the smile-toe. Adele doesn't know that Bryony has tried mascara already. She'd been expecting a dramatic transformation from stubby-lashed child to devastating teenage beauty, but it had just looked as if she'd dunked portions of her face into some kind of deadly black glue. It took the whole rest of that afternoon to get it off and she still went down to supper looking like someone had punched her in both eye sockets.

'Aunty Sally didn't wear mascara, and she was a woman in your family.' Bryony clamps her jaws together too late and the words swim out and gravitate towards the dark spot.

Actually, it's been so long since Bryony saw

her Aunty Sally that all she can really picture when she thinks of her is a pair of balloony lilac trousers that look like a nappy gone wrong. Aunty Sally was wearing them in an old photograph that Bryony found at the bottom of one of the kitchen drawers when they were pulling out the old units and putting in the new, shiny ones that Adele ordered a few months ago. In the picture, her mother looked smiley in a luminous way that Bryony has seldom seen on her actual face. Her arm was around Aunty Sally's shoulder, and between them both was a little girl with two plaits and freckles on her nose. The little girl was holding on to the lilac fabric of Aunty Sally's pants, twisting it into crumples with her small, chubby fingers. Bryony knows this is Sally's daughter, Gigi, and she's been told that she and Gigi once sat underneath Granny's dining-room table and ate a whole jar of peanut butter, but try as she might, she can't remember it. The purple-pants picture is the only photograph that Bryony has seen of Aunty Sally as a grown-up, which is strange, because there are quite a lot of family photos hanging alongside the one of Granny on the landing wall. Bryony couldn't tell whether Aunty Sally was wearing mascara in the picture or not, but she figures she wasn't. Adele mentioned the fact often enough in a tone that implied that it was some kind of insult to her very Adeleness. *I fail to see how 'finding' one's self, becoming a vegetarian and living in a 'spiritual community' to cuddle abandoned animals entitles one to waft around looking like a bag of faded washing.*

When Adele saw Bryony studying the photo, she'd whipped it away with a dark look in her eyes that halted Bryony's indignant whine at once.

'You're right,' Adele now says, and runs the tissue under each eye again, absorbing the new sparkles of wetness. 'She didn't wear any, did she?' And then her forehead crumples and she drops her head into her hands. 'Oh God. Monkey.'

Bryony looks away. She wishes that she still had that photograph. Adele often used to say that Aunty Sally had 'let herself go', and Bryony now imagines those billowy lilac pants rising up into the sky like an escaped helium balloon.

'Addy?' The slam of the front door and the sound of her father's voice float up from downstairs. 'You ready, doll?' Liam's voice grows louder as he climbs and his shoes make padding sounds on the carpet as if he's carrying something heavy. For a second, Bryony considers dashing to her bedroom so as not to see the weird colourlessness that has taken over her father's face since THE phone call, but she waits too long.

THE phone call happened just as the family was sitting down to supper on Sunday night. It was chops, which Bryony likes, and mielies, which she hates, and she was just thinking of ways to get out of eating hers when the phone rang. Adele muttered about people knowing better than to phone at supper time and went to answer it, then the family heard a strangled howl sound and Liam shot out of his chair and raced

10

out of the kitchen. Tyler and Bryony looked at each other. Tyler's eyes were so wide that Bryony could see white all around the blue bits. Then, from the telephone table in the lounge, came snuffling and shouting sounds and crying and then the sound of Liam leading Adele upstairs.

It was only after Bryony had finished both her chops and her Greek salad with extra olives stolen from Adele's plate that Liam returned to the table and announced: 'Guys, I've got some bad news. Something terrible has happened to Monk — I mean, Aunty Sally. She's . . . she's dead, I'm afraid.'

When he said it, Bryony's head went all buzzy and she had to lie it down on the table very quickly. She stared at the bright yellow teeth of her uneaten mielie with a weird, thick feeling in the back of her throat that made her think she might throw up. She didn't, although with the stench of mielie that close to her nose it was a near thing. The whole time, she couldn't stop thinking about billowing purple pants.

'Where's Gigi?' Tyler asked, and Liam told them that their cousin was unhurt and was 'in good hands'. This made Bryony think of that song about the man who's got the whole world in his hands, and how big your hands would have to be to have the whole world in them.

Since the news of Aunty Sally's death, the house has filled up with choked whispers and secrets. When Granny died from a stroke two years ago there was loads of crying and lower-lash wiping, but no heavy, white-faced, open-eyed silences. Also, nobody threw things.

11

Yesterday afternoon, when she was supposed to be doing her homework in her room, Bryony heard Adele shouting and the sound of glass breaking. Later, when she snuck into her mother's bathroom after the storm had passed, she saw that in her rage, Adele had smashed all her little jars of expensive skin lotion. Bryony had never even been allowed to touch them, and now the bathroom tiles were covered with thick glittering glass slices and gobs of pastel cream. It smelt like vanilla and roses and being clean and Bryony stood there for quite a while just breathing it in.

Since THE phone call, the house has also been full of shadows. Bryony noticed new ones this morning in between the throw cushions on the sofa in the lounge with the flowers printed on it, and behind the side plates in the newly renovated kitchen cupboards when she reached in to get out a cereal bowl. Even though it's only been three days, Bryony can't remember what the house was like before the shadows arrived. They're everywhere.

'Hey, Bry.' As her father comes up the stairs he gives Bryony a smile that looks only half defrosted. 'Mrs Ballentine is going to be taking you to school this morning, OK?'

'I know, Dad.'

'Well, get your shoes on, munchkin,' he says, and then when he sees Adele wrinkling her black linen suit at the dressing table: 'Ah, doll.' He sighs and goes over and rubs her back with one golf-tanned hand.

She flinches at his touch, which causes a little

12

worm of worry to burrow through Bryony's guts.

'It's going to be OK, Addy.'

'How is it going to be OK?'

'Jeez, I don't know, doll. It just . . . it will be in time. You know. These things . . . happen.'

'What? Massacres on a Sunday afternoon? Only in this bloody country.'

'Shush, Addy.' Liam increases the force of his back-rubbing and glances up at his daughter but she's looking at the carpet. She swipes one foot across the rug making a darker curve in the pile. The word 'massacre' leaves a new black blotch in the golden bedroom and makes her think of mascara again. She knows it's a word she's heard in History class, but just can't, for the moment, remember what it means.

'Come on, girly-pie, shoes on. Go and make sure your brother is ready for school,' Liam says in his no-nonsense voice. Bryony turns and leaves the crumpled tissue, the scalded eye-skin and the dark stink of that heavy word behind her.

★ ★ ★

I pull myself free. It's a struggle, because Bryony has become sticky (like the boiled sweets that Gigi used to suck and then take out of her mouth to glue to the sunny kitchen window when she was little and we still lived in Johannesburg), but I finally manage. From up here, the spun-ice strands of some merciful cirrus clouds hide the Wilding house from view.

I remember those silly purple pants. I

13

eventually cut them up into a skirt for Gigi when we were living on the farm and new clothes for a growing girl were hard to come by.

The last time I set foot (a real, flesh-and-blood one) in the cloud-hidden Wilding house, I was wearing a tie-dyed wrap-around skirt in shades of turquoise that I loved despite its dangerous tendency to flap open in a strong wind. Whenever I wore it, I would have to walk very sedately so as not to upset it too much, and speed was out of the question unless I wanted the world at large to get an eyeful of my panties.

But that afternoon, I ran in it.

I remember Gigi's squeal of surprise when I scooped her up off the floor of the lounge where she'd been playing with toddler Bryony, and then her look of concern when she saw my tears. *What's the matter, Mommy?* Although she was too heavy to carry in such a way any more, I clutched my daughter to my hip and ran.

As I swept through the front door, the hem of the skirt flew up and snagged on to one of the hinges. For a moment I was caught, legs bare, sobbing and fumbling with the fabric whilst trying to keep my hold on Gigi. That is when I looked back and saw Adele. She was watching my struggle from within the safety of her immaculate kitchen and her face looked smooth and white, like hard bone. She did not come to help me, or call me back and say that no, it was all right, she'd made a mistake, was just being silly. She did not rush to embrace me and tell me that she didn't mean it and that of course I was welcome here, and please forgive her for saying

14

the things she'd said. No, she just watched me as I fought to free myself from the clutch of her front door, her eyes burning fury from behind that still, ivory-coloured mask.

I had to tear my skirt to get away.

It is blissful to be out of the story. Up here, every delicious cold mouthful of Africa's cloud breath buoys me higher, and families of swallows swoop and glide inside me. But I cannot taste ozone and feel the birds without also hearing the relentless roar of the story tide. It only takes a moment before the call of that one, insistent little tale begins to build to an unbearable crescendo.

The story tugs at me like a brass hinge with threads of turquoise fabric caught between its teeth.

★   ★   ★

Bryony is impatient to get to school and revel in the recent celebrity status that a murder in the family has given her. She twitches and shifts on the squeaky leather back seat of Mrs Ballentine's car, and barely waits for it to stop before flinging the door open and sliding out on to the pavement. Before Carryn (who is only in Grade Five and lisps) can even think of walking next to her, Bryony dashes through the school gates.

As soon as she's in, she slows down to a trudge and makes her way up the drive towards Miss Botbyl's classroom with her eyes down and her shoulders bent over to indicate just how burdened she is under the massive weight of despair. The fellow inmates of Class 7B waiting in the patch of sun outside the classroom all rotate their heads towards her approach like a family of inquisitive meerkats.

Bryony, now centre stage, stops and allows her school bag to slip to the floor.

'Hey, Bryony.' Amanda's long, straight pony-tail shines like strands of sticky toffee in the sun. She takes a step towards Bryony and the lesser meerkats swivel their heads to watch. They're always watching Amanda. Bryony's convinced that a fairy godmother cast an enchantment spell on Amanda when she was born because everything she does is somehow just that little bit shinier than everyone else. *It's kind of sickening how unfair it is.*

'How are you doing today?' Amanda asks.

'OK, I guess.' Bryony keeps her voice low, as if the energy of talking is taking its toll.

'Shame,' Amanda mutters and puts a soothing arm around her shoulder. She smells of Pantene shampoo and toothpaste, and Bryony's stomach flips at the great and wonderful Amanda's touch.

'The funeral's today,' Bryony adds.

'Oh my God,' says Stacy, coming up on her other side and breathing more toothpaste into her face. 'That's the grimmest.'

'They're not going to have one of those open casket thingies, are they?' Tsolophelo asks, stretching her lips over her braces in order to bite them.

Seeing as her parents have not actually told Bryony how her aunt was killed, and enthused by her classmates' thirst for details, she made up

16

a tragic little tale in which Aunty Sally was shot in the neck and bled to death in minutes (they did the arteries in Biology last term). Now she wishes she'd given herself some story-telling wriggle room. A stabbing would've been much more gruesome. 'It's a closed casket.' Her whisper implies a corpse too horrifying for family members to bear.

'If it's today, why are you at school? Why aren't you going?'

'Mom won't let us.' This much of her tale is true. Adele says that funerals are unsuitable for children, and wouldn't even let them go to Granny's funeral two years ago. Bryony had been secretly relieved to be banned from it. Crying in front of people makes her feel strange and skinless, as if anyone can see inside of her.

'My mom said that it wasn't just your aunty that got killed on Sunday,' Angel pipes up in an eager voice. 'It was a whole bunch of people that lived on that farm in Limpopo. It was in the newspaper and everything.' The sides of Bryony's head feel suddenly cold and it's not because she can't stand Angel (who wouldn't let Bryony join in on a game of Running Red Rover once when they were in Grade Three) but because Aunty Sally's murder was in a newspaper. She had no idea.

Bryony leans her back against the wall and shuts her eyes. The conversation now seems to be coming from a long way away.

'It was an animal rescue centre that they raided, my mom said. Did you ever go there and play with the rescued animals, Bry? Were there

17

baby lions? My brother had an iguana once but it started to get aggressive and my mom made him give it away.'

'Shut up, Angel.'

'My mom says that all the farm killings in this country are actually a jellyside and something should be done.'

'A what-i-side? What are you on about?'

'Jellyside. Haven't you ever heard of it?'

'Isn't it like when lots of people get killed or something?'

'No, man, that's jealouside.'

'*Ja*, use your logic . . . you kill people when you're jealous of them, right?'

'I guess.'

'So it's got nothing to do with jelly.'

'But what about those poor animals? Do you think they're OK if all the people are dead? Do you think someone's feeding them?'

'Oh, shame!'

'Bryony?' Amanda is suddenly right up close again. 'Hey, guys, I think Bryony's going to faint.'

Bryony lets nameless hands help her down to sit on the cement floor of the corridor, not even caring that her skirt has ridden up and everyone can probably see her panties. She is thinking about how she always wanted to go and visit her aunt and her cousin at their exciting-sounding animal rescue centre in the bush, and was sure that she would one day be able to convince her mother to let her. Now she never will.

Bryony's nostrils are suddenly, inexplicably, filled with the floor polish and butternut smell of

18

her granny's old house. For the first time, she remembers the way the folds of the embroidered tablecloth had made her feel as though she and cousin Gigi were in their very own private, lacy tent under the dining-room table. She remembers the stolen jar of peanut butter. The ends of Gigi's plaits had ended up all glued together because she'd kept twisting them with her sticky fingers.

She tries to imagine what Gigi must look like now that she's fourteen, but she just keeps seeing peanut butter smeared on freckles and a red corduroy skirt that was handed down to her when Gigi grew out of it. It had itched.

Bryony bursts into tears: huge, uncontrollable ones that pump and slime out of her. The circle of girls around her opens up a little. This kind of crying is dangerous and everyone knows it.

'Someone call Dommie. Is she here yet?' Dommie is Bryony's best friend and at the sound of her name, she cries even harder.

'I think we should rather get a teacher.' That's Tsolophelo talking. Bryony can hear her still struggling not to spit through her new braces.

'Hey, Miss Botbyl's coming!'

'Miss Botbyl, Bryony's crying.'

'Bryony?' She hears the click of high heels on cement. 'All right, sweetie. Come along to the sickroom with me. We'll get you a tissue and some sugar water. There we go. Up you get.' Strong hands and the smell of perfume and suddenly Bryony's on her feet. She opens her eyes to see her hated school shoes swimming next to Miss Botbyl's elegant pointy ones. 'I'll be

19

back in a moment, girls. Please take your seats and get your homework out. Amanda, I'm leaving you in charge till I get back.'

'Miss Botbyl?' Bryony asks as her teacher leads her through the now quiet corridors towards the school office. 'What's a jellyside?'

'I've no idea. Some kind of pudding, perhaps?'

'Oh. OK then, what's a massacre?' Bryony asks, thinking back to the way the word hung like a rotting black flag in the sunny bedroom that morning.

Miss Botbyl doesn't answer, but her arm tightens round Bryony's shoulder.

★   ★   ★

Gigi has moved. Her left arm is higher up on the pillow than it was at my last visit. Her eyes, however, are still closed. Bruised grey eyelids in a pale grey face on a cloud-white pillow: she looks like a child made of storms.

I keep expecting to feel pain at the sight of my hospitalized daughter; I'm waiting for it, but anguish, it seems, is one of the things I need a pumping heart to experience. Just as I've been doing with Bryony, Liam and Adele, I observe Gigi from a clean breathless place unmuddied by emotion.

She's not here with me, listening to the stories, and she's not *in* the story, so where have the storm winds taken her? There is no one to ask, and no time to find out.

Follow me, the story howls. It screams. There's no way I can ignore it.

20

Sticky threads.
Bryony.

★ ★ ★

The garden smells of sprinklers and soil and the soft, almondy scent of the fuzzy little yellow balls that blossom on the acacia tree.

'*Noun: the indiscriminate, merciless killing of a number of human beings, or a large-scale slaughter of animals.*' Bryony whispers it a little louder now that she's outside, but the words seem no more real. Earlier, when they'd arrived home from school and Tyler had vanished into the bathroom for one of his mysterious, lengthy episodes, she'd braved his off-limits bedroom, scowled at the picture of a woman with her top slipping off that he'd recently made into his laptop's desktop wallpaper, and Google-searched the word 'massacre'. She then had to look up the word 'indiscriminate' as well, but luckily Tyler stayed in the bathroom for a *really* long time.

So now she knows. She expects to feel different, but she doesn't. Also, she still has no idea just exactly how this dictionary definition relates to her Aunty Sally in her billowing purple pants. Bryony balances on the cobbled border that edges the flowerbed, challenging herself not to touch the earth on either side as she walks along it, following the route it makes all the way round the side of the Wilding property. The further she gets from the too-silent house where her mother weeps behind one blank door and her brother listens to his iPod and looks at

21

pictures of girls in bikinis on the net behind another, the better she is able to breathe.

But the word still follows her. It follows her all along the boundary wall, round the side of the house, and to the spot where the big black plastic wheeled dustbins are housed in neat wooden cabins to hide their unsightly functionality until they're ready to be wheeled out on Tuesday and emptied by the rubbish-collecting men. Bryony hoists herself up on to the smooth slats of the dustbin house and walks carefully on the joists so as not to go crashing through on to the bins beneath.

She shuffles to the wall that borders the neighbouring garden and peers over the top of it. She sucks in her breath, because right there, kneeling on the floor in front of the plate-glass window of the back room she uses as a home office, is Mrs Matsunyane. Bryony knows that Mrs Matsunyane's first name is Lesedi because that's what it said on the letter that landed in their post box one time by mistake, and also, thanks to her previous spying sessions, she's heard Mr Matsunyane call out to her.

To Bryony, Lesedi looks too young and lovely to be a Mrs Anybody. She wears Levi jeans and tackies and colour-coordinated tops and dangly earrings, and her hair hangs in long glorious liquorice braids down her back.

Bryony's convinced that there's something *special* about Lesedi. She has often noticed the strings of earthy tribal beads that she wears around her ankles, and she's sure that there's something interesting hiding around Lesedi's neck too, because when she leans forward, there's a pointy bulge beneath her top.

Today, Lesedi's top is yellow, and Bryony can see that she has accessorized her outfit with some kind of special white make-up around her eyes and a lovely headdress of dangling beads that shiver when she moves. However, because of the way her neighbour's furniture is arranged, she still cannot see what exactly it is that Lesedi is fiddling with on the hardwood floor at her knees.

And then, Lesedi looks up. Not at Bryony, who gasps and ducks below the top of the boundary wall, but directly at me. It should not be possible, but she stares straight at me with still dark eyes that seem to gleam between their rows of curly black lashes. How does she see me? Am I a faded photocopy of my old tall, blonde Monkey shape? Am I a patch of shadow, a sliver of light? Lesedi doesn't let on, merely lowers her head in a slow, respectful nod of greeting.

With that nod I am suddenly baked red earth that has been pounded by dancing feet. I am warm aloe sap that drips from a rip in a leaf like slow-running wax from a candle. I am the petulant 'go-away' call of a grey lourie and pulse of a thousand drums.

But when Lesedi looks away, the sensation is gone.

*　*　*

Liam comes home from work early, and the hello hug he gives Bryony, who has been waiting for his return, is brief and distracted. 'Where's Ty?' he says, dropping his briefcase beside the front door.

'In his room.' Bryony slides her bare foot over the porcelain hall tile and listens to the squeak it makes.

'Go and call him, Bry.'

Adele comes out of the lounge. The two smoky ovals of her sunglasses, which she seems to have given up taking off at all since the funeral, flash in Liam's direction.

'Tell him we want a family discussion,' Liam says, and brushes his palms down the pockets of his suit.

'About what?'

'Fetch your brother, Bryony. Now.'

'OK, OK, I'm going. Jeez.'

'And don't say jeez,' Adele calls after her as she runs up the stairs, 'it's common.'

'Dad says it all the time,' Bryony mutters, bashing on the 'Keep Out' sticker on Tyler's bedroom door. *Maybe if I keep thumping it, it'll finally peel off.* Tyler's iPod is blaring through the wood at the top of its little synthetic lungs. 'TYLER!'

'What's the goddamn panic?' Tyler wrenches the door open. He's still wearing his school shirt and trousers and Bryony doesn't know how he can bear to; her uniform starts coming off in increments from the moment she gets into the car for the ride home.

'Dad's home and he wants a family discussion.'

'Oh shit.' Tyler swears a lot. Liam calls him the *angry young man*, but Bryony doesn't see what

24

on earth he's got to be so cross about half the time. 'OK then, little one, let's get this crap over with.' He follows Bryony back down the stairs and then the two of them stop, just near the bottom, as if about to pose for a family photograph.

'Right, guys.' Liam shoves his hands deep into the pockets of his charcoal suit trousers. 'We need to have a little chat about your cousin Gigi.'

Bryony thinks of the little girl with the plaits in that photograph and worries the edge of the stair carpet with her toe. Half of the smile scab came off earlier in the garden, and the toe face is disappearing.

'I know you've been concerned about her welfare, and I'm sorry we've been keeping you in the dark about this whole ghastly episode, but there have been all sorts of . . . things to sort out.' Liam glances towards Adele with a strange, fearful look on his face. Adele doesn't notice. She's too busy staring at the floor through her sunglasses. 'I guess we've been trying to protect you lot from the worst of all of this.'

'The worst?' Bryony says.

'Where is she? Gigi?' Tyler asks.

'She's been transferred from a hospital in Louis Trichardt to one closer to us. She's at the Sandton Clinic at the moment.'

'Hospital? But you said she wasn't hurt?'

'She's not injured, but she's in terrible shock,' Liam says. 'She's currently under sedation.'

'They've had to knock her out with drugs?' Tyler shakes his head and sits down on the bottom step.

25

'She's just . . . well, understandably she's feeling very lost and alone right now.'

'I bet.' Tyler starts picking at one of his toenails and Bryony gives him a little kick to get him to stop. It has no effect.

'I need you guys to be a little mature about all of this, OK? This girl has had a very hard time and, up until now, she's had no one to turn to.' Liam glances at his wife, but she continues to avoid his gaze. 'But all that's about to change because, tomorrow, Mom and I are going to be fetching her from the hospital and bringing her home.'

Finally Adele looks up at Liam, but her eyewear makes her expression impossible to read.

'To stay,' Liam adds.

'The night? Where's she going to sleep?'

'For God's sake, Bryony,' Tyler says, 'the poor kid just lost her mom and just about all the other people she knew, and you're worried about her invading your bedroom?'

'What other people?' Bryony says, thinking: *The indiscriminate, merciless killing of a number of human beings.*

'Aunty Sally and Gigi lived in a sort of commune, remember?' Adele finally speaks. They all turn to look at her as she brings a fresh tissue out from behind her back, almost as if she's performing a magic trick. She wipes under the sunglasses, and they jog up and down with the motion of her hand. 'There were quite a few people living all together at that animal sanctuary place, Bry, and it wasn't only Aunty

26

Sally who died. It's very sad. We're very lucky that Gigi wasn't there when . . . it happened.'

'Did anyone else survive?' Tyler asks. Nobody answers. 'Come on, guys, I know you're trying to protect us and all that, but one quick Google search and I'll find out anyway. We can't be the only people in the country that don't know.'

'There were two domestic workers out at church, and another woman, Aunty Sally's best friend, who wasn't there when it happened. She's very fortunate to be overseas at the moment,' Adele says.

(Simone. Of course, I remember. She left to attend a conference at Findhorn in Scotland just over a week ago. Simone has shiny brown hair; Simone dripped lavender essential oil on my finger that time I burnt it so badly. I remember sitting in the kitchen on a winter morning, clutching a mug of tea and watching her teach Gigi how to do yoga sun salutations on the stoep. Their breath made little frosty clouds in the cold air. So Simone is alive in Scotland. She's not in the story. Not yet.)

'But all the rest were killed?' When Bryony speaks the words out loud, they don't sound quite real, and she has to bite back a burst of inappropriate laughter at the weight of them.

'So, how many people — ?'

'I hardly think that we need to discuss this now, Tyler,' Liam says.

'And Gigi's coming here?'

'We're her family.' Liam rubs the new lines on his forehead and swallows hard. 'And she needs a stable environment.'

27

'Is there no one else she can go and stay with?'

'Christ, Bryony!' Tyler shouts, his face going red to match the fresh pimple that's brewing on his chin.

'I didn't mean I don't want her to stay,' Bryony retorts, 'I was only asking. It's not like you've ever hung out with her either, or anything. I bet you can't even remember what she looks like. She's practically a stranger.'

'She has nowhere else to go, don't you get it?'

'OK, calm down, both of you.' Liam's face is all sharp lines and no colour.

'I know this is a lot to take in, kids,' Adele says, 'and I am well aware that it was us . . . ' A sharp glance from Liam makes her pause. ' . . . Mostly *my* doing that kept you cousins from getting to know each other properly, but I can't take back the past.'

'No,' Liam says, and suddenly leaves the room, marching through to the kitchen with stiff, controlled strides.

'I owe my poor sister, and Gigi is coming to live with us, and that's the way it is, all right?' Adele finishes. She is shaking. The tissue flutters in her hand.

To live? thinks Bryony.

'All right,' says Tyler.

'All right.' Bryony's response is a small uncertain echo.

★ ★ ★

The spare bed in Bryony's bedroom is so hidden under an avalanche of clutter that if you didn't

28

know, you'd never suspect that there was a bed under there at all. When Dommie sleeps over, the girls usually just haul everything off it and then dump it all back on the next morning. Sometimes they don't bother, and the two of them curl up on the floor in a pile of sleeping bags instead. Bryony takes a step towards the puffy rubbish dump of a bed and notices that her hockey stick is buried within the madness. *Jeez, I haven't played hockey since last year.*

'Staring at it isn't going to get the job done.'

Bryony turns to see Adele standing in the doorway with a pile of clean bedding in her arms. Over the top of the blue duvet cover with the cherries printed on it, her eyes are finally sunglass-free and more burnt-looking than ever. Bryony wishes that her mother would suddenly smile because, although she knows that Adele used to smile quite a lot, she can't seem to remember what she looks like when she does.

'That's my favourite duvet cover.'

'Oh please, Bry, you haven't used this bedding set since you were about seven.'

'But it's still — '

'Come on, get tidying.'

'Can't Dora just do it tomorrow?'

'Your absurd mess is not something that Dora should have to deal with, Bryony; we've talked about this before. She's employed to keep the house clean, not to be your personal picker-upper.'

'I know, but it's going to take all night. And there's school tomorrow.'

'I am very well aware of that. If it takes you all

night then it takes you all night. Perhaps this will teach you to put your stuff away properly in the future.' Adele marches in, places the pile of linen on Bryony's bed, then goes over to the cupboard and wrenches it open. 'Good Lord, Bryony.'

'What?' Bryony glances at the jumbled collection of old toys, puzzle pieces and books on her cupboard shelves.

'You know very well what.' Adele opens the remaining built-in cupboard doors and then stops, staring. She lifts her hands to her face and, for a moment, Bryony thinks she's going to burst into tears again, but she doesn't. She just stands, frozen.

'Mom?'

Nothing.

'Mom?' Louder, this time.

'Right,' Adele says, and lowers her hands. 'I'm going downstairs to get a couple of bin bags. This pile of endless junk is ridiculous. We need to get half of it out of here and clear up some space for that poor child.'

'You're taking my stuff? But it's my stuff!'

'Good gracious, girl.' Adele lurches towards her daughter, and Bryony steps back until her legs are pressing against her bed. 'People are dead, do you understand? My sister is dead, and her daughter is going to need a sodding cupboard to store her goddamn clothes in, all right?' Adele, unlike Tyler, hardly ever swears. She's never hit Bryony, either, but it sure looks as though she's going to take a crack at it now. Bryony swallows down a chunk of fright.

'Yes, Mom.' Adele's face is so close that

30

Bryony can see white and pink blotches all over it as if someone has melted up a bag of marshmallows and spread them on her skin.

'I'm going to make it up to Sally.' Adele's voice trembles as she stumbles towards the doorway. 'Dear God. Somebody has to do SOMETHING.' The shout stabs right through the sound of the news channel on the TV downstairs and the thump of Tyler's music from next door, which stops mid clang. The whole house seems to breathe in. Bryony is too scared to move. She hopes that if her mom starts throwing things as she did in her bathroom the other day, she doesn't break the crystal heart bowl on her dressing table that Granny gave her for her ninth birthday; it's about the only thing of Granny's she has.

Adele grips the doorframe and sags her head against it, her fingers yellow and hard-looking, like uncooked pasta.

'Mom?' Bryony whispers.

Adele pulls back her head and lets it fall, crack, against the wood. Bryony's stomach heaves at the sound it makes.

'Mom?' Tyler is suddenly out of his sanctuary and standing beside his mother. 'Please don't. Please don't hurt yourself.' He tries to take her hands to unstick her from the doorframe, but she isn't budging. Over the top of her dishevelled hair, Bryony notices that her brother's blue eyes look just like their old cat Mingus's did that time she tried to bath him when she was five.

A sob boils up out of Bryony and she runs out of the bedroom and past them both, hurtling

31

straight into Liam who has come running up the stairs.

Bryony stares at her father. There are a hundred questions flying up her throat, but her mouth is too dry to move, and they all smash into the back of her teeth, unasked.

'Stop it, Adele,' Liam commands, pushing past his daughter and gripping the sides of his wife's head to stop her slamming it back into the doorframe. His hands on either side of her quivering, blotched cheeks look very strong and brown. 'For Christ's sake.'

'She's just upset, Dad.' Tyler hovers close to his mother, his hand still resting on her arm.

'I know she's upset. We're all fucking upset, but we've just got to pull ourselves together and deal with what is.' Liam is breathing hard, eyes shiny like glazed porcelain.

'You're not fooling anyone,' Adele hisses back at her husband through tight white lips. 'You put on a nice act, Liam, but *you're* the one who's really losing their grip.' She pulls her head out Liam's hands, nearly smashing into Tyler, who jumps backwards and out of her way as she whirls around and storms into the master bedroom. The door closes behind her with a deliberate click.

'Dad?'

'Tidy up your room, Bryony.'

3

My daughter enters the story at last, but only just.

She's out of the hospital bed, standing and walking from Liam's car towards the yellow glow of the porch light that illuminates the oversized wooden front door, but I still cannot feel her. It must be the tranquillizers making her consciousness dull, like an old bathroom tap covered in calcium scale that could do with a good polishing up.

Gigi.

*　　*　　*

The first thing that Bryony notices is that her cousin no longer wears her hair in two plaits. In fact, her hair is so thin that there doesn't seem to be enough of it to make even one decent ponytail. It is the exact colour of the carpet in the downstairs study, and hangs down on either side of her thin face like over-washed curtains that have gone limp from too much sun. She is wearing jeans and what looks like a pyjama top under an old dressing gown. It's way too big for her. Bryony thinks that she looks like a bag lady.

Gigi's eyes flick up once, twice, towards where Bryony and Tyler have been standing and waiting at the front door ever since they heard the car pull up.

33

Bryony glances at her brother, and, as if on cue, they both step aside like a pair of hotel porters. Tyler's cheeks are red. Bryony wants to say hi, but she doesn't. Tyler clears his throat.

'All right then, Gigi, in we go, darling. I've made up a lovely bed for you in Bryony's room. You remember Bryony?' Adele seems to be trying to fill the silence all by herself. Gigi doesn't say a word. She's stopped moving.

'Up you go, sweetheart,' Adele urges, coming up behind the stalk-thin girl and putting a hand on her shoulder. Gigi jumps and Adele makes a little gasping 'oh' sound and whips her hand away.

'What's the hold-up?' Liam's voice, like his wife's, is super chirpy. He walks up the path behind them, carrying Gigi's suitcase. 'Let's all go inside, shall we?'

Gigi sort of falls forward into a walk again, and passes between Bryony and Tyler like a solemn ghost. Bryony breathes in the sharp sour smell of hospital disinfectant.

'Hi,' Bryony croaks out at last, but Gigi doesn't look her way. She doesn't seem to be looking at anything but her feet. And then suddenly, *everyone* is looking at Gigi's feet — Bryony and Tyler at their sentry posts on either side of the hallway, Adele with her plastered-on smile and pink eyes at the front door, and Liam, shifting his grip on the handle of the bulging suitcase — one red rubber flip-flop flopping down on the Persian entrance-hall rug, and then the other. Flip flop, flip flop. Stop. The Wildings hold a collective breath. Gigi sways a little in the middle of the hallway.

'Oh darling, sorry!' Adele says, dashing forward like a tour guide. 'I didn't tell you where to go. We were just about to have supper in the kitchen, how does that sound?'

Gigi doesn't say anything. She just continues to stare down at the floor from between those lank, dirty hair curtains. The cord of the dressing gown is damp at the end from where it must've trailed on the wet grass during the walk from the garage to the house.

'We're having spaghetti bolognese,' Bryony says, and then immediately wishes she hadn't. It seems like such a stupid thing to say to someone whom you haven't seen in nine years and whose mom was just murdered. Gigi doesn't seem bothered, though. In fact, she doesn't seem anything. She has not moved or spoken, or even glanced around at the house. She just stands and sways. Adele gives Liam a desperate what-shall-we-do look.

'I bet Gigi isn't really hungry.' Tyler finally speaks. 'Are you?'

Gigi shakes her head. Finally, something she seems able to respond to.

'You want to go up to bed?' he asks, and she nods.

'Oh well, I suppose . . . ' Adele gives another brittle smile.

'I'll take you up,' Bryony says, and Adele turns her lighthouse beam on her daughter.

'Lovely, Bry. You do that. Up you go, girls.'

'Come, it's this way,' Bryony says to the dressing-gowned ghost as she heads towards the stairs. When Gigi turns to follow, Bryony notices that her cousin's eyes are the same kind of blue as her own, only dead-looking. The skin around them is grey.

The journey from the front hallway up the stairs and to her bedroom seems endless, the sound of their feet on the carpet not quite loud enough to cover the thumping of Bryony's suddenly nervous pulse.

'This is it.' The room has been tidied to within an inch of its life and has never boasted so many unused surfaces, but Gigi is still looking at the floor and doesn't notice.

'You can have that bed.' Bryony points to the spare one which now looks warm and delicious with the cherry-print duvet on it. The cover still bears a faint crease down the middle from where it has been folded up in the cupboard ever since Bryony discarded it for being too babyish. The one with the red swirls she has on her own bed looks too bright all of a sudden, the red reminding her of an over-ripe tomato that's gone all mushy.

Gigi shuffles across the floor, steps out of her flip-flops and climbs into the cherry-duvet bed, hospital-sour, wet-corded dressing gown and all. Her eyes slam closed. Her eyelids twitch and then go still. *If she wants to never wear mascara like Aunty Sally*, Bryony thinks, *she won't have such a problem because her eyelashes are brown.* It would seem that not *all* of the women in her family are albino lab rats. She stands at the doorway and stares at her cousin. Gigi looks younger than a fourteen-year-old should look,

36

somehow, and too skinny. She also has hardly any boobs, which Bryony thinks must be a pretty big disappointment. *I hope mine get into gear a bit more than that by the time I'm fourteen.* She gives them a tiny squeeze to check if they've started yet, and although it hurts, there's nothing to pinch but skin.

Suddenly, Bryony is very aware that if those grey eyelids fly open, Gigi will see her staring with her hands on her non-existent chest. It occurs to Bryony, then, that this will probably never ever be just her room again. She and Dommie will have to sleep downstairs in the lounge when her friend comes over and Bryony will have to do all her boob-checking and toenail-picking in the bathroom from now on. It's a horrible realization.

She switches off the light and turns to leave but then pauses, holding her breath, to see if she can hear Gigi breathing. She can't.

Great. I'm going to be sharing my bedroom with a zombie.

★ ★ ★

Bryony sleeps. In her oversized sleeping shirt that has been washed and faded over time to delicious softness, she turns over and sighs. Bryony dreams of a field of cherries (not regular ones that grow on trees, but small perfect pairs of them suspended on a field of blue, like her old duvet cover). Each time she tries to pick a cherry to taste it, it dissolves into lint between her fingertips. A little distance away she sees Lesedi from next door, dressed in full tribal gear like an extra on that TV show about Shaka Zulu, gathering the fabric cherries and plopping them into a woven basket with no trouble at all. Bryony tries to call out, to ask Lesedi how she does it, but her voice is nothing but breath.

On the other side of the room, Gigi, lying beneath her own blue cherry field, doesn't snore or snuffle or make a single sound. Her dreams, if she has any, are still off limits to me.

4

During break, Bryony and Dommie sit on a sunny patch of grass beside the tennis courts to eat their packed lunches. They kick their shoes off, despite it being against the school rules, and push their white-socked toes through the wire diamonds of the chain-link fence.

'She still hadn't moved a single muscle when I finally went to bed last night,' Bryony says, looking out towards the pine trees that block the tennis courts from the road. 'Even when I turned on the light.' The dark prickled arms of the trees move against the blue of the sky.

'She sounds weird,' says Dommie, and takes a bite of her sandwich. She always has lettuce and cheese on seed loaf, and Bryony doesn't know how she can stand to have the same thing every single day. Today, Bryony's got Marmite on hers, which is dull but workable, and she certainly would not complain to Adele about anything sandwich-related at the moment. Her mother is still lower-eyelid-wiping like crazy.

On top of the tears about Aunty Sally, and the strange fury that has gripped her mother since the tragedy, Bryony can tell that Adele is already starting to get stressed out about zombie Gigi. This morning at breakfast she heard her ask Liam: *Is it healthy for her to just carry on sleeping like that?* And he said: *It's probably the drugs, Addy*.

39

'It's probably the drugs,' Bryony says, and Dommie's brown eyes go big.

'She's on drugs?'

'Not like dagga or anything; just medication ones from the hospital.'

'Oh.'

'When I left this morning she was still sleeping.'

'Doesn't she have to go to school?'

'I don't know. Probably not for a while, what with her mom dying and everything.'

'Shame, hey.'

'*Ja*,' Bryony agrees, shaking her head, 'shame.' She tries to echo her friend's sympathetic tone, but she just keeps imagining Gigi breathing out that horrible chemical smell into her bedroom all day. *Ick*.

'Does Gigi being there mean you're not coming to my house this evening?'

'No, of course I'm coming; it's Shabbat.'

'*Ja*,' says Dommie and gives Bryony a long look. 'Of course.'

★   ★   ★

For the first time in as long as Bryony can remember, Tyler has not shut himself up in his room as he usually does the moment they arrive home from school. Today, he hovers on the landing outside her bedroom as if waiting for something. He's still wearing his school shirt and grey trousers, but his feet are bare and, for the first time, Bryony notices that his toes have a few long hairs on them, like her dad's.

40

Tyler peers around the doorframe, and watches Gigi sleep for a moment.

'Same position?' Tyler whispers.

'Same position,' Bryony replies.

'Wow, that stuff they gave her to zonk her out sure does the trick, hey?'

'*Ja.*' They glance at one another, and then both suddenly have to duck out of the bedroom to let loose a gale of snorting, spluttering laughter.

'Shit,' says Tyler, trying to stop himself. 'We shouldn't be laughing.'

'Are we not allowed to laugh ever again now?'

'No, man. It's just . . . well, is she all right, just lying there like that? I mean, she hasn't eaten anything since she got here last night.'

'Looks like she hasn't eaten anything in a while,' says Bryony, peeping around the doorframe once more. Above the cherries, Gigi's ribs rise and fall, rise and fall. *If she wasn't wearing that gross gown I could probably count them from here.*

'Shouldn't we wake her? What do Mom and Dad have to say about it?' Tyler asks, and Bryony shrugs.

'This morning, Dad just said it was the drugs.'

'*Ja,* but still . . . '

'And Mom's in her room.'

'Crying again?' Tyler asks, glancing towards their mother's closed bedroom door.

'*Ja.*'

'Shit.'

'Let's just go downstairs and watch some TV.' Bryony rubs one foot against the other, itchy to be away from the ribs and the cherries and the chemical smell.

41

'I really think we should wake her.'

'What, are you nuts?'

'She can't just lie there for days and days, Bry. What if she needs the loo or something?' The look Tyler gives her stops Bryony's giggle in its tracks. 'If she doesn't eat it could be serious.'

'She smells.'

'Bryony!'

'Well, she does. Of hospitals.'

Tyler rolls his eyes at Bryony and she watches as he pauses for a moment, clearing his throat and straightening his shoulders. Tyler steps into the bedroom, and in a few short strides he is at the foot of Gigi's bed. Bryony stays rooted to her post by the door, twisting the hem of her T-shirt between her fingers.

'Hey there.' Despite the throat-clearing and shoulder-straightening, Tyler's voice still comes out all wobbly. He reaches down and gives the raised bedding over Gigi's toe a gentle nudge. 'Hey, Gigi?'

Her eyes open. (For the briefest of seconds I can sense her vivid purple swirl of confusion and panic.)

'I think maybe you should have something to eat or something.' Now that his cousin's enormous blue eyes are open and staring right at him, Tyler's shoulders are not quite as sure-looking. 'Or something.' He pulls at the buttons on the front of his white school shirt. Gigi's expression is utterly blank. 'Um, I'm Tyler.'

'I know,' she breathes. It is the first time she has uttered a word since her arrival the night before. She blinks, swallows, and then shifts herself up a little on her elbows. Her collar-bones stand out like the handles of a bicycle beneath her pale, freckled skin.

'I could get you some toast,' Tyler says, encouraged, but Gigi's eyelids have already gone heavy, her brown lashes poking out of red rims covering up the blue within. 'Or maybe just a glass of milk?'

'A glass of milk?' Gigi makes it sound as if Tyler has just offered her a litre of fresh pig's blood. Her voice is thin and empty, like fat-free dairy. 'No thanks.'

'OK . . .' Tyler shifts from one bare foot to the other and Bryony wonders if that patch of her bedroom carpet is going to have a gross cheesy boy's foot smell in it from now on. Not that it matters, seeing as it is not, strictly, *her* room any more.

'So you're too old for milk?' Tyler says, smiling. 'Tot of whisky? Bottle of beer?'

The corners of Gigi's mouth move as if she just might smile, but it seems her face is too heavy for that. She closes her eyes and flops her head back against the wooden head-board with a clonk. It must hurt, but she doesn't seem to notice.

'Don't drink milk,' she whispers. Those bruised eyelids twitch. Tyler stands with his hands shoved into the pockets of his school trousers and waits at the bottom of the bed.

'Gigi?'

Nothing. He shrugs and turns away.

'Zombie,' Bryony mutters as Tyler walks back towards the bedroom door.

'What?'

'She's a zombie, Ty, I'm sure of it.'

43

'You're impossible, Bryony.' He grins, shakes his head. 'It's just the tranquillizers.'

'How much longer will she be on them?' Bryony imagines Gigi crashed out in her spare bed for years, gradually growing older and older, her hair eventually covering the pillow and growing down to join the carpet on the floor beneath. *Sleeping Beauty, only in a saggy dressing gown, and minus the 'beauty' part.*

'Dunno.'

'Ty?' Bryony says, before her brother can shut himself up in his room again. 'If Mom stays in her room until supper, tell her I'm at Dommie's, OK? I have to get there before sunset.'

'You know you're not Jewish, right?' he says, smiling, his eyebrows lifted up and lost in the floppy blond of his fringe.

'I *know*.'

'You're sure the Silvermans don't mind you gate-crashing their religion every week?'

'I'm not gate-crashing, Tyler, Mrs Silverman invited me.'

'Once. She invited you once. I don't think you've missed a single Friday night dinner at their place since August.'

'So?'

'It's just weird.'

'*You're* the weird one.'

'You going to convert or something?'

'Shut up.' She turns to hide her red cheeks, and starts running down the stairs.

'Good Shabbos, Bryony,' Tyler calls out after her.

'Shut *up*!'

44

The afternoon hangs still and yellow and full of the sound of ticking clocks. Bryony is tired of staring at the motionless Gigi, and it's still too early to go to Dommie's house, so she balance-walks along the cobbled flowerbed border in the garden once more. Today, her journey takes her all the way out of the front gate. She shuts it behind her, blocking out the garden, and stares up the street towards Dommie's.

It isn't a real street; real streets are not paved with russet-coloured bricks in a neat herring-bone pattern and dotted with wrought-iron curlicued lamp posts and street signs, but the designers of Cortona Villas had obviously been trying to capture the quaint charm of a Mediterranean village. They might have suc-ceeded better if the entire complex had not been landscaped by someone who clearly had the wrong brief, because the plantings maintain a distinctive indigenous African flavour: spiky aloes, succulent elephant plants and pebbles flank the paths, and between each two adjoining driveways stands a pale-green-barked, white-thorned fever tree.

Bryony hovers beneath the delicate fluttering shade of the fever tree that grows between the Wildings' driveway and the Matsunyanes'. She drops to her haunches and fingers the warm white pebbles lying at its base. Soon she has a small collection, the most circular ones that she can find, and folds the front of her T-shirt up into a little pouch in order to carry them.

'*The indiscriminate, merciless killing of a number of human beings,*' Bryony whispers, and with each word she drops a round pebble into her shirt with a soft click.

'What've you got there?' The voice startles Bryony and she jumps, sending the pebbles tumbling out of the cloth and scattering across the bricks of the driveway. She turns to see Lesedi Matsunyane standing by her own garden gate and staring at her. She wears a long skirt with a picture of the Johannesburg skyline printed on it, and from beneath its hem, Bryony notes a pair of bare brown feet.

'Um. Nothing. I wasn't going to take them . . . '

'Interesting.' Lesedi smiles and walks closer.

'I wasn't — '

'The way the stones fell.' Lesedi comes beside Bryony to peer down at the scattered pebbles and Bryony breathes in the smell of warm soil and cinnamon. After studying the pebbles for a moment, Lesedi glances sideways at Bryony with a tiny frown line between her perfect brows. 'Hmmm.' And then, at last (I have been wondering if she will do so again), she looks up at me.

This time Lesedi's attention brings with it the ozone smell of approaching thunder and the sensation of a sun-warmed lizard skittering over my scalp.

'How did they fall? Why's it interesting?' Bryony asks, thrilled at Lesedi's fragrant proximity and the sudden mystery of the fallen pebbles.

'You have a guest?'

'Yes!'

'Hmmm.'

'How did you know we have a guest staying?' Bryony stares hard at the pebbles, but they just look like oversized mint imperials scattered on the paving in no particular pattern at all.

Lesedi is about to answer, but she checks herself, and starts again: 'I saw your mom and dad arriving home last night with a girl in the car.'

'Oh. She's my cousin, Gigi. I'm Bryony, by the way.'

'Pleased to finally meet you, neighbour-Bryony.' Lesedi's formal handshake makes Bryony blush. 'I'm Lesedi.'

'Hi.' Bryony's voice is a squeak.

Lesedi looks down at the pebbles again and the frown between her brows deepens. 'You must be careful,' she says in a soft voice. 'Be careful.'

'Of what?' Bryony breathes. For a long still moment, nothing moves but the pattern of dappled shadow cast by the slender fever tree branches above their heads.

'Of messing around with 'communal area' property,' Lesedi says in a different tone. She smiles and walks back towards her garden gate once more. 'The Body Corporate of this place is run like a military institution. You might get court-martialled for even *looking* at these stones.'

'Oh.' Bryony smiles back, wondering what a court-martial is.

'Well, I'd better be on my way then, Bryony. See you around.'

'See you around, Lesedi.'

*   *   *

47

The candlelight strokes the stems of the silver knives and forks and glints off the hairclips that Shane Silverman has borrowed from his sister to hold his yarmulke on. When Dommie's mother waves her hands above the twin flames and then raises them to her face as if pulling the light right into her temples, an electric shiver races down Bryony's spine and all the little blonde hairs on her arms stand up on end.

'*Barukh atah Adonai Eloheinu melekh ha'olam . . .*' Bryony breathes in the throaty, mysterious words as Mrs Silverman sings them, and shuts her eyes. *Something magical is happening. I just know it.*

Bryony resents her parents for not being Jewish or, in fact, for not being Catholic or Native American or Zulu or anything interesting at all. The annual, tense flurry of decorations, food preparations and arguments with extended family members over who's doing what at Christmas is no substitute for a connection to something ancient and powerful as the Silvermans seem to have. *So unfair.*

Bryony wants magic; and this low-lit dining table with its plaited loaves nestling under lace napkins like fragrant babies waiting to be named is not quite the same thing as the Hogwarts Great Hall, but here at least she can believe that such things are possible.

★   ★   ★

My intrusion on the Silvermans' Shabbat dinner feels impolite, and I hurry to pull myself free of Bryony's story. The noise begins its relentless buzz the moment I leave the prayers and chink of cutlery on china, but I continue to head for the darkening sky. Straight away it rushes at me and pours right into me, filling me up till I am the entire horizon stretched from end to end across the earth.

Nocturnal creatures stir and step out into the cooling air to sniff at the scents that the day has left behind and I can almost feel the soft pressure of their footsteps: dusty paw pads, claws that dig and the delicate, tiny-boned toes of mice.

At the rescue centre in Limpopo, out behind the kitchen, we used to keep a large chicken-wire cage full of mice. Caring for them ensured that we could provide regular meals for the small wildcats, snakes and birds of prey that passed into our care, and with a bit of luck, out again and back into the wild.

When we first moved from Johannesburg to join Simone on her farm in the northern part of Limpopo, watching those silky little pockets of fur with feet at each corner dashing up the tree branches and ducking into the hidey-holes of their enclosure was torture for me. All of that industrious living and whisker-twitching for what: to end up as nothing more than a mini-meal for something with bigger teeth?

Even though Gigi was only five when we arrived, she had no such dilemma. I remember her in a tiny pair of denim dungarees and city sandals lugging a bucket of food from the kitchen to the mouse cage, and then, later that same day, watching Phineas feed a small selection of the rodents to Bratboy, the milky-tea-coloured caracal whose arrival at the sanctuary had coincided with ours. Bratboy had been brought in with a raging attitude and a foreleg that had been horribly damaged in a gin trap. He had spent the first few days of our stay under partial sedation as Johan, the resident conservationist who had abandoned his veterinary practice in favour of tending to the creatures that Simone took under her wing, cleaned out his wounds and tried to reset his leg.

On the morning of Bratboy's first meal, Gigi had stood a sensible distance from the fence and watched the snarling cat crouch low, his muscles bunched beneath his caramel coat, and wolf down his living dinner. There was nothing but fascination on her round, recently sun-pinked face.

'You're a smart one, aren't you?' I overheard Johan say to my daughter a few days later at the caracal cage. Johan had that overly tanned, rough-skinned look shared by just about every conservationist I'd recently met and, beside him, Gigi looked smooth and newly minted. 'It's not everyone who understands that ending up as lunch no way diminishes the little life in question.'

'Huh?' Gigi said, clearly uncertain about *diminishes*.

'That's why I'm not a vegan like everyone else at this place. Some things are lunch for other things, and those things are lunch for even bigger things. It's all just a part of the natural order of life.'

'OK.' Gigi poked a slender piece of straw into

the caracal enclosure and Bratboy flattened his tufted ears back over his head and showed her his impressive collection of pointed teeth. She bared her teeth back at the animal before turning to Johan. 'So will I end up as something's lunch one day?'

'Well, that all depends . . . ' Johan said with a serious look on his face.

'On what?'

'On whether I've had enough breakfast or not!' Gigi squealed with delight as Johan lifted her up with his scabbed, strong hands and pretended to gobble down her dimpled elbow. Bratboy snarled at them both from behind the wire of his cage.

⋆　⋆　⋆

Two months after that, Johan burst into the kitchen while I was giving Gigi her breakfast.

'You,' he pointed at me, 'come.' I stared at him in astonishment. Since my arrival on the farm, Johan had been nothing but shy and painfully polite to me. 'Quickly,' he barked, 'I've just had a call. There's a young wild dog not far from here. It's eaten from a poisoned carcass. If we move fast, we might be able to save it.'

'But Gigi . . . ' Everyone else was out, there was no one I could leave her with.

'Bring her.'

The three of us bounced against each other in the boiling hot cabin as Johan floored the bakkie over the rutted dirt roads. *Careful*, I wanted to say, but the determined set of his jaw stopped

51

the words in my throat.

'Wild dogs are pack animals, so there's probably more than one of the poor things dying out there. Bloody farmers, man.' His fingers on the wheel were white. 'Lacing carcasses with poison. The wild dogs have almost been totally wiped out because of shit like this.'

I was too busy praying we'd survive the hurtling drive to even think of asking him to watch his language in front of Gigi.

'There,' he pointed to a patch of darkness in amongst the trees. The bakkie squealed to a stop. 'Stay here, both of you.' He leapt out of the vehicle and ran to the back.

'Are you going to kill it?' Gigi's eyes widened when she saw Johan heft the dart gun onto his shoulder.

'No, lovey, just going to give it a little something to put it to sleep so we can try and make it better.' He rifled in the med pack. 'This is a low dose sedative with muscle relaxants mixed in. Sal, I need you to prep the activated charcoal solution for me. Black powder, lukewarm water. OK?'

I nodded. My hands were shaking. Gigi and I watched Johan march off into the bush.

'Mom?' Gigi shook my shoulder. 'Come *on*, you need to mix the charcoal stuff.'

In a daze, I climbed onto the back of the bakkie. My fingers slipped on the plastic water bottle. I could see Gigi watching me through the window, urging me on. The sun hammered at the back of my neck. I wanted to throw up.

Suddenly Johan crashed out from between the

trees. 'Got her. She's down. Checked and she's bleeding from the nose, pinpricks on her gums. Puking brown stuff. Definitely a blood thinner.' He jumped back into the driver's seat and turned on the ignition. 'We need to get the antidote into her. Hold tight, Sally!' I clutched the side of the bakkie bin as we went plunging deeper into the bush.

When Johan killed the engine again, an eerie quiet seemed to have descended on the landscape, as if it was holding its breath. Johan kneeled down beside the brindled body in the grass. I could see a dark red patch in the dirt by the animal's black brush of a tail.

'Her bum's bleeding,' Gigi whispered. She jumped down from the bakkie and ran to crouch down beside Johan.

'Gigi, get back here!' I yelled.

'Shame. Poor puppy.' She reached out and touched one of the wild dog's large, rounded ears.

'Seriously, Gigi, now's not the time for your nonsense. I want you back in the car in two seconds, young lady.'

'No. I'm not going to.'

'Gigi — '

'Hush, Sal, we need her.' Johan came over to the bakkie and began collecting meds.

'To do what? She's a child, for goodness' sake.'

'I've got to get a drip catheter into this animal, fast.' Johan's brown, sweaty face was inches from my own. His gaze was steady on mine. 'She needs fluids. She needs a gastric tube in her gullet, and activated charcoal down her throat.

We have to monitor her vitals. We're on our own out here, and let's face it, you have no experience. This animal needs all available hands.' He handed my daughter the clear bag with the drip solution in it. 'You're going to hold this while I put the needle into her hind leg, OK, Gi?'

'You're insane! She's five years old, Johan.'

'Mom!'

'Sal, I'm going to need that charcoal solution.' He bent down to insert the needle into the animal's leg. 'You OK with this, soldier?' he said to Gigi. She nodded her head. Earnest. 'Just stay back there away from the toothy end and keep holding that drip up nicely while I inject the antidote, there's a good girl.' Another calm nod.

I collected the gastric tube and the activated charcoal solution with numb fingers and clambered down from the bakkie. I tried to relieve Gigi of her drip duty, but she hung on to the little bag with such fierceness that I backed off and crouched down beside Johan instead. I gave the wild dog's flank a tentative pat. Its dusty fur was slightly sticky. Wirier than it looked.

'Is she going to be OK?'

'Here's hoping,' he muttered. I looked up at Gigi, but her eyes were fixed on Johan, trusting, watching his every move as he inserted the gastric tube between the animal's terrifying teeth.

I sat down hard in the grass with my head swimming and blood pounding in my ears. Johan administered the charcoal with Gigi resting her small hand on the wild dog's rump and whispering comforting words in the direction of the round-tipped ears.

'Nice one, girls.' Johan ruffled Gigi's hair and turned to look at me. 'What a hot-shot ER team you guys have turned out to be, hey?' The warmth of his smile made his eyes crinkle up like crazy in the corners. It was impossible not to smile back.

When Simone returned and heard of all this later that evening, she dropped to her haunches and pulled Gigi into a tight hug. 'What a brave girl! Aren't we lucky to have a pro like you helping us out here?' Gigi nodded, pink with pleasure.

'Yeah, I'm so proud of you, love,' I said, but when I placed my hand on her warm head, she pulled away from me, scowling.

'*You* didn't think I could do it. *You* didn't think I was good enough.'

'Oh come now, Gigi, I was just being a worried mom. You might've been hurt, you know. I wanted to spare you from seeing something awful happen to that doggy.'

'Well, I helped save her, so there,' she retorted, and flounced off to follow Simone into the depths of the house.

I blinked, unreasonably hurt and hating to show it.

'Kids can be so harsh,' Johan said. I whirled round. I didn't even know he'd been in the room. 'She shouldn't talk to you like that. She's no idea what a great mom you are.' He leant back against the wall and gave me another of those warm crinkly smiles.

'Please. I'm hardly a great mom.'

'But you are. You're . . . ' His gaze dropped to his feet. His boots were scuffed and stained, and there were burrs clinging to the laces.

'Johan.' It was Seb's voice, calling from outside. Johan hesitated a moment, and then walked out of the kitchen, leaving me alone with prickles of tears in my eyes and a strange cold pulse in my temples.

5

In the quiet before dawn, Gigi wakes. I feel her consciousness as a sudden sharpness in the room, as if someone sliced into a fresh lemon. And just like that, she's another way into the story at last.

She blinks at the darkness, disorientated, staring up at the little glowing stars that Liam once glued all over Bryony's ceiling. Slowly, her thoughts gather and congeal into a hard little ball, and when they finally make sense, they erupt into the room on a wave of hoarse sobs.

When her body stops heaving, Gigi lies on her back, stomach aching, and for long, motionless minutes endures the cloying feeling of her hot tears and sweat gluing her hair to the pillow until she can't stand it any more. She flings off the covers and swings her legs off the bed; it is the fastest she's moved for days, and her head swims. She glares across the room in the direction of Bryony's even breathing and then launches herself upright, wobbling for a moment before heading off to find the bathroom.

I am struck by how the familiarity of my daughter has been altered into strangeness by the new sadness she carries inside her. She must be the same Gigi that used to sit in the gazelle enclosure with a book and polish off a whole bag of litchis, letting the spiky little skins and shiny pips build up into a pile on the ground beside her, but she is wearing my death like a dark shawl around her shoulders that makes her hard to look at and impossible to know. Again, I wait for that old stab-in-the-guts agony that used to come when I saw her hurt. But nothing. No guts to stab. Not any more.

Gigi stands at the small bathroom window. The night air is a relief on her sweaty neck and, for a moment, she lets her forehead drop against the cold glass. She can just make out the cement courtyard at the back of the house, and the skeletal metal tree of the washing line one storey down. *If I fell, how many bones would I break?* She scowls and turns from the window. *Not enough.*

She digs trembling fingers into the ragged pocket of the dressing gown and pulls out the plastic vial of pills with its printed hospital label. She gives it a small shake, frowning at the sparse rattle. She should save the remaining tablets and ration them out slowly, but carrying this dark, aching *thing* inside her for even one moment longer is unthinkable. She uncaps the bottle and tips two little discs into her palm before popping them into her mouth. She's only supposed to take one, but one doesn't stop the dreams.

She drinks long and deep from the basin tap before tiptoeing back to bed.

★ ★ ★

'Elbows off the table, darling.' Adele has not made much of a dent in her 'Saturday Special' fried eggs and bacon breakfast, but this only

58

means that she has more time to look around and nitpick over Bryony's manners. Bryony removes her elbows from the yellowed pine with a sigh and glances at her brother, hoping to share a furtive eye-roll. Tyler doesn't notice; he's too busy shovelling forkfuls of food into his face as if he's in some kind of breakfast race. 'Don't gobble, Ty. Anyone would think I hadn't taught you any manners at all.'

'Jesus, Addy. It's Saturday; take a break, for heaven's sake,' Liam snaps, and Bryony looks up to see him give his own, barely touched 'Saturday Special' a vicious stab with his fork. Her father loves bacon and eggs and weekend morning breakfasts; or at least he always did. Bryony glances at the empty chair and a hopeful-looking set of cutlery and an empty juice glass placed before it. No Gigi. Her absence at this table is so pronounced now that it is starting to become a solid entity; more real, in fact, than the sleeping girl in her bedroom upstairs.

'It's ridiculous, is all I'm saying,' Adele says.

'Addy.' The warning note in Liam's voice makes Tyler look up from his plate at last. Bryony takes a big mouthful of her toast in order to swallow down the flutter in the back of her throat. It won't go down.

'No, honestly, Liam. The child just cannot go on sleeping indefinitely. It's not healthy.'

'Healthy?' Bryony starts as her father rises to his feet. A smear of vivid orange free-range egg yolk slimes across the tabletop behind his dropped knife and fork. 'She was practically catatonic when they found her, Addy. She'd been hunched over her dead mother for who knows how long. The blood had dried over the both of them, for Christ's sake.'

The unmanageable chunk of soggy marmalade toast still squatting in Bryony's mouth suddenly tastes like rusted metal.

'Liam, not in front of — '

'What do you want from the child? She's taking the time she needs to recover; who are we to tell her when she's ready to get up and face it all?'

'Well, it won't be much longer,' Bryony says, and everyone turns to stare at her. 'I looked in the bottle of pills that I found on the floor by her bed. There's only about four left.'

'Right then, there you have it,' Liam snarls into the heavy silence. 'She'll be up and about in no time, Adele.'

'I'm not being insensitive to what she's gone through, for God's sake, I just worry about her lying there like that stoned out of her mind.'

'Like a zombie.'

'That's enough, Bryony,' Adele snaps. 'Eat your breakfast.'

You eat your breakfast. Bryony glares meaningfully at her mother's full plate, but the grilled tomato makes her think of a scab and she looks away fast. *What must it feel like to be covered all over in dried blood?*

'I'm not really hungry any more,' Bryony says, and Adele responds by making a horrible gasping sound and bursting into fresh tears. 'But I'll eat it anyway. It's OK, Mom.' Bryony hurriedly picks up her half-eaten slice of toast, but Adele just shakes her head, squeaks the chair back from the table and leaves the kitchen.

'Well done, Bryony,' Tyler mutters.

'Oh, can it, Tyler,' Liam says as he follows his wife out of the room, 'stop being so goddamn holier-than-thou all the time.'

And then it's just Bryony and Tyler and four plates of half-finished food and a stripe of late-morning sunlight across the wooden table.

'I bet she's put a curse on us.'

'What are you on about now, Bry?'

'Ever since Gigi got here, all anyone can do is fight.'

'That's not *her* fault. She's not even awake. She can hardly be blamed for this family's bullshit.'

'I guess.'

'You're one weird kid, you know that? You always think someone's cursing someone.'

'So maybe they are.'

'Maybe you should lay off reading those books about witches and wizards and stuff all the time? It's turning your head.'

Bryony watches her brother finish the last few mouthfuls of his food. She shifts on her chair, and the skin on the back of her bare legs stings as it sticks to the varnished wood. 'Did you know about the blood thing, Ty?'

'What?'

'About Gigi being covered in Aunt Sally's blood?'

Tyler wipes his mouth and then tosses the crumpled paper napkin into the centre of his egg-streaked plate. 'No, I didn't.'

'How long do you think she was sitting there before they found her?'

'Listen, Bry, I wouldn't give it too much thought, OK?' The unexpected kindness in his voice causes a slithering feeling in Bryony's stomach.

'OK.'

'She'll be fine. We'll all be fine. Just put your head down and wait for the crap to pass.' Tyler gets up from the table and ruffles the top of his sister's head as he passes behind her chair.

'Hey! You're messing it up,' she says and removes the hairclips she put in earlier that morning; they are silver with yellow pineapples on them, a colour that Adele is always telling her she can't pull off. Bryony stares at the miniature plastic fruit for a moment, and then jams the hairclips into the pocket of her shorts. *Stupid*, she thinks. *Everything's just stupid*.

★   ★   ★

I leave Bryony sitting alone at the kitchen table.

Suspended within the centre of the story roar I feel around for another thread to follow instead; the house is full of them, woven tight in some places and unravelling in others. I hunt for Gigi's, but again, the pills she's taken make it impossible to find.

I pick up a navy-blue thread in amongst the tangle. This one feels familiar and solid and carries with it the faint smell of mown grass and aftershave. I follow it up the stairs and into Bryony's room where Liam is kneeling on the floor beside Gigi's bed.

'Gigi?' he whispers, but she sleeps on, lost in her chemical void. Liam smooths the grimy hair back from her forehead, revealing a pale constellation of freckles. *Are you in there, Gi?* He finds the pill bottle on the floor by his knees and takes a moment to read the label. 'You're still OK, Gi, aren't you?' It's not a question; it's a plea.

You were always such a sweet kid, just like your mom. She was the sweet one and now . . .

The force of his feeling side-swipes me and pulls me under, a powerful wave that tumbles me till I rip my skin on grainy sea sand and there's a searing salty pain in my mouth, my nose and my lungs — I am drowning. Such grief.

Oh Liam.

I drop the navy-blue thread. I flee the Wilding home as fast as I can.

The story-sound hisses at me like an enraged, trapped animal. I clutch at shadows, blind and screaming, to try and block the noise as I race down streets, through shopping mall parking lots, around corners and across school hockey pitches, until, finally, I stop.

I know this place.

The houses along the tree-lined street are old, nothing like the ones in Cortona Villas, but they have been brought up to date with expensive sandstone cladding, sleek brushed-steel house numbers and electrified fencing. The house where Adele and I grew up is still surrounded by a large white wall, but the black iron gates that used to rattle when we swung on them as we waited for Daddy to come home from the office have been upgraded to electronic ones.

I remember how cold the metal felt that one long afternoon in my second last year of high school when our parents told me and Adele that Dad had been diagnosed with cancer. I remember feeling weirdly disconnected from my body as I walked out of the house with this new, icy news inside me. I crossed the brown crunchy winter lawn, strode past Mom's roses, which had been pruned back to nothing but thorny sticks poking out of the flowerbeds, and stopped when I saw fourteen-year-old Adele clutching on to the gate and looking out at the street, just as she used to do when we were little.

She'd come outside in her slippers, and I could see the outline of her newly curvy torso through her thin jersey. She must've been cold.

I came up beside her and climbed on to the gate too. Her nose was pink and her cheeks were wet. She didn't look at me. A car drove past. Inside it, there were people carrying on their normal lives with no clue that our dad was sick and might die.

'Assholes,' I said.

'Yeah,' Adele agreed. She was shivering.

I shuffled closer, unwound half of my scarf, and tucked the one end around her neck.

'Thanks.'

'Sure.' My voice wobbled.

'I hate this.' Adele leant her forehead against the chilled metal bars.

'Ditto.'

'Nothing's ever going to be the same again, is it, Monkey?'

64

'No.'

'Think he's going to . . . ?'

I was glad she didn't finish her question. The word was as impossible to hear as it was to say. It hung between us and clung to us both, just like the woolly scarf.

'I don't know, Addy.' I put my arm around her shoulder, and that's how we stayed until the sky started to go orange at one corner. The bars of the gate had chilled our fingers into stiff claws. We walked back to the house holding on to each other to stop the scarf from pulling and strangling us both.

Now I plunge through the iron ribs of the new gate and into the green garden. The first thing I notice is that the tipuana tree is gone. I remember the vast reach of its strong curvy limbs, the perfect thumbprint rows of leaves, the whirling helicopter seed pods, and the exuberant yellow, crumpled-tissue-paper flowers that used to litter the ground beneath it.

Adele and I used to hate walking under the tree because of the foamy bugs that lived on the branches that would spit drops of insect goo into our hair. But it was fun to climb. I loved scrambling up as high as I could go and looking down over the surrounding gardens.

My most memorable tipuana-tree-climbing occasion happened years after my bark-scrambling days were done. I was already well into my second semester at university.

It was the day Liam challenged me to a climb.

Had we still been in high school, Liam would've been the jock (he'd been captain of the school cricket team, for heaven's sake) and I would've been the weird, arty chick who read poetry, and we would probably never have exchanged a word, but although he was studying towards an LLB, and I was doing a Bachelor of Arts, we sat beside each other once in our only joint class: English Literature.

As I was walking home from the bus stop after lectures, I heard the grumble of an engine and turned to see a rather clapped-out old Ford Sierra slowing down beside me. Inside it was the gobsmackingly unattainable blond god who'd sat beside me in Eng Lit 101 earlier that day.

He leant out of his open window and squinted against the sun. 'You live on this street?'

'Ja.'

'Me too. Number seventy-seven.' He looked up at me, shading his eyes with one hand. 'Did you walk all the way from the bus stop?'

'Yeah, it's not so far.'

'I can give you a lift home tomorrow if you want, just meet me in the campus parking lot if you fancy a ride. Look for the dodgiest car in the lot.'

'Um, OK.' My breath came in shallow little gasps.

''K. See you then.' He grinned and drove off.

The next day, I waited by his Ford Sierra and, as promised, he drove me home. The next day, he did the same. At first, we sat side by side in silence, but then, quite suddenly, we were talking. We talked about our classes at varsity and the lectures we liked or didn't like, the people we had been to school with, our families,

66

our first pets, our first dates and, just like that, we were friends.

Soon, Liam was parking his Ford Sierra in my parents' driveway and following me inside the house, rather than dropping me off outside the black iron gates. Most days, he'd stay till just before dinnertime.

After three months, we still had not run out of things to say to each other, although sometimes the delicious torture of sitting beside Liam overwhelmed me, and I would go dry-mouthed and silent. He smelled like freshly mown grass clippings, and occasionally the fine golden hairs on his lean, tanned arm would brush against mine.

One afternoon, while we were making the most of the end-of-summer sun on the stoep, Liam challenged me to a climb up the old tipuana tree.

'You're on!' I said, and we both jumped up, jostling into each other and laughing like kids as we ran towards the tree, racing to be first to scramble up the trunk.

'I'd forgotten how much fun this is!' I yelped as I swung myself up on to a swaying branch, my hands stinging on the uneven bark.

'Wow, you're like a total monkey-girl,' Liam said, laughing. 'I get the nickname now.'

'Hey, guys, what on earth are you doing?'

I looked down to see Adele standing on the lawn below. She smiled up at us, beautiful in her brand new dress; her hair (so much thicker than mine) curled alongside the slender blue ribbons that tied over her shoulders to hold it up.

'Watch out for the spitting bugs, Monkey!' Adele called, but I was watching Liam. He was staring down at the curved shadowy gap between the bodice of her dress and her creamy skin in such a way that, for the first time in my beloved tipuana tree, I experienced the nausea of vertigo. I tugged at my own, sensible, high-necked T-shirt. I was pretty sure there were sweat stains in the pits. Monkey-girl.

'Hi, Adele.' Liam grinned down at her and my nausea grew. Holding my breath, I shuffled my way along the branch and started lowering myself to the one beneath.

'Hey, where're you off to, Monks?' Liam said. 'You're not going to leave me here by myself, are you?'

I turned to look back up at him, my chest softening with hope, but his eyes were not on me: they were riveted on my younger sister who, although still in high school, was already more womanly than I would ever be.

I remember trying to graze away the hurt by pushing my fingers hard into the rough bark as I hurried to reach the ground, but I was biting back tears by the time my feet thumped into damp, bug-spitty grass.

When Liam and Adele officially started going out several months later, I told myself that it didn't matter. But every time I saw him with my sister, it was impossible to maintain the lie: I was in love with Liam Wilding and it was killing me.

6

Bryony is back on top of the wooden slatted dustbin cabin at the side of the house. The painted plaster of the wall between the Wildings and the Matsunyanes is chilly beneath her fingers as she grips on to it to look over. Lesedi is wearing the beads on her hair again, and she's not alone. There is another woman kneeling on the floor by the picture window with her back to the glass. The woman's hair has been brushed out into a puffy African halo and her rotund backside squashes out over a pair of calloused bare feet that look as if they've walked miles carrying heavy loads. There is something familiar about those feet. Bryony squints harder, scrutinizing the black pleated skirt with little roses printed on it and the shiny black pumps placed side by side on the wooden floor when, suddenly, the guest-woman turns her head.

Bryony gapes at the familiar profile. *It's Dora!* Even with her hair all puffed up instead of the sky-blue doek that she always wears when cleaning the Wilding home from Monday to Friday, Dora is unmistakable. *What's she doing at Lesedi's? Why's she all dressed up like she's going to church?*

Bryony squirms. The unfairness burns like a thousand little ant-bites on her skin. Her room has been colonized by the sleeping zombie, her parents are fighting, she's not Jewish, and now, to top it all off, Dora gets to sit on those sunny Matsunyane floorboards without her shoes on. Bryony wants to be the one invited into that room; she aches to bask in Lesedi's perfect-toothed smile and be privy to all the secret goings-on next door.

She clambers down from her spying post, skinning her knee on the edge of one of the wooden planks. She crouches down, eyes squeezed shut, and tries to swallow down the pain. 'Shit,' she says, and can suddenly understand why Tyler swears all the time; it seems to lessen the sting.

Bryony inspects her injury: the wrinkled skin on her kneecap has been scraped white with little speckles of blood welling up in patches. Bryony touches the red beads with her tongue and tastes metal and dust.

If Dora can be Lesedi's friend, then why can't I? She stands up, testing her knee as she straightens her leg. *I'm going to make her like me.* She strides back towards the house, newly resolved. *Something good has to happen soon.*

★ ★ ★

As much as I want to have Lesedi look at me so that I can feel complete and deliciously empty all at the same time once more, I pull away and up into where the story noise is solid sound. Down below, suburban Johannesburg sprawls beneath me like a forest. In amongst the dense green I spot the bright red baubles of the flame trees and the first jacarandas in vivid lilac bloom. I remember what it was like to drive on the streets beneath the jacarandas where the tar was carpeted in soft purple trumpet-shaped fallen flowers. If your car tyres crushed them from just the right angle, the trapped air in their bases would escape with a glorious popping sound. It was like driving through a giant bowl of Rice Krispies.

Adele hated jacaranda season because of all the bees that would hover over the flower-coated ground. They hid inside the blossoms until disturbed by your footsteps, when they would zoom out and zip around your ankles. Adele always felt ambushed by the bees, as if they were lying in wait for her instead of just going about their innocent, pollen-collecting business.

Once, Liam picked her up to carry her over a jacaranda-strewn bit of road. I was so busy staring at the way her hands clutched on to the back of his brown neck, her fingers so carelessly rumpling his hair, that I forgot to look out for bees myself, and was stung in the soft curve at the back of my left knee. I cried out in surprise and pain, but they were laughing too much to hear me. I had to bend and contort to scrape the pulsing sting out of my reddening flesh with the edge of my student card. It ached for the rest of that afternoon.

7

This time, when Gigi wakes, she knows that there's no going back to the numbness. She clutches the empty pill bottle so tightly that the plastic warms, almost seeming to become a part of her hand. She listens to the morning birds outside the window. No more dullness; I can sense all of her.

At home on the farm, the dawn chorus had been a symphonic riot of sound, but here it is sparse enough for my daughter to make out individual calls. *Wood pigeon, bulbul, weaver, hadeda, lourie* . . . she forces herself to focus on identifying each bird, but despite her efforts, her mind begins to slip, gathering speed as it plummets towards the thoughts she can no longer hold at bay.

Gigi sees viscous blood, like ink leaked from a red pen, pooled around the scuffed wooden legs of the kitchen table. She can smell it now, too, just as she could then (just as Jemima could, from her enclosure outside). Gigi remembers sitting on the kitchen floor and listening to the cat's frantic pacing and scratching as the meat and metal scent of blood overwhelmed them both.

'Gigi?' She turns her head to see that Bryony is awake and staring at her from the bed on the opposite side of the room. In the dim bronze light of morning, her young blonde cousin looks strangely featureless, nothing but pupils hovering above a pillow. Gigi closes her eyes once more and tries to slow down her breathing, but she is so rigid with tension that fresh sweat seeps out of her skin and into her already soaking sheets.

'I know your pills are finished,' Bryony whispers. 'I heard you taking the last one in the middle of the night.' Gigi doesn't respond, but Bryony can see the frantic movements of her cousin's eyes beneath their grey lids. 'Does this mean you're going to get up now and have breakfast with us?'

'What day is it?' Gigi croaks, eyes still squeezed shut.

'Sunday.'

A week. I have been dead a week. Gigi's story thread, a bruised, dark red, whips round and snakes back into the past. I follow.

Last Sunday, Gigi had woken early and gone outside in her pyjamas to practise her sun salutations alone because Simone was in Scotland. Gigi liked to do her yoga and think of Simone performing the same flowing moves half a world away in an icy stone castle by a loch somewhere.

As she stepped off the stoep, the crumbly orange soil of the driveway was cool between her toes. She could've put her mat down in the clearing beneath the lucky bean tree where she and Simone usually performed their morning asanas, but the close proximity of Johan's cabin made it impossible to feel the calm she craved.

She walked all the way down the curving dirt drive to the gate, unlocked the padlock and headed left towards the dam.

The dew clinging to the tips of the grass stalks caught the early sun, making the pathway look as if it was flanked by a thousand tiny light bulbs. When she finally arrived at the rickety deck, she unrolled her yoga mat with a flap that sent a flurry of birds winging upwards out of the reeds. She could feel the shape of the wooden planks through the mat beneath her hands. Downward-facing dog.

Gigi doesn't want the memory of the day to progress beyond that quiet moment, but it does. It races all the way to the gathering storm clouds on the hill, the farm gate flapping open and the acrid smell of excited male sweat that hovered like a strange new poison sprayed over the yard.

Gigi makes a high, helpless sound like some strange engine starting up. It makes Bryony's stomach plunge and churn.

'Are you all right?' Bryony asks. She grips the hem of her duvet with fingers that are suddenly icy cold. 'Do you want me to call my mom?'

'No!' Gigi howls. Her face is purple now; scrunched up and shiny like a newborn's. She convulses on the mattress and then wrenches the duvet up and over her head. Bryony stares at the white feet that are now coverless at the bottom of the bed. *They don't look real.*

'I'll just get you a glass of water,' Bryony says and stumbles out of bed and runs to the bathroom. She forces her impending tears to stay in as she fills a glass at the bathroom tap. She has no right to cry; she can't even remember what Aunty Sally looked like, except for those silly purple pants from the photo.

When she gets back and quietly places the glass of water on Gigi's bedside table, the shuddering mound of bedding has gone still. Bryony notices that there is some kind of reddish sand stuck in the groove around each toenail of Gigi's slender unreal feet. *The indiscriminate, merciless killing of a number of human beings.*

At least, I hope it is sand.

★   ★   ★

Bryony picks at the peeling paint on the bedroom doorframe and watches Adele tiptoe towards Gigi's bed. The duvet lump is still motionless. Her feet must be getting cold.

'Gigi, sweetheart? It's Aunty Adele.' No response from the lump. Bryony winces as a shard of dried doorframe paint that she's been picking at stabs under her fingernail.

'I've brought you some cereal, OK, love? You need to sit up and have a bite to eat. It's muesli. Nice and healthy.' Adele gives the lump a brave smile. 'I remember that your mom was very into her health food.'

Bryony slides the paint shard beneath another fingernail, testing to see how hard she can push it.

'Gigi, I just want you to know that we all understand how upset you are, and what a horrible thing you've been through, but we worry about you. You really are going to have to eat something.' The duvet mound remains utterly still. Adele turns and, once more, Bryony notices how thin her mother's skin has become lately, like paper that's gotten wet. *Maybe it's from all the crying.*

'I'm heading out to Woolworths to get some groceries now, Gigi, but I'll be back again soon,' she says, and then to her daughter: 'Bry, you going to come with me?'

''K.' Bryony follows her mother out of the room and down the stairs, relieved to be away from the duvet mound. 'Is Gigi going to be all right, Mom?'

'Of course she is. She just needs a good meal.'

Bryony thinks back to her father jumping up from yesterday's breakfast table: *She'd been hunched over her dead mother for who knows how long. The blood had dried over the both of them, for Christ's sake.* She remembers how the goops of egg yolk from her dad's knife had later solidified into shiny yellow scabs on the kitchen table. *Yellow yolk. Red sand. Toenails.*

★ ★ ★

'She didn't eat it, Mom.' The muesli bowl is heavy in Bryony's hands as she offers it to Adele to check. It feels as if it is filled with cement rather than a disgusting lump of congealed cereal. Her mother's lips pinch together.

'Maybe she just doesn't like muesli,' Tyler mutters as he flicks through the TV channels and back again, sound muted. 'Wouldn't blame her. The stuff's gross.'

'What's gross?' Liam asks as he walks into the room. He's still wearing his golf shoes, and Bryony notices that there's a small clump of soil and grass sticking to the bottom of the left one.

She smiles up at him, but he doesn't seem to notice. Bryony wants to ask *did you have a good game, Dad?* because that is what she usually does, but she doesn't.

'The muesli that Mom tried to make Gigi eat,' says Tyler, eyes still glued to the TV.

'You gave her muesli?' Liam asks Adele. His nose is pink from the sun and there are still sweat patches darkening his pale blue shirt.

'I tried,' Adele says. 'Sally was always on some kind of healthy organic mission, so I thought it would be the kind of thing Gigi'd be used to.'

'With milk?' Liam asks, forehead crinkling even further.

'Well, of course with milk, what else?'

'But Gigi's a vegan,' Liam says.

'A what?' Bryony asks, but no one answers. Tyler is looking at Adele, who is looking at Liam, who is suddenly looking at the turf clump on his shoe. There is a long, horrible silence.

'And just how exactly do you know that, Liam?' Adele finally asks in a sharp, frightened-sounding voice. The room is very quiet except for the whispering murmur of the muted TV. 'Because the child hasn't said a word in three days. In fact, she's barely been conscious.' Bryony wishes she could put the bowl down; it's starting to feel odd and slippery between her fingers and it would make an awful mess if it fell on the kelim rug. 'And you've either been at work or at your beloved golf course since she got here . . . So please, how is it that you're on intimate terms with the child's lifestyle choices?'

'Christ, Addy,' Liam mutters, lifting his golf

cap and rubbing a hand through his damp, flattened hair. 'It was on her hospital chart.'

Adele looks down at the knot her fingers are making in her lap. 'Well, seeing as you're the expert, you can tell her that she's expected to join us for dinner at the table this evening.'

'Addy, I don't think — '

'I promise she won't have to eat anything with a face, or anything that came out of a cow.'

'It's a bit soon — '

'But she will be up, and she will be at the table.' Adele's voice is very calm and hard, like smooth stone. Bryony swallows, and adjusts her grip on the muesli bowl. The warmth from her hands is making it give off a sick sour smell. *Out of a cow.* There's another long silence. Tyler and Bryony share a brief look.

'You're probably right, doll,' Liam says at last, turning to leave the room. 'The poor kid has to eat sometime.' *Did you have a good game, Dad?*

★   ★   ★

Liam goes into Bryony's bedroom and closes the door behind him. For a long moment he stands, motionless, staring at the pale blue, cherry-patterned lump. There's a small tuft of mousy hair protruding from the top of the duvet, and at the sight of it, he almost bends double in sudden, overwhelming pain. He breathes hard through his mouth and straightens up again.

'Gi?' He walks over to sit on the floor beside Gigi's bed. 'Do you remember that song, that one by Toto that your mom would just listen to over and over again? The one about rains in Africa?'

Liam notices the dirt on his golf shoe for the first time. Staring back across the room to see where he's left a few marks on the carpet on his way over, he clears his throat, and then begins to sing.

His voice is almost a whisper, the tune barely discernible. Halfway through the first verse, Gigi's hand slides out from beneath the cherry duvet.

Liam takes the warm fingers in his own. They're long and skinny, just like her mother's. He hums his way through the chorus.

He is quiet then; for a long time.

' 'Wild dogs in the night.' ' Gigi finally mutters, her voice muffled through the bedding. 'That's the next line.'

'Oh *ja*. I remember now.' Liam squeezes the hand. 'Thanks, Gi.'

'My mom loved that stupid song.'

'I know.'

'It's totally corny and ancient and the lyrics don't even make sense.'

'I know, but your ma was a sucker for that stuff, hey?' Liam waits. He can hear the faint sounds of Tyler's frantic channel-switching from downstairs.

Gigi lowers the duvet cover from her face and Liam tries not to recoil at the greyness of her skin. Only her eyes show any colour: vivid blue rimmed with lilac and dark pink. 'I have to get up, don't I?'

'It would probably be the best thing, Gigisaurus.'

79

'Your wife was in here earlier, she seemed kind of stressed out.'

'Your Aunty Adele is seriously worried about you, my girl. I don't think we'll survive the fallout if you don't at least try to join us for supper.'

'She tried to feed me milk.'

'She won't again. I talked to her about that. She knows you're a vegan now.'

Gigi lies back on her pillow and stares at the ceiling stars for a moment. 'I guess I must stink like a hog,' she mutters at last. 'Can I have a bath first?'

★ ★ ★

For a brief second, when Gigi walks into the kitchen, Bryony's not sure who she is. The warmth of the bathwater has pinked her cousin's skin, and with her hair all clean and her dressing gown gone, she looks almost normal.

'Hi, Gigi, just in time . . . ' Adele chirps as if Gigi has been having dinner with the Wildings for weeks and her presence in the kitchen isn't a rare, astonishing thing. 'Could you please help Bryony cut the tomatoes for the salad? That knife's a bit too sharp for her.'

'No it's not.'

'Hush, Bry, you cut yourself last time, remember?'

'That was the other knife, the red one.'

'Well, that's the one I'm talking about. The brown one's useless on tomatoes.' Adele marches over and yanks open the knife drawer. Bryony notices that her mother's fingers tremble as she pulls out the sharp serrated knife and hands it, red plastic handle first, to Gigi. 'This thing's devilish, but it's the only one in the kitchen that doesn't reduce tomatoes to mush.' Adele gives a sort of smile and whisks herself back to the stove. Gigi does not move. The two round fat tomatoes wait patiently on their wooden board, intact.

'Here.' Bryony shoves the wooden chopping board closer to her cousin and then Gigi's previous kitchen experience seems to kick in, because she suddenly picks up a tomato, places it at the desired angle, and touches the knife to the shiny skin. Then she stops. She closes her eyes. On the other side of the kitchen, Adele rattles the lid on the pot of rice.

'In segments . . . Like an orange,' Bryony whispers. 'That's how we normally do them for salad.'

Gigi doesn't say anything, but she opens her eyes again and starts cutting the tomato at last. In segments.

Liam enters and hovers at the kitchen doorway, looking in. He clenches his hands into fists in the pockets of his chinos. Bryony notices him first, and flaps a wet lettuce leaf in his direction.

'Hey, Dad.'

'Hey.' He shifts from foot to foot, not looking at her.

'Ah, Liam, could you just — ' Adele begins, but her request is cut short by Gigi, who flings down the red knife, runs across the kitchen and

81

crashes into his chest. Bryony stares, mouth open.

'There, there,' Liam says in a soft voice, and he lifts his hand to give Gigi's shoulder blades a tentative rub. Bryony tries to think back to when her father last hugged her; it was the day he told them that Gigi was coming to stay. She uses the tip of one finger to squish the edge of a lettuce leaf into the corner of the countertop. It bruises transparent, leaking watery lettuce blood.

'I got up, Uncle Liam,' Gigi says, and bursts into tears.

Bryony darts a glance at her mother and notes that her face has gone melted marshmallow pink and white again.

'Good girl,' Liam whispers. He has a helpless sort of look on his face. 'It's going to be all right, Gi, it's going to be all right.'

'Well.' Adele steps back, holding a pot lid up in front of her like a small, stainless-steel battle shield. For a moment, the only things moving in the kitchen are the steam rising up out of the rice pot and the up-down, up-down of Liam's hand on Gigi's white T-shirt. 'Go and call your brother, Bryony,' Adele finally barks. 'Dinner's nearly ready.'

★   ★   ★

'She knows you, Liam.'

'Adele — '

'No. Stop dodging.'

'After all that's happened in the last week, is one of your bloody interrogation sessions really

82

necessary right now?'

'Stop turning this all around on me.'

'I'm just saying that things are crazy, and we need to support each other at a time like this, not start making up ridiculous crap all over again.'

'I made nothing up, Liam. Sally told me herself.'

'Oh, don't start. I know this story, Adele, believe me.'

'I'm sure you do.'

'What's that supposed to mean?'

Silence. Bryony waits on the other side of their bedroom door, taking tiny sips of breath so as not to give herself away.

'Why does that child act like you're her long-lost friend?'

'She needs someone, Addy. She's just lost everything, for God's sake.'

'And that someone just happens to be you? By chance?'

'Look, I know how much you want to be close to Gigi to make up for all the stuff that happened with Monkey in the past, but you've got to give her time, doll. She's here, she's got a safe place, just let it happen.'

'Cut the trite bullshit. That's got absolutely nothing to do with what I'm talking about here, and you know it.'

'Trite bullshit? What happened to the grief and the guilt and the 'wanting to make everything right again', hey?'

'She was my sister, of course I still feel — '

'Look, I can't do this right now, Addy.' Liam's voice breaks and then stills again: 'I'm sorry.'

Bryony jumps back from the door as she hears Liam approaching from the other side. She scampers across the dark passageway in her bare feet, and then crouches behind the bathroom door, heart thumping. She listens to her parents' bedroom door open, her father walking out, and the soft click as it closes behind him. She waits until she hears the TV downstairs before venturing back to bed.

★   ★   ★

Finally, they're all asleep.

Even Gigi, exhausted from battling to act like a normal human being all through dinner and then pretending to watch the Sunday night TV movie while her thoughts ran riot inside her head, manages oblivion without any chemical assistance.

While they sleep, the threads go slack, and the story quietens a little, allowing me some time to drift high above the orange city lights along with the Joburg dust on Africa's night breath.

Then I let the wind take me north to where the air is thicker and hotter, the crickets louder, and the stars huge and milky in the charcoal sky.

I let it carry me home.

The warmth of the dark Bushveld pulses beneath me, but as soon as I get near enough to the farm to pick up the faint familiar scent of baobab tree bark, serval scat and thatch, a strange force surges up and pushes me back. I hover at its perimeter, unable to discover if Jemima still leaps and pounces on invisible prey in her enclosure, or if the little Thomson's gazelle with the gimpy leg still sleeps in the stall beside Seb's retired racehorse, Polonius. Are Phineas and Lettie still living in their tiny tidy house beside the old water tank? Do they still wake every morning to tend the rows of morogo and beans in their veggie patch, and harvest ivory-skinned pumpkins from the giant vine that sprawls over the compost heap? I cannot get close enough to find out. It would seem that the farm gates have been secured against me with something far more powerful than the chunky old chain and padlock that we used to use.

The first time I drove up to those wonky wire farm gates with Gigi slumped and sleeping against her seat belt in the back seat, I thought I was just visiting.

'Come and stay for the weekend, Monkey,' Simone had coaxed. 'It's always good to get out of the city and just *be*. Come, you'll be amazed at the clarity you'll find.'

I was frazzled at the time; Adele's excommunication had steadily sent all sense slip-sliding out of my life, and I was rigid with confusion about what to do next. 'Come,' Simone insisted, and so I went.

I'd been driving on dirt roads for what felt like days, rattling my old Opel's bug-spattered windows and jolting its suspension on the rutted dirt roads, when I finally saw the lone baobab that Simone mentioned to watch out for, and then the gates that heralded the entrance to the farm. I knew I was at the right place because Simone had tied a scrap of pink fabric on the wire, just as she'd told me she would. The incongruous floral flag flaunted itself like a showgirl against the sensible greens and browns of the bush. I turned off the engine, climbed out to open the gates, and froze in shock. The silence was so thick it was almost edible.

That astonishing silence was also the first thing that Liam commented on when he came to visit, many months later. By that point, I'd finally surrendered all thoughts of going back to my old life in the city, quit my shitty PA job, moved all my stuff to Simone's, and ensconced myself and Gigi within the small community of conservationists, esoteric wanderers, international volunteers looking for an 'African experience' and healers that passed through the sanctuary she'd created on the land her family had left her years before. I had finally lost the lilac look around my eye sockets, managed to get a light tan on my arms, and was even meditating in the mornings (which in my case, meant sitting with my eyes closed and listening to that rich, layered bush quiet for as long as I could keep my mind from lurching off into thinking about Liam or Adele).

'Man, but it's *quiet*,' Liam exclaimed as he extracted his long body from the shell of his dust-coated Mercedes. I had known he was coming, and had spent the morning in a state of nerve-wringing anticipation, nursing a thundering tension headache, and now, at the sight of his crumpled jeans, crumpled smile and a funny-looking fluffy grey rhino with a bow on it that he'd brought for Gigi, I burst into huge, heaving sobs.

'Well, it *was* quiet,' he said, hugging me and then pulling back with a grin once my crying had died down. 'What are you doing out here in the bundus, Monkey?'

'Living,' I said, wiping my wet face on the sleeve of my grubby T-shirt.

'I guess I can believe that,' he said. 'You look good.'

'I am.'

'Are you sewing up wounded leopards and doing physio on crippled zebras?' he asked as I led him towards the house.

'To be honest, we mostly handle the smaller, less glamorous predators that get caught in farmers' traps,' I said. 'I'll introduce you to my charges in a bit.'

'Jeez, you don't have much security out here, hey? Is this place safe?'

'Oh boy, listen to the paranoid Joburger!' I laughed. 'Would it make you feel any better if I told you I only took the padlock off the gate this morning because we knew you were coming?'

'A padlock? That's your security? You never heard of farm murders, Sal?'

'Of course I've heard of them, Liam.'

'Well, you don't seem to be taking them very seriously; it's happening all the time, especially here up north. There's a whole damn hillside of little white crosses on the road from Joburg to Polokwane. You must've seen it.'

'Crosses?'

'*Ja*, man, each one represents someone on a farm who has been murdered. They're offing people all the time out here, Mugabe-style.

Zim's just over the hill, in case you hadn't noticed.'

'You sound like a throwback from the apartheid era or something, Liam,' I said, scowling. 'Heavens above, this is the new South Africa, and I think we should take a more positive approach.'

'Positive? If you can find something positive about having a bunch of assholes come into your home to wipe out your whole family, then you must be smoking some really strong stuff out here in your hippy commune.'

'Liam.'

'Jesus, man, I heard how they killed this one old lady by holding her down and shoving a hot iron on her chest.'

'Stop it. Talking about stuff like that just creates bad energy.'

Liam shook his head at me, squinting against the light.

'We're trying to live in harmony with things out here, Liam. Negativity creates fear, and fear brings things to be fearful of.'

'Christ, listen to you!' He gave me a gentle smile, but his blue eyes were grave. 'Any minute now you're going to whip out a guitar and sing 'Kumbaya' at me.'

'Please, you know I can't carry a tune in a bucket,' I said. 'And we're getting electric fencing soon, so stop panicking.'

Suddenly, Liam gripped my arm with his large, warm hand and drew me to a stop. 'You're OK, are you, Sal? You haven't resigned yourself to some kind of wacky Bushveld purgatory just because Adele went ballistic, have you?'

'Purgatory? Have you looked at this place?'

He did so, then, taking in the muddy white-washed farmhouse with its mended wooden doors and the odd collection of paddocks, wire enclosures and cages nestling between the trees. In the centre of the yard, the lucky bean tree was just starting to flower, and its bare branches were bristling with vibrant crimson spikes. Beyond the clearing, the lush long grass glowed tall and green and singing with life, and in the distance, you could just see the smoky outline of the Soutpansberg.

'It's bloody gorgeous, Liam. You can practically chew the oxygen out here,' I said, and Liam shook his head and smiled.

'I guess it's very *you*, Monkey.'

'I guess so.'

We continued walking towards the house.

'And this place belongs to the same Simone from way back when in Joburg? I remember her from when we were in varsity. What's *she* doing out here in the bundus?'

'Her family has owned this plot of land for decades; it used to be a working farm once. When her grandparents passed on, Simone was going to sell it, but then she met Seb, a conservationist who was looking for a place to start a community of like-minded, earth-conscious souls. So they moved out here and started this sanctuary for rehabilitating wildlife.'

'Including Monkeys.'

'*Ja*.' I grin. 'Hey, monkeys are wildlife too.'

'Tell me about it.' He shot me a sideways look,

and then darted his eyes away again when our gazes met. 'So this Seb . . . he's a . . . ?

'Conservationist and energy-healer.'

'Of course. Does he play the guitar?'

'Oh shut up, you cynical old capitalist!' I said, and as I punched Liam lightly on the arm, I suddenly realized just how different being in his presence had always made me feel. I may have started sleeping better and gotten some sun at Simone's, but I hadn't felt so light inside since before that afternoon when Adele threw me out of her house. Then I remembered how, later that evening, I'd thrown my torn turquoise wrap-around skirt into the bin with the eggshells and sodden teabags and other used-up rubbish of my life.

'Oh,' I gasped, and Liam turned to look at me, brows drawing together.

'Ah, Monkey,' he said. 'I know. This whole mess is bloody impossible, isn't it? I've stopped trying to talk some sense into Adele, to be honest; it just makes her nuts if I so much as mention your name.'

I said nothing, the breath still snagging in my throat.

'Not surprising, I guess, considering my part in the whole debacle. She doesn't know I'm here, of course. She'd have a mental breakdown if she knew I'd even spoken to you on the phone.'

'So you're . . . '

'On a golfing weekend.'

'Ah.'

'Not a total lie; there's a great golf estate not

90

far from here, as luck would have it. I'll be staying there tonight.'

'Oh,' I say, keeping my voice bright. 'That's cool.'

'*Ja*,' he said. 'Cool.' He stepped on to the stoep, and the sudden shade made it impossible to see the expression on his face. 'Now where's my little Gigisaurus?'

8

When Bryony walks into her bedroom after school and sees Gigi sitting motionless on the cherry duvet staring at the bitten ends of her fingertips, she feels all itchy with irritation. Bryony marches to the cupboard, wrenches it open, and hunts for a pair of shorts and a T-shirt. At her back, her cousin (who does not seem even remotely related to the girl who ate peanut butter beneath Granny's dining-room table all those years ago, but is rather a coalescence of those strange new shadows that appeared in unexpected corners of the house after THE phone call) doesn't move a muscle.

Bryony changes in the bathroom, leaving her school uniform in a heap in the corner, and then runs down the stairs and outside into the garden.

The afternoon heat is solid and resolutely breathless, and in the distance a thick duvet of steely-grey storm clouds coats the horizon. She shifts her shoulders against an ache she can't quite define and makes her way to the front gate to wait beneath the fever tree. The stones are warm at her feet and, above her head, the leaves hang limp in the still air. She waits for five long minutes. There is no sign of Lesedi.

Little beetles of impatience skitter up and down her bones and force her back into the garden and all the way up to her spy post on top of the dustbin housing. She crouches down behind the wall and looks over. Her shorts feel prickly, and a slime of perspiration coats the back of her legs. The Matsunyanes' place is closed up and silent. Nobody's home. She puffs out a breath that lifts the fringe from her sweaty forehead for a brief blissful moment before it falls back down again.

Bryony rises up on her haunches and tests the top of the wall, resting her palms flat on the dusty plaster before putting more weight on them, and then finally swinging her whole body up. From this exciting new vantage point, she has a far better view of the Matsunyanes' garden. The lawn is smooth and bare, a bland, unfinished mirror image of the colourful flowerbeds, rockeries and borders of Adele's landscaping on the Wilding side. It looks like it's waiting for something.

Bryony stretches out a toe and prods the replica wooden slatted structure covering the Matsunyanes' dustbins. She climbs down on to it, and then even further, sucking in her breath at the tickle of forbidden grass beneath her feet. After a heart-thumping pause, she creeps towards the plate-glass window that she's spent so much time watching from over the top of the wall, and stares into the room. There's a desk in the corner, a puffy brown leather chair which looks as if it's been exiled from a lounge suite in some other more important room, and a large cabinet with lots and lots of little drawers in it. Against the back wall there are strange dark folded shapes: some like heavy winter coats hung up on pegs, and others that look like rolled-up rugs leaning upright. Bryony cups her hands to block the glare on the glass but she cannot make out what the peculiar items are.

She notices a strange kind of feather duster leaning against the wall in one corner. Its handle is decorated with patterned rows of beads, making it seem a bit too fancy for housekeeping. The feather duster part doesn't look quite right either. Bryony peers closer, and then suddenly twitches backwards from the glass. *It is hair!* A whole clump of some kind of hair, as white as her own, is tied on the end of the beaded stick.

Gooseflesh springs up on her arms and legs. She glances back around at the empty garden. The storm clouds have moved in with stealthy speed and now cover almost all of the sky, turning it a bruised greeny-grey. The gust of wind she so longed for earlier now tugs at her shorts and lifts her sweaty fringe from her forehead. Bryony shivers.

It's going to start pouring any minute, and despite the clotted feeling at the back of her throat from seeing that hair 'feather duster', Bryony risks one more look into the room. As she stares in, one of the coat-like objects on the back wall begins to move slowly. It is gradually unfolding and slipping from its peg.

Bryony freezes.

The folds of the dark fabric slip down to reveal a sliver of what looks like a white painted face. Little prickles of heat spring out all over her scalp. *It's a person.*

The cloth drops a little further: two slit eyes, a straight nose and, finally, a dark gaping mouth.

Bryony has stopped breathing. A sudden blast of wind pushes her closer to the window as if it wants to smash her right into the glass just as the dark cloth finally falls to the floor.

It's just a mask! One of those creepy African masks. Bryony almost giggles in relief. She rests her forehead against the cool window and gulps air at last. But then, just as she is about to leave, the mask, as if desiring to join the blanket that once covered it, suddenly slips off its hook and crashes to the floor. Bryony leaps backwards, stumbles, and then wills her legs to move.

She runs with blood pounding in her ears. The first drops of warm rain start to splatter down and her feet skid on the dampening grass. Above the garden, the clouds open and the storm breaks. Bryony chokes on lungfuls of rain and hurtles towards the safety of the wall, running straight into the edge of the dustbin cover, oblivious as its sharp corner bites into her chest. She struggles for a grip on the wood, unable to see anything but the rain.

It moved. It fell, just as I was looking at it. It saw me! Panic has turned her muscles into cottage cheese, but at last she scrambles up on to the Matsunyanes' dustbin housing and drags herself up and over the wall. Bryony lands so hard on the dustbin cover on her own side that one of the slats cracks and, for a moment, the splintered wood yawns like ragged teeth beneath her foot.

Bryony yelps and throws herself down to the muddy ground before sprinting towards the house, her wet blonde hair plastered to an almost transparent sheen across her scalp.

I do not follow.

No. Something calls to me from that room with the masks and the beads and the hair, something that promises silence. I allow the call to rush through me and all at once, although I can still see the rain and the grass through a shifting skin of shadow, I am no longer just in the garden; I am no longer sure where I am.

The charcoal-coloured wind swirls and parts and the white wooden mask that so frightened Bryony seems to hang in the air before me for a second before it resolves itself into a painted face. I notice dark smooth skin between the cracks in the white face-paint. Black eyes with curly lashes. And then, a slow smile. Lesedi.

I see you, Ancestor.

I feel the words. They come at me from everywhere, resonating into the very centre of me and echoing far, far out to the edges of the black sky.

For a moment, I am Africa's rain, nectar-sweet, thumping on to and soaking into brown earth. I am rank cowhide, dusty, twitching, covered with flies. I am river sand, washed caramel-sugar-clean by the waters of a flooding spruit.

Why have I not left? I send my own wordless question back. It pulses and beats like the wings of a hundred birds around the white-painted face. *Tell me. Why must I follow the noise? Why am I still here with all the human mess and the aching and the past?*

A shard of lightning flicks down.

I understand your frustration, Ancestor, I know what it is to have to follow a path that has been thrust upon you by forces you cannot see or understand.

The storm is both around and within me. For a moment it *is* me. Africa's thunder shakes through me like laughter.

You need to stay until the end.

I'm dead. What more of an ending do you want? I wait. For a long moment, there's nothing but the rain.

And then: *Gigi.* My daughter's name is a wild wordless song that rises up on the wind and, for a moment, it is one high, clear note on the tumultuous air.

What about Gigi? What am I supposed to do? But there's no reply.

Softly at first, barely distinguishable from the sound of the storm, the story noise returns. It banishes the white face and the voiceless voice, building to a scream until it is everything. Urgent.

I follow where it calls me. There is nothing else I can do.

★　★　★

Bryony hurtles in through the kitchen door and smashes straight into Tyler.

'Watch where you're going, Bryo — . . . Jeez, you're soaking.'

'Was caught in the storm.' Streams of water race down Bryony's bare legs and puddle on the kitchen tiles.

97

'No kidding,' Tyler says, glancing down at the spreading wet patch on his school shirt. 'Are you OK?' Bryony doesn't answer. 'You're shivering like a maniac.'

'I know,' she mumbles through chattering teeth.

'What's up? You look kind of weird.'

Bryony shakes her head, and her blue-tipped fingers dig into the flesh of her arms.

'Go and get changed. You're going to catch pneumonia or something.' Tyler frowns. 'Are you sure you're OK? You look like you've seen a ghost.'

'There was something . . . weird . . . I dunno . . . ' she manages through chattering teeth. 'I saw . . . '

'You're not making much sense, Bry.'

'It was . . . There was this mask and I think . . . it was like there was a spell on it.'

'Well, that should be right up your street then, hey? Spells and stuff? Remember how you used to be so obsessed with Harry Potter that you used to try and get us all to call you Hermione?' Tyler grins. 'You even wrote 'Property of Hermione Granger' on all your school books, remember?' Mentioning this is usually the perfect way to elicit a blushing scowl and a slap from his sister, but she just continues to stare at him. Her eyes, with their wet spiked lashes, are open very wide. Tyler feels a squeeze of discomfort deep in his stomach. He trots into the scullery, drags a dry towel from the laundry basket, and then places it around his sister's quaking shoulders. 'There. That better?' She nods, wrapping herself up tighter.

The towel seems to return Bryony to some kind of normality. Her gaze flickers over the kitchen. She notices an opened jar of peanut butter on the kitchen counter. Her expression hardens. 'Hey . . . ' she says. 'What are you doing?'

'Making a sandwich. What, is that a crime now?'

'But you *hate* peanut butter.' She glares at Tyler, narrowing her eyes at the blush rising up his neck. 'You're making it for *her*, aren't you?'

'What?'

'For Gigi. You're making her a sandwich or something.'

'So? What if I am?'

'Why bother? It's not as if she's going to suddenly talk to you or make you her best friend or anything.'

'She already has been talking to me; so there.' Tyler turns his back on his little sister, embarrassed at how childish he sounds. He busies himself with cutting a slice of bread and jamming it into the toaster.

'What did she say?' Bryony is too curious to maintain the accusation in her tone.

Tyler shrugs. 'Nothing much.' He swirls the knife inside the jar, working it into the stiff peanut butter, and Bryony notices that the veins on his forearm pop up as he does so.

'Did you ask her how come she knows Dad?' she whispers, and he darts a quick look at her.

'No.'

Silence.

'Well maybe you should.'

'*Ja*, maybe.' The toaster pings. 'Now go and get changed, for heaven's sake; you look like a drowned rat.'

★ ★ ★

Gigi finishes the toast, taking bite after mechanical bite until her mouth is left dry and sore. She's glad that Tyler handed her the plate and then left the room, because for a moment she thought he would stay and watch her eat. Something about the way he looks at her from beneath his blond lashes makes her feel too sharp-edged, too alive. She knows that he's trying to be kind and make her feel less of a stranger in this large, expensive house, but his attention brings too many memories hurtling to the surface. They close her throat and fill her mouth with bile.

Gigi darts a look across the bedroom to where Bryony, now in dry clothes, is rubbing her hair with a towel. There's a slight frown between Bryony's pale eyebrows, and she's a million miles away, barely even noticing Gigi at all. After all the horrified looks shared over her head, the worried whispers and the sympathetic smiles of the past week, Bryony's naked dislike is an honest relief. Gigi doesn't want to be asked if she's OK, she doesn't want to have Adele place a trembling tentative hand on her shoulder; it all makes her feel too full, as if she might split open and spill out a thick stinking stew of guts and dark mud all over the floor.

Gigi sits surrounded by Bryony's abandoned Barbie dolls, grubby soft toys and Justin Bieber posters stuck on askew with oily lumps of Prestik and wonders if she remembered to close the window in her own bedroom back home. If she didn't, the monkeys will have gotten in again, probably knocking the curvy kudu horn and the collection of bones and stones that she keeps on the windowsill to the floor. She wonders if the monkeys (who have little black faces and grey bodies, like Siamese cats) will notice the crack in the corner of her room near the ceiling that looks like a map of the Nile, and swing on the frothy bridal extravagance of the mosquito net that's tied up and screwed into the creosoted wooden beam above her bed.

Gigi shuts her eyes and curls her body over her folded arms to try and contain the longing. She tries to remember every detail of the painting of Buddha, which was painted on the wall by her bed by an artist friend of Simone's called Angela who came to stay on the farm last year. Angela was a small, loud American who'd been living on retreat in India for years before she came to volunteer at the rescue centre, and she'd worked the letters of Gigi's name in Hindi to swirl with the clouds in the sky above Buddha's head.

Angela had already returned home to the States by the time the men came. Simone was in Scotland. Phineas and Lettie were at church. It had just been Johan, Seb and her mother in the house.

101

Gigi grinds her teeth together, hard, and fights for air.

She tries to breathe back the plant sap and dung and dust scent of home, but all she can conjure up is the salty tin smell of blood.

9

'Hey, Dommie, do you remember when we both pretended to be Hermione Granger?'

'Oh, *ja*.' Dommie grins and rolls her pencil across the large, smooth expanse of the art-room table they're sharing. 'We were such dorks.'

'I know.' Bryony takes her own pencil and draws a soft, curved line across the sheet of paper. They're supposed to be make sketches of ideas for the 'What South Africa Means to Me' inter-school art contest, but all she can think about is yesterday's storm and the way that ghastly white mask seemed to stare at her before it fell from the Matsunyanes' wall.

She adds another pencil curve to the first, creating the outline of the pointed chin just below that awful open mouth, and then scribbles firmly over all of it.

'Bryony, don't waste paper, please. If you've made a mistake, use an eraser to rub it out,' Miss McCrae says as she swoops past the desk trailing a cloud of cloves in the wake of her gypsy skirt. 'Just think of the poor trees, dear.' Bryony dutifully turns the piece of paper over and readjusts her grip on the pencil.

'Man, I can't believe I spent so much time trying to make my hair frizzy to be more Hermione-ish,' Dommie says, smoothing the corkscrew curls that she now wears scraped back into a brutal ponytail to keep any sign of frizz from springing to life. 'I must've been out of my mind.'

'Uh-huh.' Bryony places the tip of her pencil on the page. 'But all that magic stuff that we were so into . . . '

'Oh, remember when we made those bamboo wands? We put all sorts of weird stuff inside them. We were so sure they would work.' Dommie giggles, remembering how they used strands of Bryony's silver-pale hair as a substitute for unicorn tail.

'Do you think that maybe . . . I dunno . . . there really are people who can do spells and stuff?' Bryony asks. 'Like for real?'

Dommie looks at Bryony for a long moment, one hand still on her curly hair, pencil poised over her paper.

'Bryony? Are you planning on presenting a blank sheet of paper as your design entry?' Miss McCrae asks as she and her spice cloud drift past their desk once more.

'Um, no, I'm just . . . thinking.'

'All right then, but think a little faster, dear, there's only half an hour to the bell.'

Bryony bends over the desk and quickly moves the pencil across the page. She's drawing the mask again. She can't seem to help herself.

'What do you mean, 'people who can do spells'?' Dommie whispers once their teacher has moved on.

'Just . . . like put curses on things, or make things move from a distance and stuff. Like some kind of witch, or something.'

'Jeez, Bry, sounds like you're watching too

104

much TV, as my dad would say.'

Silence. Bryony begins to fill in the mask's dark open mouth, pushing the pencil harder and harder into the page.

'Oh my. That's rather interesting,' Miss McCrae says, coming to a stop behind Bryony's shoulder. 'A tribal African mask, is it?'

'Yes.'

'Ritual and mystery. Nice idea for the beginnings of a theme, Bryony. Although, I must say, you've made it look rather scary.'

'Ritual?'

'Oh yes. Tribal masks are not just African decor items, dear; they've been used for centuries in all sorts of ceremonies.'

'For what?'

'Oh, I don't know, making rain and talking to the ancestors, that sort of thing. Sangomas and what-not.' Miss McCrae smiles and moves off again.

'You mean witch doctors?' Bryony asks in a strangely loud voice. 'Magic?' The murmurs and scratching sound of pencils cease as girls all over the room turn to stare.

'Well, I suppose so,' Miss McCrae says into the silence. 'But the term *witch doctor* is not the same as a sangoma, Bryony. Witch doctors are believed to be like the bad guys who put curses on people, and sangomas are the good guys, the healers.' And then she claps her hands lightly together. 'All right now, come on, everyone; back to your work.'

'What's up with you?' Dommie mouths, but Bryony just shakes her head and shrugs. She tries to smile as if nothing is wrong, but the

105

corners of her mouth don't seem to be working properly.

★ ★ ★

Bryony is on top of the dustbin housing once again. Over the wall, in the Matsunyanes' ground-floor back bedroom, Lesedi, wearing her headdress with the dangling white beads and a stitched blanket over her shoulders, throws her head back and starts making a strange noise. Bryony can only hear faint edges of it from her vantage point, but it seems to be a chant, and it goes on for a while. Bryony gapes, riveted. The man in a suit whom Bryony watched Lesedi welcome ten minutes ago is sitting across from her, on the other side of a woven rug. As with Dora before, he has removed his shoes. Lesedi holds what looks like a straw bag with an open top. She shakes it and shudders and empties the contents out on the rug. Bryony cranes forward to see what falls out, but can only make out small white and brown objects. They don't look worth all the fuss.

(I know what Lesedi is doing. She's throwing the bones to read messages in the way the pieces fall. Seb used to have a friend called Mike who was one of a few white male sangomas in the country. Mike was one of my favourite guests ever to visit the sanctuary when I was still Monkey. He was soft-spoken and freckled, and wore his traditional garments and blobs of white face paint with quiet authority that stopped the astonished stares almost at once. Gigi was in love with his hair, which he wore in gingery

106

dreadlocks that bounced when he walked. She bugged me to allow her to do the same with her own for weeks after his visit. I remember him saying to Simone once: 'Throwing the bones is no different from you reading your Tarot cards. They're a way to focus energy, to enable the diviner to step aside from all their own headstuff and let something bigger speak through them.')

Bryony's heart is thumping behind her ribs. She pulls back from the wall and climbs down to the ground. She wants to go inside and do something normal — even homework would do the trick — but she finds that she cannot. Instead, she follows the flowerbed all the way to the gate and goes out to stand beneath the fever tree. After long minutes, her pulse slows and her breath comes more easily. She picks up a white pebble, studies the tiny veins of grey threading its powdery surface, and then puts it down again. Finally, the Matsunyanes' front gate opens, and the man she watched in Lesedi's room emerges. He is sweating in his smart suit, his face glowing like chocolate about to melt in the sun. He presses the button on his remote control, and a shiny car in the guest parking bay responds with a cheerful 'blip'.

'Hi,' Bryony says, and the man jumps, startled, unaware that he was being watched.

'Hi.' The man glances from left to right, and then speeds up to a trot as he nears the sanctuary of his BMW.

'Hey, Bryony!' Bryony spins around to find that she's being watched too. Leaning on the gatepost and wearing a pair of khaki cargo pants and a crisp white T-shirt is Lesedi herself. (For a moment I am dew glittering on grass tips and filigree spider's webs, and all the dusky space in an evening sky.) Lesedi smiles across at her little blonde neighbour. 'Are you planning on making *all* my clients feel so uncomfortable?' she says and Bryony blanches.

'Clients?'

'Oh yes. I thought you'd have figured it out by now, standing at your fever tree sentry post.' Lesedi winks and crosses her smooth brown arms over the front of her T-shirt. 'I've got a little illegal concern going on here, but you know that already.' Her eyes go round with studied concern. 'Hey, you're not spying on me for the Body Corporate, are you? I know it's against the rules to run a business from home in this perfect, precious little place, but I'm not causing any harm, am I? And anyway, what's a businesswoman to do?'

'Um.' Bryony's mouth is dry and her voice comes out in a croak. 'I don't know.'

'So you won't tell on me then?'

'No.' Lesedi smiles one of her warm delicious smiles again and Bryony notices just how perfect her teeth are. Like a Colgate ad. 'I don't even . . . No. Of course.'

'Cool. Thanks.'

'What do you do? I mean, what sort of business?'

'I guess you could call it counselling. Possibly consulting . . . Helping people is a good way of putting it.'

Bryony thinks back to the mask, the beaded

headdress and the woven rug, Miss McCrae's comments in Art class, and her latest bit of Google research done on Tyler's laptop before she came outside to climb the dustbin housing.

'So you're not a sangoma, then?' she blurts, blushing a violent pink the moment the words are out of her mouth.

'I see you *have* been spying, little Bryony.'

'No I — I didn't . . . ' Bryony nudges one warm pebble with her smile-toe.

'Shush, it's OK. I admire the desire to seek the truth; it shows an innate belief in the need for more justice in the world.'

'Does it?' Bryony's not sure what Lesedi means, but it certainly isn't the telling-off she expected. She looks down to where the bottoms of Lesedi's cargo pants crumple up over her bare feet and notices that her toenails are painted a delicate shell pink. As far as Bryony's aware, sangomas wear skins and gall bladders tied to their manky hair and hang out in dark little shops in the centre of town full of crocodile guts and dried leaves. She also once heard someone say that sangomas sell tapeworm eggs to people who want to lose weight and the worms then hatch in their tummies and eat half the food they swallow. And then, in case that's not disgusting enough, when the worm gets too big, you get a special poison to drink which makes you poo the whole horrible thing out of your bum and flush it down the loo. *Gross.*

Bryony stares at Lesedi's pretty toes and giggles. Tapeworm poo and pale pink pedicures just do not mix.

'I was only kidding, of course,' Bryony says. 'I obviously know you're not one of those.'

'Do you now?' Lesedi's voice is calm and unreadable and Bryony's grin falters. She remembers the hairy, beaded feather duster leaning up against the wall of that peculiar room; wasn't there something similar in one of those internet pictures?

'Well then, Bryony-with-the-cousin-who's-come-to-stay, in that case, I'd like to offer you a little advice . . . ' Lesedi steps closer, and Bryony nods, her throat inexplicably tight. 'You might find you do better in life if you trust your instincts rather than your eyes.' The word is almost a hiss, and as she says it, Lesedi opens her own very wide so that the creamy white shows all around the brown.

Bryony gulps. Even the tips of her fingers seem to be sweating.

'Go home now,' Lesedi whispers, and as she does, a gust of wind rushes through the quiet townhouse complex, sucking up sand and fallen leaves with its hot breath and sending them dancing up the faux street.

Bryony doesn't need to be told twice. She bolts back into the garden, and the wooden garden gate shudders on its hinges as it slams shut behind her.

10

'So, Gigi, tell me how you're feeling today?'

Gigi feels as though she's going to throw up. She stares hard at the blond wood of the small table at the side of her chair. On it is a floral tissue box with one white tissue pre-pulled out of the slit at the top. The corner of the white tissue poking up looks clean and expectant. Gigi clenches her hands into fists, and then forces them open again. They feel very hot through the denim of her jeans.

'Is there anything you'd like to talk about?' Dr Rowe asks after minutes of silence have ticked by. 'How are you fitting in at your uncle and aunt's place?'

'OK, I guess.' It's the first thing that Gigi has said since Adele walked into the bedroom an hour and a half ago and announced in a no-nonsense voice that it was time for her psychiatrist appointment. In fact, it's the first thing she's said all day. The sensation of Gigi's voice croaking out makes her instantly nauseous. She shuts her mouth quickly to swallow it down.

'Are you managing to get any sleep, Gigi?' A shrug. 'Aren't the pills any help? Remember, the ones I prescribed to you while you were still here at the hospital?'

'They're finished,' she says, and Dr Rowe's eyebrows lift, just a tiny bit. He considers his young patient for a moment before speaking again. 'I see.'

'You could give me some more, you know . . . ' Gigi looks up at Dr Rowe at last. 'Like make out a prescription.'

'Well, yes, I could; but that probably wouldn't be a very good idea considering you seem to have relied rather too heavily on the last lot. How many did you take a day?' Gigi shrugs, staring back down at her hands.

'Medication can be very handy in helping us cope when things get too overwhelming, but it doesn't actually make any of the bad stuff go away. All that pain still has to be dealt with at some point, doesn't it?'

Another shrug. Gigi twists her hands together, watching how this makes the skin on her fingers go mauve and then white.

'You might find some relief if you tell me a little about what happened that day, Gigi.'

Silence. (I notice that my daughter's story thread is all bunched up and twisted into knots. It's the colour of spilled wine, and just as sour, and it fills the room from wall to window, ceiling to floor, winding tight around her throat.)

The afternoon sun beats against the western window of Dr Rowe's hospital consulting room, but they're protected from its heat by the bluish UV glass. Dr Rowe dislikes the way the glass makes the world outside seem strange and overcast, like something from a sci-fi movie, but it's either that or swelter.

Dr Rowe glances down at his file: the girl had been crouching beside her mother on the kitchen floor when the police had found her. The mother had been dead for hours, her face beaten into a

112

purple, inhuman pulp, and her clothes slashed and bloody. Cause of death: asphyxiation from strangulation. The other victims, two white men, no relation to the patient, had been lying on the floor a little distance from the woman, both of them bound and gagged. Cause of death: loss of blood due to laceration with what appeared to be a machete. According to the report, Gigi was found to be unhurt and intact, and it was later revealed that the blood that had dried to a rusty crust along the one side of her face (right in her nostrils and inside her left ear) and had solidified her clothes on to her body like rigid bandages, had not been her own.

She'd made no statement to the police, hadn't spoken at all, in fact, so there was no way of knowing how long she'd been on the floor like that holding on to her mother's lifeless hand. It was a domestic worker who had finally alerted the police and called them out to the scene. The weeping Phineas Radebe had also identified the three bodies, seeing as no one could get anything out of Gigi at all.

Dr Rowe rubs his hand across his forehead and looks across at the girl. His stomach churns. There'd been too much melted cheese on his tramazini at lunch; he should've scraped some of it off.

'OK, Gigi, I am not going to press you to talk about this when you're not ready to.' Gigi's fingers twist and twist in her lap. Dr Rowe glances back down at his notes and sees that she did, in fact, say something before they took her to the hospital. She'd asked Mr Radebe if he could feed someone, or something, called

Jemima. 'Perhaps you can tell me a bit about what you feed Jemima?'

Gigi glances up then, her eyes searching his kind face for a second before darting away again. Dr Rowe doesn't smile. He knows that Gigi doesn't want smiles.

'Mice.' Her voice is flat. 'Jemima's a serval.'

'Ah, glorious creatures, those.'

'You know what a serval is? Lots of people don't.'

'True, but I happen to be a very keen nature buff. Tell me, do they really jump as high as the books say they do? I've never seen it myself.'

'Ja,' Gigi says; she reaches across and touches the waiting tissue with the tip of one finger. 'Jemima can leap higher than my head, from like just standing still.'

'Wow.'

'And she does somersaults and stuff, twisting and turning in mid-air. She's a real show off.'

'It sounds like the two of you are pretty close.'

Silence. Dr Rowe shifts in his chair, trying to ease the gas that is building in his guts. He really should've ordered the tuna.

Gigi is holding herself terribly still, taking tiny sips of breath so as not to break apart into sharp little pieces. She focuses on the corner of tissue till it seems to expand and fill the whole room with bleached whiteness. Her eyes ache.

In and out, little sips of breath.

'Gigi?'

But Dr Rowe has been in the business long enough to know that his patient is not going to say any more. Not today.

114

Adele sits in her car in the parking lot outside and waits for her niece to emerge from the building. She closes her raw eyes and leans her head back. Her body aches to sleep, but her haranguing thoughts won't let her. In her lap, her hands are clenched into fists, her fingernails going from pink to white to mauve.

Purple fingernails.

Adele and I always used to share nail varnish when we were teenagers. She liked to paint her toenails, and I used to colour-in my fingertips, under the misguided impression that it made my long hands look less monkeyish. I remember how Adele once spent fifteen whole minutes selecting a shade of nail varnish from the array of little bottles at the big pharmacy in the mall. She'd asked Mom to take her there especially, so that she'd have the most options to choose from. The rich, bluish burgundy shade that Adele finally picked looked to me like dark, clotted blood, but from the satisfied look on her face I imagine it must've made her feel edgy and darkly alive.

She bought the nail varnish on the afternoon before her fourth date with Liam. I'd been numbering their encounters as closely as she had, so when I walked into the lounge to find her sitting in front of the TV but not seeing it, I knew she was waiting for night to fall. We were both counting the minutes till she would be with him again. I watched her from the doorway, saw how she kept glancing at her socked feet with

115

those freshly painted burgundy toenails beneath. Clearly, she was planning for Liam to see her naked feet. How much more of her nakedness was she going to share? The nail varnish was worldly-looking, dangerous. Sexy. My stomach clenched and then fluttered and then clenched again. The flickering light from the TV danced over my sister's face, but I couldn't read her expression. I wanted to know what she was thinking. Did she have the same breathless feeling in her chest that I got when I thought of him?

Suddenly, I jerked to life. I marched up to the sofa and ruffled her hair from behind.

'Sally!' she yelped, spinning in her seat to scowl at me. 'Come on, man.'

'What?' I was all innocence. I climbed over the back of the sofa and slid down to sit beside Adele. 'What's with the face, Addy?'

'My hair, you putz. I just blow-dried it.'

'It looks great.'

'Well, it did before you messed it up.'

'Oh please, it's fine.' I picked up the TV remote. My own hair was overdue for a wash. Adele wrinkled her pretty little nose. Could she smell it? 'I can't believe you're watching this drivel, Addy.' I changed the channel, turned up the volume.

'Oh my *God*.'

'What now?' I asked.

My sister had gone pale. She was staring at my fingers. Each one was tipped with a bluish burgundy nail. 'You used my new nail polish.'

'Oh yeah. I saw it in your room and thought

I'd give it a go. It's a bit hectic. I'm not sure what you were thinking with that one!'

Adele glared at me. The edges of her lips went white. I could see she was furious.

'What? You've never had an issue with me using your things before.' We shared clothes and make-up and books all the time, always had. Why was this so different? Why did I get the feeling she wanted to scream and slap the TV remote out of my hand?

Adele got up off the couch and stormed out of the room.

'What's up now, for goodness' sake?' I called after her. Adele didn't answer. I could hear her in the bathroom, hunting for something in the cabinet. Then there was a long silence. Even from the lounge I could smell the sickly acetone stench of nail polish remover.

★   ★   ★

Adele has been sitting in the car for over an hour. Her bottom feels numb, and her legs are stiff as she forces them to work the pedals. The car jerks out of the parking space, and Adele feels absurdly nervous, as if the teenager sitting in the passenger seat beside her has suddenly transformed into a driving instructor and is evaluating her every move. She glances across at Gigi and the misery on her young face is palpable. Adele fights the urge to reach over and stroke one of her clenched hands.

When they emerge from the underground parking and into the brilliant sunlight, she slips on her sunglasses, and the sensation of the plastic connecting with the bridge of her nose brings back that now familiar, over-full pulsating inside her temples. She wonders if Gigi also feels her grief in overwhelming waves of physical sensation, like a sickness.

But perhaps it's different for Gigi, because there's no guilt.

Adele grips the steering wheel as hard as she can and clenches the muscles in her belly to try and stop the regret from rising up to settle in its familiar spot at the back of her throat. Before her sister's death, Adele had no idea that the state of 'missing Monkey' had become an integral part of who she was, flavouring her every breath with a lemon-pip bitterness for nearly a decade. And now it all seems so ludicrous: all she had needed to do was to pick up the phone to end the ache; all those days, all those chances . . . but not any more. Now the taste is permanent. One day, she will die herself with its ugly sharpness still coating her tongue.

'I wish . . . ' Adele begins; stops. She clears her throat, hoping to dispel the embarrassing voice wobble. 'I wish we could share it, Gigi.'

Gigi's eyes don't move from her hands. She gives no indication that she's heard Adele at all.

'I mean, we've both lost someone we care about. Maybe it would be easier for us both if we could talk about your mom a bit. Share the memories we have of her.'

Gigi turns to Adele, her red-rimmed eyes almost metallic in their hardness. Her mouth twists.

118

You're right, Adele thinks. *I have no right to poach your memories after throwing her away like I did.*

Alongside the guilt that has taken up permanent residence inside her gut, there's a hollow new hunger for this girl to allow her in. As Adele steers the car through the boom gates of Cortona Villas, she resolves to do more, to try harder. Gigi must love her. She must.

Gigi stares out of the car window at the rows of immaculate, identical Tuscan-style houses slotted safely into their adjacent manicured gardens. None of the window frames are peeling, none of the door lintels are uneven, and the roofs are all neat geometric patterns of reddish clay tiles. At the farmhouse, tufts of greying straw were always slipping out of the thatch over the eaves. She loved walking around the house and pushing them back in, relishing the satisfaction as each reed slid back in to join its brothers. From the looks of it, nothing is out of place here in Cortona Villas.

Hidden behind their smooth blank walls, identical garden gates and electronic garage doors, each villa gives very little away . . . but there's something different about number 22. Gigi leans closer to the window, fighting the tug of the seat belt against her collarbone. Up against the electronic garage doors of number 22 is a pile of dusty twigs and leaves and those at the bottom of the heap look grey and crumbly with age. A pile like that would be quickly displaced by the constant opening and closing of the garage door, but instead, it has a staid, settled look about it. Number 22 Cortona Villas is vacant.

Gigi sits back into her seat and puffs out the breath she's been holding.

★   ★   ★

Gigi sleeps and dreams of dusty leaves.

Across the silent bedroom, Bryony squirms beneath her duvet. (She's got the cherry one tonight. Earlier, she ambushed Dora at her ironing board and left specific instructions to put it on *her* bed, and to let Gigi have the old one that once used to be on Tyler's. It has racing cars on it.)

The back of Bryony's neck is slick with sweat and her fingers clench and unclench at her sides. In her dreaming, the bedroom is hollow and huge, and someone, somewhere, is playing a tribal-sounding drum in a constant, irregular rhythm that sets her teeth on edge. Bryony dream-walks across the room to her cousin's bed. Two white feet are sticking out of the bottom of the bedding, their soles rimmed with orange sand. She pulls back the duvet: the bed is empty, save for two bloody torn-off shins with the feet attached.

She runs, screaming, searching for her mother, her father, Tyler, anyone! Room after room, corner after corner . . . the house is empty but for the throbbing drum. Finally, Bryony bursts out of the front door and into the night air, only to find that her way is blocked. It's Lesedi. The woman stands beneath the porch light dressed in

120

Aunty Sally's billowing purple pants, with ribbons of tapeworm draped across the skin of her bare chest and shoulders. Her face has been painted in some kind of white make-up, and when she grins, the tapeworms all lift their flat segmented heads and grin along with her. Lesedi opens her mouth to speak, and although Bryony is terrified, she knows that whatever is about to be said is very, very important.

Bryony wakes, rigid, with tears leaking from her eyes and into her hair. She huddles over on to her side and hides her face into the cool cotton cherries. Her heart is thumping, echoing the drum that pounded through her nightmare. She aches to get up and go to her parents' bedroom for comfort as she used to do, but for some reason she does not. She lies as still as she can, waiting for the thumping to stop and praying for morning to come.

11

The Wildings have started eating their dinner in the TV room, chewing their food in the flickering light of the screen in preference to the mortifying silence of the dinner table. Adele has instructed a mystified Dora to cook special recipes for Gigi from the new book she bought at Exclusives called *Vegan Delights*. Poor Dora, baffled by the notion of meat-free, keeps adding chicken stock in along with the pulses and vegetables because that is what she's always done, muttering to herself over chopped bringals and split red lentils about having to cook a whole extra dish every night for the grumpy girl who has never even said hello. Gigi doesn't notice that her dinner is tainted with death; since *that day*, death, it seems, is a flavour she's getting used to.

Tonight, the single-seater in the far corner of the TV room that Gigi usually chooses is occupied by a scowling Bryony. Liam and Adele share the one couch (pressed as far into the opposite sides of it as possible) and so Gigi has to sit beside Tyler on the other. He lounges with his legs sprawled wide, and his one bare knee keeps bumping into hers, wobbling the plate of mush that balances on her lap.

Gigi steadies the plate and glances across at him, but he's staring intently at the screen, and his floppy blond fringe hides his eyes. Gigi tries a small mouthful of her food, swallows it, takes another. Bump, bump goes Tyler's knee. She can feel the hairs on it, new man-leg hairs that tickle. She shifts her body as far away from the bumping as she can and, for a few minutes, eats in peace. Then the knee is back. Not a bump, this time, but a slow press of skin against skin. Gigi goes ice cold inside, and suddenly her mouth tastes as if it is full of blood. She tries to edge away from the knee, but the sofa arm hems her in.

She suddenly remembers how dusty her mother's splayed legs had looked in the afternoon sunlight as it had poured into the farmhouse kitchen through the open door. Her bare knees had been oddly fleshless, like those of a bird. A heron. Gigi fights the urge to hurl her plate to the floor and run from the room; instead she sits frozen but for the tears that slide down her cheeks and roll into her neck.

Bare legs; bright bloody smears on the bluish pale skin of her mother's skin.

Gigi starts to shake, and the fork rattling on her plate makes Tyler turn from the TV at last.

'Gigi?' His knee vanishes, leaving a cool patch on her leg below her shorts. His eyes go very wide when he sees the state she's in. 'Shit, are you OK?'

'Gi?' Liam jumps up from his seat and comes over to her, gently removing the rattling plate from her lap. 'Come, angel. It's all right, come here.' He cradles her back with his hands and helps her to her feet. When she puts her arms round him, her skin looks very white against the sun-baked brown of the back of Liam's neck.

Bryony, Adele and Tyler watch in silence as Liam leads the sobbing Gigi from the room. Over the sound of the TV they can hear him murmuring comfort to her as they climb the stairs together.

'Well, I guess it's a good thing that Gigi has *someone* in this house that she feels comfortable with,' Tyler mutters, placing his own unfinished plate of food on the floor beside Gigi's abandoned one. He rubs his hand over the knee that made contact with her smooth, warm leg. There's a strange, hot ache in his belly when he thinks of the girl's arms around his father's neck. He tightens his hands into fists.

'I mean, what's with the two of them anyway?' Tyler asks his mother. Adele's face is pink and her eyes very bright. 'How come she knows him better than the rest of us? Did Dad used to visit Aunty Sally and Gigi on that farm where they used to live?'

Adele finally swallows the lump of chicken that's been sitting in her mouth since Gigi began her sobbing fit. It leaves the same bitter taste that she's come to associate with guilt, but has now taken on a far more familiar flavour from her past: pungent, salty betrayal. She tasted it first the day, all those years ago, when Sally told her the truth and Adele banished her from the house. It was vivid on her tongue later that same evening when she'd made Liam promise her he'd never contact her sister again.

'Who the fuck knows,' she says and Tyler's eyebrows shoot up into his fringe.

On the single-seater chair in the corner,

Bryony pulls her legs up underneath her body and holds very tightly on to the edges of her dinner plate. The shadows have grown and thickened. They've seeped out from between the sofa cushions and ballooned out from the folds in the curtains, and even when she squeezes her eyes shut she can see them. *They're here to stay.*

★ ★ ★

Upstairs, Gigi sits on the racing-car duvet and sips on the glass of water that Liam has brought her.

'You feeling better now, Gigisaurus?' he asks, and she gives him a shaky nod in return. 'You're doing really well with all this, hey? Such a strong girl, just like your ma.'

'I don't feel strong.' Her fingers squeeze around the glass.

'Me neither.'

'You miss her, too?'

'Like crazy,' Liam whispers.

'Everything is so bloody stupid.' She's gripping the glass so tightly now that she can no longer feel it between her fingers. 'I just want to go back in time — '

She suddenly remembers the vegetable smell of the water beneath the deck as she spread out her yoga mat, then the open padlock and the gate swinging wide on its metal hinges . . .

'*Ja*,' Liam agrees, thinking back to when he still had a choice: Adele in her high-school uniform with her slanted eyes that promised secret, thrilling things; or Monkey in those funny

125

baggy T-shirts she used to wear to varsity, her own round eyes so sincere that looking into them had made him feel confused and uncomfortable inside his own skin. 'Doesn't work like that, I'm afraid, my girl.'

'I know that,' Gigi snaps. 'I was just saying.' She sets the glass down, hard, on the bedside table. The silence in the room is suddenly awkward. 'Shouldn't you go back downstairs to be with your family?'

'You're family too, Gigi . . . '

Gigi shrugs.

'But you're probably right. I'm in quite a bit of trouble.'

'Well, then perhaps you shouldn't have lied to them about not knowing me.' Gigi looks down at the bedding, tracing the outline of a racing car with one finger. She thinks of the soft, frightened look on Adele's face that keeps emerging from behind her kind smiles. 'I'm not stupid, you know. I've noticed.'

'Look, things are complicated — '

'You grown-ups just love that word, don't you? It's like an excuse for everything.'

'Gigi? I don't — '

'Mom always used to use it after you left the farm after one of your *visits* and I would ask her why she was crying.'

'Crying?' Liam takes a step towards the bed, and then stops. He suddenly doesn't know what to do with his hands.

'She would be all fine and busy with the animals and meditating with me sometimes and stuff, and then you would come and it was like starting all over again for her. Back to the beginning when she was all messed up. You should've just left her the hell alone.'

Liam sways a little on his feet. All the blood seems to have drained out of his head.

'What was the point? I mean why did you keep coming anyway? You guys never had an affair or anything even though you were like nuts about each other. You never even held hands. I know. I used to spy on you.' Liam opens his mouth to speak but nothing comes out. 'Pathetic.'

'Shut up,' he snaps out at last. 'You don't have a clue about half the stuff you're talking about.'

Gigi dips her head to hide the fresh brimming tears. *All those visits and never there when she needed you. Not there when the men came in.* She doesn't want to cry again. She hates herself for crying again. She reaches down deep within for the strange new hardness that has begun to grow there, and slips inside it where all is numb and still and black.

Liam no longer sees the girl hunched over on the bed in front of him. He battles for breath, vision swimming, and waits for the frantic rise and fall of his chest to calm before leaving the room. He pauses on the landing, and then wipes his sweating palms on his shirt and heads back down the stairs.

★ ★ ★

Gigi's outburst releases me, and although I know the respite will be brief before I have to enter the fleshy mess in the Wilding house once more, I flee back to northern Limpopo where the air tastes thick and sweet and vibrates with insect buzz and the liquid burp of frogs. Although I still can't get home, I surrender to the memory of it. I can see exactly how Gigi looked at ten as she dragged Liam off to see the tiny pawpaw tree she'd nursed into a sprout from the glossy discarded pips of a long-ago breakfast. He'd barely have time to extract himself from the car and she'd be on him: grabbing his arm, grinning up at him, jumping up and down at the sight of him, all the things that I longed to do, but couldn't.

'You know how I don't have a dad?' she'd begun after we'd waved him off once again, and stood together in the stillness left behind by his latest car. 'So does that mean I can choose one?'

'Well, you've got loads of dads here, hon,' I said, sliding the padlock through the two ends of the heavy chain around the gatepost and clicking it shut. 'There's Seb, and Phineas, and Johan, and even Hugh.'

She pulled a face. 'I don't even know Hugh. He's only been here like a few days, Ma.' She took my hand and we started to walk back up the long drive (which was really only two ruts cut by car tyres through the ever-encroaching vegetation). 'And he'll leave again, just like the other overseas people.'

'True.' Simone was always inviting fellow inner-peace searchers to live with us and volunteer at the shelter for a while. The foreigners loved it on the farm with the animals and the quiet, and would always leave brown from the sun, and skinny from all the vegetables and beans and physical work, promising to return. 'OK, not Hugh then.'

'But the others aren't my real dad either.'

I had only known Gigi's real father for two weeks, a silly holiday romance in Cape Town that ended with a bout of nausea and a panicked trip to the chemist for a do-it-yourself test. I remember Adele's expression at the news, her cry of *Oh Monkey, you did it on purpose, I bet! Ever since Tyler was born you've been dying for a mini-monkey of your own.*

'No, but that doesn't really matter, Gi, they love you just the same.' The sun baked down on us, and I could feel the moisture springing out at the base of my skull and making my head itch.

'Can I have Uncle Liam for my dad, then?' My hand was boiling in Gigi's grip. I longed to pull it away from her, but forced my fingers to relax.

'He's already your uncle, silly-billy. He can't be both.'

'Oh.'

My feet kept skidding around on the sweaty rubber soles of my flip-flops, and my toes were coated with fine red powder from the dusty path. I huffed out a breath of silent frustration.

'Are you cross, Ma?' Those little wet fingers pressed and tugged.

'No.'

'You *look* cross.'

'I'm just hot, Gigi, for goodness' sake. Let's get a move on, shall we?'

'You're always so grumpy when Uncle Liam leaves.' She let go of my hand and for a second it felt cool and free.

'Well, so are you, Miss So-and-so.'

'*Ja*, but you're *much* worse than I am.' Her feet stamped in the dust, and a baby acacia sapling with a full coating of thorns snapped beneath her sandal and scraped hard over the top of my foot.

'For Christsakes, child. Now look — '

'Don't swear, Ma. Right words and right action, remember?' The thorn scrape stung as it filled with salty sweat.

'Don't you start quoting the frigging Buddha at me, Gigi, I'm not in the mood,' I hissed, and she sucked in her breath and stormed ahead, arms folded across her chest.

'Maybe I can just choose my mom as well, then,' she muttered.

I kept forcing one leg in front of the other through the stifling afternoon. Gigi stomped up the veranda steps ahead of me, but I stopped just short of the beckoning shade. The itch of incessant heat crawled all over my skin.

12

The Wilding house is filled with the restless quiet of no one sleeping. Tyler has thrown off his bedcovers, but is still somehow too hot. Maddening slicks of sweat glue his body to the sheet, and although the window is wide open, he can find no relief from whatever it is that burns inside him.

In the adjacent room, Gigi lies on her back with her eyes squeezed shut and her hands clenched into fists and Bryony blinks at the dark, trying to swallow down the rising certainty that the shadows in the room are deepening. *Stop being silly, Bryony.* But they are. Over on Gigi's side of the room, the darkness has intensity and weight, and when Bryony slides out of bed, she has to edge her way past it to get to the door and the relief of the upstairs landing.

She stands for a moment, feeling the familiar itch of the carpet beneath her toes and staring at the vague shapes of doorways in the gloom. She can just about read the 'Keep Out' on Tyler's, and make out the chip in the paint of the bathroom door from the time last year when she bashed into it when taking a forbidden ride on his skateboard. Her parents' door is a blank oblong at the end of the landing that gives nothing away. She takes a step towards it, and then freezes when she hears a noise from downstairs.

Suddenly, last night's nightmare is vivid once more, and her heart squeezes still before speeding up to a thundering madness. Lesedi draped in segmented tapeworms. The thumping of an unseen drum.

She almost darts back into the bedroom, ready to dive under the warm duvet and tuck it tight over her head, but the memory of Gigi's bloody, legless dream-feet stops her cold. Bryony turns and, with her arms folded into a shield across her chest, tiptoes to the top of the staircase and peers down it. The porch light shines through the blocks of glass on either side of the front door and makes yellow patterns on the hallway tiles. She heads downstairs towards the relief of that light, but just as she reaches it, the noise happens again and Bryony gasps.

There's someone in the TV room! She tries to quieten her breath but she seems to need to suck in more and more, and it rasps in and out like a hurricane.

'Addy?' someone says.

'Dad?' Bryony follows her father's voice, lightheaded with relief. 'Dad, why are you still up . . . '

And then she sees the bed made up on the couch. She recognizes the pillow from her parents' bedding set. Her father blinks up at her from beneath one of the sleeping bags that she and Dommie use for their sleepovers. His hair is all messed up on the one side, sticking up in a little cockatiel tuft over his left ear.

'It's OK, Bry,' he says, shifting himself up to sitting and giving her a weak smile.

'But why are you . . . why aren't you sleeping upstairs with Mom?'

'We had a little fight, darling, but don't worry, everything will be all right.'

Bryony shifts her weight from foot to foot and wishes that she'd come downstairs to find a burglar instead. Or even a witch doctor covered in disgusting tapeworms. Somehow this is worse.

'What are you doing up, Bry?'

Bryony wants to tell of the nightmare bloodied feet, but her father, with his mysterious connection to her cousin, has become a stranger lately, and telling him something so private is suddenly impossible. *Maybe this is how Mom is feeling. Maybe that's why Dad's sleeping down here.*

'Are you and Mom going to get a divorce?'

'Don't be daft, Bry, it's just one little night on the couch in years and years of good stuff. Sometimes people don't get on so well for a bit, but it doesn't mean anything. You'll understand when you're older.' He rubs a hand across his head, but the tuft springs straight back up again. 'Now back to bed, young lady.'

'I don't want to go back to the bedroom. Gigi is . . . ' Bryony rubs her hands over her goose-bumpy arms and thinks of the clotted darkness over Gigi's bed.

'Gigi is what?'

'Nothing.'

'Come on, off you go. It's late, my girly.'

'I know.'

'Goodnight, Bry.'

'Goodnight, Dad.'

But rather than going straight back to bed, Bryony goes upstairs and crouches outside her parents' bedroom door. She leans her forehead against the painted wood and thinks of her mother behind it, alone in the vast bed. She remembers how Adele looked like a patch of dense shadow that morning of the funeral, and how her irritating tears seemed to threaten to dissolve her away completely. The crying for Aunty Sally has stopped now, but the tears seem to have evaporated away something vital inside her mother, leaving less of her behind.

Bryony tries to remember what things were like before her cousin came to stay, but she just cannot.

★ ★ ★

I wait with Bryony outside the door in the dark passageway, and think back to the way Adele looked the day I tore my turquoise skirt.

She had just had her hair cut into a new style that feathered around her face, softening the angle of her jaw, and making her big eyes seem to slant upwards even more. I remember watching my beautiful sister cut sandwiches into triangles as I tugged at the open edge of my wraparound skirt which, just that morning, had seemed so pretty and radiant a thing to wear. Beside her well-cut trousers and white cotton blouse it now looked daft and childish, like something pulled from a dressing-up box. A familiar hot wash of jealousy jumped into my mouth, and I grabbed a Romany Cream from

134

the pile she'd laid out on a plate for the girls and jammed it in to help push the feeling back down again. Choking on chocolaty biscuit crumbs, I went to the cupboard and got out the tea things. I knew the layout of the kitchen as if it was my own. It was always like this when we were growing up, I was as much in her room as I ever was in mine. I remember how I used to try on every new item of clothing that she ever bought, regularly going through her cupboards to find the items still with their tags on. She never minded — or, at least, she never told me that she did. Was I ever going to grow up and stop thinking that all of Adele's things were a little bit mine, too?

He'd married *her*, for heaven's sake.

The sound of Gigi and Bryony's giggling rose to a crescendo in the adjacent room as my daughter taught her younger cousin some new thrilling game.

'Sounds like those two are going to be great pals,' Adele said.

'Let's hope nothing gets in the way.' I plonked the cups and saucers on the countertop and reached back into the cupboard for the teapot.

'What do you mean?'

'Oh you know, boys and things.'

'Heavens, I should think that they've got some time before boys become an issue, Monkey.' She laughed as the water gushed from the tap into the kettle. I tried to laugh too, but I couldn't. Suddenly, there was no way I could hold it in any more. My heart thumped.

'Did you know, Adele?' My voice came out

135

light despite the furious ache behind it. My sister turned to me and smiled.

'Did I know what, hon?'

'That I was in love with him?'

'What on earth are you talking about?' Her smile slipped a little.

'Liam. I'm talking about Liam.' I gave my head a little shake as if it was nothing, but my heart was galloping in my throat in the wake of my unexpected words.

'You were in love with Liam?' She sets the full kettle down on the side of the sink with a clatter. 'When?'

'Oh, it was just when he and I were in university. Forget about it. Ancient history.' My laugh was brittle and ridiculous.

'Did you feel like this after he and I got together?'

'Ag, leave it, Addy, I shouldn't have said anything.' Perhaps from speaking the truth that I'd nursed in secret for so long, my jaw seemed numb and oddly disconnected from the rest of me. I watched my sister's fingers, with their lovely manicured nails, clutching around the white plastic body of the kettle. They shook, and a small splash leapt out from the spout and landed on her top, turning a patch of the delicate white fabric see-through. The pink of her skin glowed through it.

'Sally?' Adele's eyes looked enormous, too big for her head.

'I shouldn't have mentioned it. I don't know what got into me.' I battled to force a smile out; failed.

'Did he and you ever . . . did you . . . ' She placed the kettle down on the countertop, and something in that careful movement of her arm, the sliding of her muscles beneath her creamy skin, made me want to reach out and snap it in half.

So I hurt her with words instead: 'We kissed once.'

I remembered the feeling of his mouth on mine as if it was yesterday. His half-closed eyes with their gold lashes were so large and vivid in close-up.

It was two years since we'd first met in English Lit. Adele had finished high school and she and Liam had been living together in a rented garden cottage for almost a month. Without my sister, it was just me and Mom rattling around at home, and I'd often find myself overwhelmed by sudden waves of frustration. I hated the house without my dad in it, even though he'd been dead for over two years; I hated my bedroom with its styleless mix of childhood and teenage detritus that seemed to have no bearing on the person I wanted to be; and I hated Adele's room for being so empty. I'd find myself wandering through it, picking up items and then putting them down again, lost in the familiar place I'd grown up in.

Campus was no better. Every time I spotted Liam, I was breathless all over again, and then furious at myself for being so. Simone kept trying to set me up with other guys, but I was hopeless at pretending I was interested, and each feeble encounter fizzled into nothing. And then, late one afternoon after lectures, I bumped into Liam in the corridor.

'Hey, we haven't hung out in ages.' He grinned at me. 'I guess since Addy and I got that place together, it's been . . . I miss you, Monks. Come on, let's get a drink.'

Two hours later, we stumbled out of the campus bar clutching each other and laughing about nothing as we made our way to his car.

'My Monkey,' he said, despite the fact that I wasn't his at all and he was already hers. 'I wonder if I've picked the wrong sister.'

'Liam.' His name was liquid in my mouth as I fell against him and inhaled the giddy-making special scent of Liam armpit and masculine deodorant. 'You're being silly.'

'Am I?' He stopped walking and turned me round to face him. He was no longer grinning. My heart shuddered. Little darts of heat spiked between my legs and then we were kissing. The moment his tongue was in my mouth I wanted all of him everywhere and I knew I'd never be over him. With a small jolt of shock, I realized I would have him, steal him, if I could, even whilst he was my sister's.

When he pulled away, I was voiceless. I could barely move. 'Need a lift home, Monkey?' I shook my head, and he drove off and it was over. Just like that.

I wonder if I've picked the wrong sister. It was enough to give me hope.

'You kissed Liam?' Adele's voice was sharp-edged now.

'Well, no, actually . . . ' Just once, I wanted to

be the one with the guy in love with me and not her. 'He kissed me.' I wanted her to ache as I'd been aching. 'And it was a real kiss,' I added, 'enough to make me think he felt the same way as I did, if you really want to know.'

Adele curled her arms over her partly see-through top and took a step backwards, knocking into one of the barstools. Suddenly, I wanted to breathe the words back in.

'How could . . . ' She blinked at me. 'I don't . . . ' She hugged herself tighter. 'One kiss? That was it?'

'Yes.' For a second I hoped she was going to laugh it off, to turn back to the tea-making and carry on as if I'd never spoken. But the little sneer that curled the corner of her mouth told me that nothing was ever going to be the same again.

'Poor old Monkey. I bet you wanted him to carry on, didn't you? You wanted to shag him. You didn't even care that he was with me, did you, you fucking slut?' Her voice cracked with fury, and her face fired up to a vicious pink.

'It wasn't like — '

'Ever since we were kids, you've always been wanting what *I've* got, always trying to insinuate yourself into every little part of my life without actually getting on with your own.'

I staggered backwards as if I'd been slapped. I wanted to grab her, shake her, stop her, but the stinging truth of her words paralysed me.

'You still want him, don't you? After all these years, after *everything?*'

The question came as such a shock that I

couldn't lie fast enough to make it stick. I just stood, speechless.

'So tell me, Sally' — her voice became low and menacing — 'what exactly *are* you doing here in my house every bloody afternoon?'

'I come to see you. The girls love playing together.' This was the truth, but I could see that it no longer mattered. For a long, silent moment, we just stared at each other.

'Sweet silly Sally,' Adele said. 'Harmless little Monkey. What a pile of shit. You're a sneaky, conniving bitch, aren't you? Look what you've done. Look what you're doing right now.'

'I was never sweet *or* silly,' I shot back. 'It's only *you* who thought that. In your opinion, I've always been nothing more than a sideshow to your fabulous fucking amazingness. Perfect little tarty Adele, getting everything she always wants, using Sally when it suits her, but only if she stays in her place in the shadows so that you can strut your stuff in the centre of the bloody stage.'

'You'd like to think that, wouldn't you? You'd like to think you matter, but you're a joke, Sally. Your whole existence is a pathetic joke. Waiting around for years for Liam to notice you? What a waste of a life.'

I gaped at her, suspended over nothing but blackness as the floor spun down and away from me. 'You don't mean that?'

She opened her mouth to speak, but paused when we heard the front door open and close, then fast, hard footsteps coming towards the kitchen.

'Hey, pretty ladies.' Adele and I both turned as

Liam strode into the room and straight through to the laundry. 'Had to pop home quick before that meeting . . . got some bloody thing or other on the front of my shirt. Typical.' We could hear him moving around in the laundry. 'Did Dora iron the blue one with the little stripes, Addy?' Both of us were breathing hard, as if we'd just run a race. Liam walked back into the room and then froze when he saw the looks on our faces. 'What . . . '

'Sally just told me, Liam. About the time you kissed her.'

Liam looked at me, and for the first time since it happened, I could tell that he remembered that kiss too. For an unguarded moment, the hot, wonderful, guilty memory of it was written all over his face.

For years I'd been waiting for that look, that acknowledgement of his desire for me, but now it was the final blow that brought my world crashing: when I glanced at Adele, it was clear that she'd seen it too. She tried to step backwards, but she was trapped by the kitchen counter. She covered her mouth with a trembling hand as the other one waved at her side, as if she was trying to push the truth away, send it back where it came from. Liam looked from me to Adele and back again, panicked.

Adele burst into tears. Liam and I both started forward on an automatic impulse to comfort her, and then both stopped. From beyond the kitchen, we could hear Gigi's sweet voice and Bryony's toddler laugh. Nobody moved.

'My whole family,' Adele sobbed. 'My whole

goddamn life. That's what you're trying to destroy here.' I wasn't sure if she was speaking to me or Liam. From the look on his face, it was clear he wasn't either. Then she turned to me. 'But I'm not going to let you.' The tears had stopped as fast as they'd appeared. She wiped her wet cheeks with the back of her wrist. 'Get out.'

'What? Adele, don't be daft, you've got nothing to worry about.'

'Out.'

'Addy, listen to me . . . ' But the crying pink had drained from her face leaving it pale and frozen-looking. 'I don't want to wreck your family, you *know* I don't.'

She drew herself up. She looked vast, immovable. 'You're never to come back here, do you understand?'

'You're really throwing me out?'

'Go and live your sad little life somewhere far away from mine.'

'Jesus, Addy!'

'I mean it.'

'But we're family — '

'Please. Like 'family' matters so much to you?' she hissed. 'You've obviously been dreaming of wrecking mine for years.'

'That's absolutely not — '

'Don't you ever come anywhere near me or my kids or Liam again.'

The finality of her words seemed to stop time. For a moment, Adele and Liam and the whole room solidified into a vast, unified entity whilst all the bits that made me, me — bones, heart, blood and skin — began dissolving away to nothing.

A spasm of sobs shook me where I stood. Adele's expression didn't change; her eyes were ice. I looked to Liam, but he was staring at the floor by his feet.

'This can't be happening.'

'Get Gigi and go. Now.'

And so I turned and ran, turquoise wrap-around skirt flying, out of the kitchen, through the front hallway and into the lounge to wrench my daughter from her game. One of my feet skidded on a small plastic animal that was lying on the Persian rug beside Bryony's chubby knee, and I nearly went crashing to the floor.

Later that evening, after I had scrunched up my shredded skirt and thrown it into the dustbin, I noticed that my ankle was swollen up from where I'd twisted it. I bent down, with my face so close to the bin that the smell of rot almost choked me, and pressed my fingers into the tender puffy flesh as hard as I could.

13

'Tyler.' Bryony leaps up the stairs after her brother and jams one of her feet into the gap before he can close his bedroom door on her. The door bounces off the hard leather of her school shoe and she's glad that, for once, she didn't take them off in the car on the way home.

'What?' Tyler asks with an impatient frown.

'I don't want to go into my room,' Bryony whispers.

'Gigi won't bite, you know. She's a vegetarian, remember?'

'Oh, ha ha.'

'Come on, Bry, you're being daft. Just ignore her.'

'You wouldn't say that if she was in *your* room all the time,' Bryony hisses.

Tyler's face goes pink. 'Look, just deal, OK? I've got homework to do,' he says, and kicks her foot out of the way before closing the door.

Bryony stands in the middle of the landing and takes a long, slow breath. Usually, she would just have to endure Gigi's presence long enough to grab some clothes before racing outside to spy on Lesedi, but after their encounter beneath the fever tree the other day, and then the ghastly nightmare, the mere thought of seeing her neighbour makes her want to throw up. Her toes squeak against each other as she wiggles them inside her shoes.

She glares at Tyler's irritating 'Keep Out' sign for a moment before suddenly clenching her fists, pivoting round on her heels and marching into her bedroom.

Gigi is not there.

Bryony stops short and stares at the racing-car duvet cover on the spare bed; it is smooth and flat for the first time, quite clearly a product of Dora's expert bed-making skills. Gigi is not on it, or under it, or curled up under her own bed (Bryony checks to make sure) or in the cupboard or hiding behind the curtains.

A laugh bubbles out of her as she kicks off her shoes, tugs off her socks and flings herself down on to the carpet. She raises her feet into the shaft of sun that burns through the window and smiles at the way the edges of her toes turn transparent pink against the light.

★   ★   ★

Gigi goes from room to warm, empty room, leaving a trail of flip-flop footprints in the fine layer of dust that coats the floorboards. In the absence of occupants and furniture in the empty unit of number 22 Cortona Villas, the wood seems to have exhaled its essence into the air and the whole place smells of sun-soaked timber. Gigi breathes in deeply, reminded of the smell of thatch back home.

Breaking in was easy. The garden gate had been left unlocked so that the Body Corporate garden service can continue to keep the lawn mowed and the pool clean, and the second Gigi had closed it behind her, she'd had more than enough time and seclusion to scour the outside of the house for a possible way in. One of the windows in the kitchen had not been properly latched. She'd pushed against it to loosen the catch and then pulled it open and wriggled through the small gap on to the cool granite kitchen counter, jumping to the floor with a soft slap of flip-flop on tile.

And now number 22 Cortona Villas is hers.

After exploring the ground floor, Gigi climbs the stairs, marvelling that even though the house has a layout identical to that of the Wildings, without any furniture or curtains it seems vast and echoey. Upstairs, she goes from room to room, peering out of the windows and opening cupboards, lightheaded with the relief of being alone and unobserved at last.

(But she isn't unobserved, of course. Fleshless and endless and still strangely free of feeling, I am at my daughter's side.)

Finally, she sits down in the corner of the large, sunny master bedroom, figuring that should anyone wander into the garden below, she'll be invisible up here. The moment that she stops moving, however, Gigi feels strange, as if all her veins and nerves are still in motion beneath her skin. She scratches her arms. She pulls on the ends of her hair and rubs the rubbery-feeling skin on her face before dropping her head into her hands.

Everything itches.

A stripe of cool shadow inches across the room and slowly slides across her body.

But still, Gigi burns.

Using a sharp splinter of meranti pulled from a piece of damaged skirting board, Gigi slowly pierces a number of angry, aching lines on the skin of one calf. Dots of blood seep out of the raw carvings, and she tries to rub them away so they won't stain her jeans when she rolls them back down.

The sound of engines filtering in from the faux street outside has been steadily intensifying as large, glossy cars return home to their identical garages. She knows she needs to leave. With shaking fingers, Gigi wipes the splinter clean, tucks it back into the patch where she pulled it from the skirting board, and gets to her feet.

She goes downstairs on legs numb with pins and needles, and slips back out of the kitchen window of number 22 just as the sky is starting to go powdery grey on the edges. She hovers behind the garden gate, waiting for a pause in the homecoming traffic before easing it open and darting out of the tiny gap.

Feigning a casual evening stroll, she heads back in the direction of the Wilding house, unaware that her exit has not gone unnoticed. Lesedi, sitting in the passenger seat of her husband's GTi as they head out to Spar to buy the milk that she forgot to get earlier, turns her head just in time to see the girl shut the gate of number 22 behind her. Lesedi notices her skinny arms and clenched fists and the dust patterning the child's jeans, and narrows her eyes at the hurt she can sense beneath.

Then Lesedi sees me.

I am the sharp hooves of goats trotting along a dusty mountain track and the whisper of hot wind in the slender, knotted limbs of the fynbos shrub.

And then the GTi moves on.

★ ★ ★

In an effort to become more likeable, Adele promised herself that if Gigi returned safely, she wouldn't ask where she'd been. So, despite the fact that she has spent the last hour in a state of white-lipped terror at the girl's mysterious absence, all she says when Gigi walks through the front door and into the entrance hall is: 'Dora's been making you a butternut risotto for supper. Sounds yummy, hey?'

Gigi does not look at her aunt. She shifts from foot to dusty foot, clearly desperate to dash upstairs and burrow into her bed once more, but Adele has placed herself at the bottom of the stairs, and stands like a linen-clad, quivering barrier to entry.

'I think I might even have some of it myself instead of what the rest of them are eating.' The cheery words sound ridiculous the moment they are out of her mouth. Adele bites her lip.

'I kind of need the loo,' Gigi mutters.

'Oh,' says Adele, her resolve slipping, and allows Gigi to edge past her to get to the stairs. The girl smells of dust and timber.

'There was a call for you while you were out,' Adele says, and Gigi freezes.

'A call?'

'A long-distance one. From overseas.'

'Simone!' Gigi turns round and her cheeks flush. 'Is she going to call back? Did you get her number? Can I speak to her?'

Adele takes a step backwards. The naked neediness on Gigi's usually impassive face is startling. 'I didn't know when you'd be back,' Adele says pointedly, 'so I told her to call again tomorrow.'

Gigi nods and blinks away tears.

'You've got an appointment with Dr Rowe in the morning . . . ' Adele continues. She wants to add: So don't pull a vanishing act, but she just smiles. ' . . . so I told Simone to call around lunchtime.'

'OK.' Gigi turns away and starts to climb the stairs once more. She grips the banister. There's a circle of brown dirt on each knuckle, and some dried blood around her fingernails from when she wiped it off her leg.

'It's the same Simone that was friends with Sal when we were kids, you know,' Adele calls after her, trying to engage her niece in a little more conversation. 'I knew her when she was growing up. She was always a real sweetie.'

Gigi pauses for a moment, and then continues up the stairs.

* * *

Simone.

When I arrived at the Limpopo farm with all my bags, clutching an over-used, soggy tissue in

149

one hand and my daughter's dimpled fingers in the other, Simone swooped Gigi up in her arms and hustled her off to show her around, leaving me some much-needed space to sob myself senseless in my dressing gown inside my new, strange bedroom.

She ran the sanctuary, organized volunteers and fund-raising, talked to the local farmers and rural communities about conservation, cooked for the humans, prepared food for the animals, cleaned out cages, drove all over Limpopo to collect injured creatures, and still had energy to sit for hours into the night and talk to me when I needed it. I remember how tender she was with my daughter when, clutching a small, stiff, rust-feathered body in her palm, she sobbed over her first loss: the sudden death of the hoepoe chick she'd been hand-rearing.

Exactly one year after our arrival, another bedraggled female in need of rescue found her way to the sanctuary. She was a young serval with a gold coat spotted with black, enormous ears and a mangled hind leg. Her mother had been killed by a trap just a few metres away from the one in which she'd been found.

After she'd been stitched up, the serval kitten, whom Gigi had promptly named Jemima, slept in Simone and Seb's room so they could bottle feed her every three hours. On the second morning of her stay, Jemima developed a horrible infection, and Simone's care duties suddenly doubled with dressing changes, medicines and monitoring. She must've been exhausted, but you'd never have known it. She

150

still looked fresh-faced and lively, and whizzed around as usual, tending to various tasks, and then dashing indoors to feed and comfort the squealing cat.

'Hey, Mones, why don't I take over Jemima duties for a bit,' I said one afternoon as we cleaned out an enclosure that had housed the black-backed vulture with a damaged wing that we'd released back into the wild that morning. There were droppings on top of droppings on every surface: a thick crust of stinking white. 'Just to give you a break for a few days.'

'Oh no, don't take her away from me.' Simone smiled and wiped her wet face with the back of her wrist. 'It's so rare that I get to treat any of these guys as pets.' Most often, we had to keep our distance as much as possible. Animals that are too familiar with humans are especially vulnerable in the wild, but Jemima's injuries would prevent her from ever being able to fend for herself out there. She was here to stay. 'I'd be bereft without my serval cuddles.' I thought of Jemima's small fuzzy face and large appealing eyes and felt a little pang.

'Well, then let me finish up here. You go and have a cup of tea and chill, or something.'

'That sounds — ' She was interrupted by a loud wail and the appearance of a sobbing Gigi.

'I fell.' There was a large bloody scrape in the smear of dust coating her left knee.

'Oh dear!' Simone dropped her scrubbing brush and we both went to Gigi's side. I inspected her knee. Nothing a plaster wouldn't fix.

'How did this happen?' At my question, Gigi pointed a shaking finger towards the paddock. 'I told you not to try and ride Polonius again until Seb organized that saddle from the van Rooyens.' This was not the first Polonius-related injury in the past few days. 'Goodness, Gi, we've got enough wounded creatures to worry about without little girls going and doing daft things to themselves every two seconds.'

'It's *not* every two seconds,' she howled at me. 'And it hurts.'

'Polonius is an old dear, but he's still a great big animal, Gi. You're going to have to promise your mom and me to stay away from him until we get that saddle, OK?' Simone wiped tears and orange dirt from my daughter's cheeks with the hem of her T-shirt. 'Seb will give you some proper lessons, I'm sure. All right, peachy-pie, let's go and get you cleaned up.'

'I've also hurt my elbow, see?'

'Ow, that looks nasty. Come on, time for a bit of Savlon and some Rescue Remedy.' Simone hugged Gigi and looked at me. 'Unless your mom . . . '

'I'm sure Gigi's in the best possible hands.' I picked up the scrubbing brush. 'I'll stay on vulture poo detail.'

'Thanks, Sal.' She took Gigi's hand. 'Gi, you'd better watch to make sure I don't put the Rescue on your knee and the Savlon in your mouth!'

Gigi laughed through her tears, and let herself be guided towards the house.

When Jemima was older and had moved out into a large enclosure of her own, I spent as much time with her as I could. She was affectionate and playful, and seemed to be an even better salve for my hidden wounds than those Simone could administer with her talks and tea. I remember sitting beside Jemima's long body and watching Simone and Gigi chatting together about something over by the kitchen door. How was it that Gigi seemed to fit so well into the curve of Simone's arms? Unlike Jemima, who was deliciously yielding beneath my hands, whenever I held Gigi, we were somehow all angles.

What will Simone say to soothe her now?

14

At four in the morning, Bryony is dragged from deep sleep. She lies alert, wondering what could've woken her. Then she hears a strange, long, deep hiss of breath. She forces her eyes to open and blinks across the room, waiting for the dawn shadows to resolve into shapes she can recognize.

Gigi is out of her bed, hunched on the carpet in a painful-looking, twisted position. She does more of that weird breathing and moves into another position, and then another. It looks to Bryony like her cousin is doing some kind of peculiar dance, breathing like Angel at school (who has sinus issues) with each bend and stretch. Bryony holds herself motionless and watches in silence, fascinated.

Then all of a sudden, in the middle of a move that involves standing on one leg with the other stuck up in the air behind her, Gigi slumps down on to the carpet. Her straight spine droops, and she holds her hanging head with fingers that grip her scalp like claws.

'Why am I bothering?' It is a furious whisper. Bryony holds her breath.

'Everything is bullshit.' Gigi's fingers tighten into fists and she bangs them on the sides of her temples, again and again. It looks like Gigi is trying to smash her head open like an egg. Bryony squirms beneath her bedding, wondering how to make it stop without letting on that she's been watching. The fists keep pounding.

Bryony lets out an enormous fake sleep-sigh and makes a noisy performance of turning over in her bed. She stares at the wall and listens hard; all she can hear from the room behind her now are gasping, shuddering breaths. There are no more head-smashing sounds. It must've worked.

Bryony closes her eyes, but the image of her cousin banging her hands into her skull keeps repeating on the inside of her eyelids.

★   ★   ★

The entire car ride back from Dr Rowe's office, Gigi jiggles and shifts in her seat until Adele feels mildly bilious. She is relieved when they pull into the garage and Gigi shoots like a cannonball out of the passenger seat and into the house. Adele stays in the car with her seat belt still on and closes her eyes.

She tightens her hold on the ignition key, feeling its sharp ridges and smooth plastic pressing into her flesh. She doesn't need to open her eyes to slide the key back into the ignition because the action is so automatic and familiar. It slots into place with a click.

She turns the key and the engine hums back to life.

Adele opens her eyes and stares at her fingers curving over the steering wheel. She gives the accelerator pedal a tiny little push with her right foot, and the car whines eagerly in response. She

155

bites the side of her lip until it stings and swells, and then, very quickly, she turns off the engine once more, undoes her seat belt, and lurches out of the car on unsteady legs. She closes the car door with great care, and leans on it for a moment before heading into the house.

She walks with her back very straight.

★ ★ ★

When the phone finally rings, Gigi, who has been sitting beside it for the past half-hour, nearly jumps out of her skin. She lifts the receiver with both hands as if scared of dropping it.

'Hello?'

'Is that Gigi?' At the sound of Simone's voice, Gigi clutches the phone tighter and rocks back and forth. Tears gallop down her cheeks and plop on to her T-shirt.

'It's me,' she finally answers. 'Hi, Simone.' Gigi hears Simone blow her nose loudly with a Scottish tissue.

'So you're staying with Liam's family, Gi?' Simone asks in a voice that doesn't sound quite right. Maybe it's the long-distance line.

'Ja. In Joburg. I miss home, though, Mones.'

'Me too. Scotland is freezing. You just wouldn't believe how cold. I've been doing my morning yoga in my winter pyjamas with a tracksuit over them, a beanie *and* a scarf. Can you picture it?'

'Ja.' But Gigi can't; she's suddenly not sure what Simone looks like at all. She forces the fractured bits from her memories together: smooth brown hair, dark blue eyes that are sometimes green, a scattering of dark freckles on thin, tanned shoulders from being in the sun too much, and the smell of geranium oil. Gigi doesn't think she's ever seen Simone in anything resembling a beanie and a scarf.

'Oh, and I thought you might like to know that the animals are all doing really well in their new homes.'

'New homes?' Gigi draws her feet up on to the couch. 'They're not at the farm any more?' She'd been imagining that all their charges at the sanctuary have been looked after all this time by Phineas and Lettie, possibly with help from various conservationists from the surrounding reserves who'd always been popping round for some reason or other.

'No,' Simone says. She blows her nose again. 'Luckily, I managed to sort out various different relocation arrangements for them. The folks in the area have really rallied. They've been so kind.' Simone's voice wavers a little. 'Polonius is still with Phineas, though.'

Gigi is silent. She cannot picture the farm without the animals on it. Just about every moment of every day up until *that one* had revolved around their care. *Did someone take the mice?* Without Jemima and the other predators to keep their numbers down, they could be breeding ferociously. She winces at the mental image of the mice becoming a furry, writhing mass pressed up against the wire mesh of their cage.

'Gigi?'

157

'*Ja.*'

'Was it . . . Are you . . . ' Simone takes a big, shuddering breath. 'They told me you weren't hurt, that you weren't there when they . . . I'm so glad, sweetie.'

'*Ja.*' Gigi forces a dry swallow.

'And you're getting some help which is good. Dr Rowe, is it?'

'How do you know?'

'I spoke to your Aunt Adele yesterday when I called.'

'Yes, well, I've just come back from him, now,' Gigi says, not mentioning that, once again, she'd refused to speak to the psychiatrist. *Sometimes, refusing to open up in any way can cause an unmanageable build-up of pain inside, Gigi. Think of it like a poison. A wound that if not cleaned out will turn septic.*

'That's good, Gi. I'm a great believer in therapy.'

'So you talked to Adele?'

'*Ja.* We knew each other as kids, you know, when I was friends with your mom. She was so little the first time I met her. She used to call me Sea-Moan, like I was some kind of sea monster.' Simone lets out a tinny giggle, but Gigi is silent on the other end of the line. Simone tries a change of tack: 'I guess that after all the horrible drama that happened between her and your mom, I wasn't sure what to expect, but Adele still seems really lovely. Your mom would be so happy to know that she's taken you in. She was always hoping for a reconciliation.'

'Was she?' Gigi is thinking about the way her mother had looked at Liam when she hadn't

158

thought anyone was watching.

'And you get to be with dear old Liam, someone familiar. It's such a comfort to me to know he's there for you.'

'Uh-huh.'

And then suddenly, Simone's voice suddenly goes all high and breathless and her next word is a sharp wail: 'Seb!' Without meaning to, Gigi pulls away from the receiver as Simone begins to weep. Her own eyes are dry now, and she sits very still.

'When are you coming back?' Gigi finally whispers, and then has to repeat herself to be heard over the crying.

'Oh, sweetie, I miss you like mad. I'll be there soon.' She listens to Simone doing some more nose-blowing. 'I just couldn't pull myself together in time to sort out arrangements to be back for the funerals. I have to build up a little more strength to face it all. There's so much I need to sort out.'

'When's soon?'

'Soon, Gi, that's all I can tell you at this stage. I have to book another ticket, and I just haven't gotten my act together yet. I will be back, don't you worry about that.' Simone tries to make her voice sound eager, but it's shrill with fear. Gigi doesn't notice; the tension that has been holding her body rigid all morning vanishes, and she slumps backwards against the sofa cushions. *Simone, coming home.*

'I can't wait to see you, Mones.'

'Me too, sweetie. Listen, I've got to go, this call is costing me a fortune with my shabby little

159

rands, but I'll call you again next week, OK?'

'OK.'

'I must say, I can't wait to escape from this endless cold. It's not even proper winter here yet, and my fingers are already blue.'

'You need to come back, Mones.'

'I will. I am. Soon.'

★　★　★

Lesedi shuts her eyes. Across from her, Mrs Radebe sits with her hands on her knees, staring at the scattered bones that lie on the mat between them. Lesedi has noted where the different pieces have fallen, but the message is muddy, and she's not satisfied that they will give her anything concrete to tell her client. She will need to go deeper. She listens to the sound of Mrs Radebe's breath. The soft huffing of air becomes a breeze that she can feel blowing right through her, tickling each cell as it passes. Lesedi sinks into the familiar sensation. Her eyelids flutter as fragmented images begin to form behind them.

Instead of sensing Mrs Radebe's hidden self, as she usually would when her *umoya* comes through her during a consulting session, Lesedi sees a house.

A small frown appears between her brows. She shakes her head. It is a house in Cortona Villas as it would be seen from a front gate. The house is an echo of Lesedi's own, also painted a sun-baked cream with dark tan trim in the standard Cortona Villas style, but there are pots of lavender at the front door. Adele Wilding is

160

very fond of lavender; Lesedi can smell it heavy on the air every time they cross paths. *Yes. The house is the Wilding house next door.*

'Aye,' whispers Lesedi. Mrs Radebe sucks in a breath and waits.

Lesedi takes a mental step backwards and stares at the house. The blonde girl child looks out from the window of a room on the first floor.

'Bryony,' mutters Lesedi.

'Eh?' Mrs Radebe says. This isn't how the sessions with her sangoma normally go.

Then Lesedi glances up above the red-tiled roof of number 35 Cortona Villas and sees the dog-cloud.

'*Hau!*' Lesedi cries, and Mrs Radebe shuffles backwards on her knees, terrified.

The dog-cloud is black and boiling, as if over-full of unshed anger, and it squats low above the roof as if waiting to rip through the clay tiles with its vaporous claws. The wisps of darkness that give the cloud its unmistakable canine shape shift and part and resolve into a wide snarling mouth filled with pointed fog-teeth that drift together on the wind.

'What is it? What do you see?' Mrs Radebe whispers.

For Lesedi, a vision of a black dog is a warning sign. It always has been, since her very first days of working with Ma Retabile, the sangoma she was guided to apprentice when she first followed her calling, ten years ago. A black dog symbol can warn of many things, from a coming argument with a family member to an international crisis.

161

But seeing the black dog in the clouds? That forecasts murder.

Lesedi knows that this dog-cloud vision has nothing to do with Mrs Radebe, who is having trouble with a wayward daughter who wants to drop out of school. So what darkness awaits the little white girl next door?

She opens her eyes.

'I am sorry, *usisi*,' she says to the quivering Mrs Radebe. 'There has been some interference with this reading. I saw something but it was not for you. Are you OK with it if we start again?'

'*Yebo*,' Mrs Radebe says with relief. 'What was it?'

'A warning for someone else came through. Sometimes things like this can happen. We will now continue with the problem of your daughter, OK?'

'Yes, please.' Mrs Radebe moves back to her spot on the edge of the mat. 'Thank you, sangoma.'

* * *

When Bryony comes home from school and darts into her bedroom, the little fizzles of excitement about having her room back to herself again like yesterday dissolve. Gigi is back in her spot on the racing-car duvet cover; but instead of sitting slumped and staring at nothing, she is cross-legged with a bizarrely straight back, hands curled into strange shapes on her knees. Her closed eyes flick open when Bryony bangs her way into the room.

'What are you doing?'

'I *was* meditating.'

'Oh.' Bryony is startled to get a response; she has stopped expecting answers from the silent Gigi.

Maybe it's the small spots of pink that now colour her cousin's cheekbones or a relaxing of the muscles around the eye sockets, but Gigi looks different. Softer. There are fewer shadows.

'What's meditating?'

'Never mind. It's too complicated to explain.'

'It doesn't look complicated. It looks like you were just sitting around with your eyes closed.'

Gigi laughs.

Bryony, en route to her cupboard to begin the obligatory hunt for something other than her horrible school uniform to wear, stops in her tracks. She's never heard Gigi laugh before. It's just a girl's laugh, the sound that someone in her class might make, but quite alien coming out of the zombie.

'I spoke to Simone,' Gigi says. 'She's going to be coming back home.' Bryony stares at her, astonished. 'She's kind of like my real family, you know. And even though the animals are gone, we'll get more. There's always going to be creatures that need looking after.'

'So you're going to go back and live with Simone?'

'Of course. When she comes back from Scotland, that is,' Gigi says, grinning. 'Awesome, hey?'

'Cool,' Bryony agrees. 'I'll get my room back.'

'And I'll get my life back. It's a win-win situation.'

'But the farm ... after what happened

163

. . . won't it be creepy going back there?'

Gigi shakes her head, but her new smile is receding, and Bryony can already see some of the shadows returning to their regular places beneath her skin.

'It won't be easy,' Gigi says in a small voice, 'but Simone always says you have to get back on the horse straight after you fall off.' She gives her head a little shake. 'Simone will be there. She's good at healing things. She will heal the energy of the place somehow.'

'How can a *place* have energy?' Bryony snorts, but then immediately remembers Lesedi's mask room next door and the way just looking in at it had made her feel.

'Can't you go outside or something?' Gigi says, shutting her eyes once more and resettling herself into her meditation pose. 'I really need to be alone to clear my mind.'

'I was going outside anyway,' Bryony mutters, and huffs out her breath as she grabs her shorts out of the cupboard.

Behind her, Gigi tries so hard to clear her mind that her jaw clenches and she starts to quiver.

⋆   ⋆   ⋆

Once again exiled to the garden, Bryony walks, then stops, then walks again. It is hot and bright, and the sky, which should be sporting a greenish mass of clouds for the regular afternoon storm, is clear and blue. She is so busy planning how she will rearrange her room after the mysterious

Simone comes to reclaim Gigi (there will only be one bed in it, for a start) that she scarcely notices what she is doing until she finds herself around the side of the house and up on top of the wooden dustbin cover once again.

The board that she snapped the last time grins at her with splintery teeth. She hasn't told her mom and dad that she broke it, and so far, no one has said a word. She figures that maybe the distraction of her cousin in the house is good for some things after all. She shuffles past the gap to get close to the wall, but before peering over on to the Matsunyane side, she pauses.

The image of the tapeworm-draped figure from her nightmare billows up in her mind.

Bryony wraps her arms around her knees, curling over her tight little ball of fear. She tries to slow her breath. Just as she is about to climb back down to the safety of the garden below and forget she ever came up here, she hears the glass sliding door of the mask room swish open on the other side of the wall.

'Hello.' It's Lesedi's voice. Who is she talking to? Bryony listens to the soft sound of footsteps on the grass approaching the wall from the other side and freezes. The footsteps stop. 'Bryony?'

She gasps. There's no possible way that Lesedi can have seen her.

'I know you're there,' Lesedi continues.

Bryony doesn't answer.

'Right.' Lesedi's voice sounds so close that even through the layers of brick and plaster and paint, Bryony imagines she can feel her breath moving across her skin. She shivers. 'I'll just say what I have to say, and you don't need to answer, just listen, even though you've decided that you know who I am,' Lesedi says.

Bryony lets the air out of her lungs very slowly. Strange colourless patches swim in front of her eyes.

'There is something dark moving into your home,' Lesedi says.

Although the sky above is clear, distant thunder cracks and rumbles and Bryony thinks of the shadows in the cupboards and behind the sofa cushions. She squirms when she remembers the way the night gloom seemed to condense and intensify over her cousin's bed. All the little hairs on her arms stand up at once like an army of silky filament soldiers.

'I don't know what it means, Bryony,' says Lesedi, 'but it is coming.'

Bryony tightens her arms around her knees, squeezing the scared-feeling as hard as she can to try and turn it into anger. 'Are you trying to get me back for spying on you by scaring me?' she asks in a small, breathless voice. 'Because don't. I didn't mean to do anything bad.'

Silence from the Matsunyane side. The air smells of cut lawns and ice, just as it does when it's going to hail.

'Adults are always trying to *stop* kids from being scared, aren't they?' Lesedi speaks again. 'There are no monsters in the cupboard, nothing bad is going to jump out from under the bed . . . but they're wrong.'

Bryony is now unable to draw any new air into her lungs.

'Fear is an instinct that is there to protect you,' Lesedi says. 'But, like all of us, you need to ask yourself if you're fearing the correct thing, or ignoring the truth because you think you already know how the world works. It's so easy to decide that a familiar thing is harmless and a strange new thing is bad, but . . . ' Lesedi's next words are lost as a flock of huge, grey hadehas fly overhead, their urgent cries swallowing up the sound: 'I am not the one you should be afraid of, Bryony.'

Acrid sweat has suddenly jumped out all over Bryony's skin. She blinks away the mental image of tapeworms slithering out through the eye holes of Lesedi's white mask. Gathering her strength, she slides to the edge of the wooden dustbin cover and then drops down to the ground with a thump, her hands slamming against the baked clay soil to steady her landing. A little lizard skitters off into the grass.

'You can stop telling me about dark energies and things because I don't believe in any of that stuff.' Bryony scrambles to her feet. 'It's just make-believe.' She races back to the sanctuary of the house, calling as she runs, 'Everyone knows that magic is just for witches in books!'

I linger by the wall for a moment after Bryony has gone.

Sawubona, Ancestor.

I am the pale yellow sap of an acacia tree, rising upwards, spreading outward into thirsty branches and biscuit-dry leaves. I am thick white thorns, like shards of hollow bone, stabbing blindly at the sky.

167

Stay awake, Ancestor. Soon, they will need you.

* * *

Just before sunset, Bryony goes over to Dommie's house for Shabbat dinner. As the two girls wash their hands together at the bathroom basin, jostling for elbow space and flicking water at each other from the tap, she tells her best friend about Gigi's morning exercises, leaving out the bit about the head-smashing because just thinking about it makes her feel a little sick.

'A zombie, doing yoga!' Dommie crows. 'I can just imagine the movie.' And both girls crumple into a giggling, useless heap. It takes ten whole minutes before they can compose themselves enough to sit down at the table.

The candles are lit, the plaited bread is waiting beneath its linen napkin, and Mrs Silverman chants her prayers in her beautiful voice, but Bryony waits in vain for the feeling of quiet wonder to overtake her as it used to. The sip of wine tastes sour in her mouth, and when she glances across at Shane, the clips holding his yarmulke on look suddenly silly.

She bows her head and bites her lip and realizes that she doesn't *want* it to feel like magic any more. Now that she knows there's a real witch living next door going on about darkness and monsters and things, Bryony just wants to go home where the TV will be on and her brother will be watching it and playing StarCraft on his laptop at the same time, and her mother

168

will be warming up a Woolies ready meal because Dora has weekend nights off and her dad will be reading a magazine about golf. She sits on her hands to stop herself fidgeting and waits for the dinner to be over.

15

Bryony wakes before the sun comes up. Outside, she can hear the first birds starting. It's Saturday, she could be sleeping late, but lately she's begun to dread sleep. Lesedi was in her nightmares again. This time, she had been wearing a mask shaped like the head of a black dog, and had been trying to break in through Bryony's bedroom window.

Bryony is relieved to hear Gigi stir, and she watches as her cousin slides out of her bed on the other side of the room and begins to do another yoga session on the carpet. Bryony lies motionless and observes through half-closed eyes, unconsciously syncing her breathing with Gigi's loud inhales and exhales.

Bryony is afraid that Gigi is going to start hitting herself again, but once her cousin has finished doing her sun salutations, she just climbs back into bed.

★   ★   ★

'Saturday Special' breakfast could hardly be called special where Gigi is concerned; she doesn't eat scrambled eggs or bacon, and doesn't even have butter on her toast. Bryony watches the slow smearing of apricot jam that Gigi applies to her slice, and takes a big fat sinfully meaty mouthful from her own.

Tyler is shovelling as usual, with his elbows on the table, but Adele doesn't say anything, she's too busy watching Liam. Bryony has noticed that now Gigi is no longer talking to Liam any more than she is to Adele, the bloodless look has left her mother's face. Bryony sees her father glance up, catch her mother's eye and give a slight nod. He clears his throat.

'Gi?' he begins, focusing hard on cutting the ribbons of fat from the edge of his bacon. 'Your Aunt Addy and I were thinking that perhaps you would like to start school on Monday.'

'Who the hell would *like* to start school?' snorts Tyler, but no one glances in his direction.

'What do you think of that then?' Liam asks, finally giving his niece a cautious smile.

'I guess.' Gigi shrugs, her face impassive. Simone will be back soon, and Gigi will go back with her to the farm and carry on her life and it will be as if all this horrible time spent with the Wildings, school or no school, will never have happened. She takes another bite of toast.

'We've made a few phone calls to the high school that's affiliated to Bryony's primary. They're willing to take you in, even at this late stage in the year.'

'Will she have to write exams? She won't know half the stuff in time.'

'Shsh, Bryony.'

'Saint Scary's?' Tyler wrinkles his nose. 'Those chicks are all so stuck up.'

'You're just saying that just 'cause they don't want to talk to *you*, Tyler,' Bryony retorts, and her brother flushes luminous pink.

171

'We'll need to get you a uniform,' Adele says. 'I don't suppose you've got school shoes in amongst your things, have you?'

Gigi shakes her head, not saying a word about the fact that she's never owned a pair of school shoes in her life. Everything she learned about history, biology, literature and science, she learned from Johan, her mother, Simone and Seb at home.

'Pity. Well, no big deal, we'll get you a pair when we go to the mall later on.'

'Yay, shopping,' Tyler sneers.

'Calm down, Ty,' Adele says with a smile, placing a hand on his arm, 'nobody's going to force you to come with.'

'No. I'll come,' he mutters, glancing quickly at Gigi and then away again. 'There's stuff I want to get, too.'

'Well, I've got a game lined up,' Liam said with a grin. 'Sure you don't want to join me instead? Those clubs I got you for your birthday have hardly been touched.'

'No thanks, Dad,' Tyler says, staring down at his plate. 'Not really in the mood for golf.'

★　★　★

The mall, so unlike the shabby little thing that Gigi used to visit with her mother and Simone on their annual clothes-buying expeditions, is absurd in its immensity. The overwhelming light and sound and humanity make thinking impossible. Gigi walks beside Bryony through the crowded corridors and stares at the gleaming

172

floor tiles. How do they keep them so shiny with all these people walking on them all the time? She feels slightly seasick, but is surprised to find that this strange barrage on her senses is a welcome relief. It makes a change from the clawing feeling that will not stop scraping on the inside her own head.

'The school uniform shop is this way,' Bryony announces, veering left, and Gigi scuttles to keep up, unsure if she'd be able to find her way out of the place should she get lost.

Inside the school outfitters, the racks of dull fabric mop up the sound and light, making the store quiet and stuffy compared to the rest of the mall, as if to prepare the shoppers for the school experience that will inevitably follow a visit here. Adele chats to the shop assistant, and a tunic is duly brought forth for Gigi to try on in the dark little changing room at the back.

The fabric feels itchy against her skin, and the whole thing stiff and difficult to move in. Gigi has to leave the cubicle to see herself in the mirror, and when she does so her body seems to move differently.

I feel like someone else.

She looks like someone else, too. In the drab brown tunic and collared pastel shirt she seems anonymous, as though she could be anyone. It's a uniform made for disappearing in. Gigi tilts her head at her reflection, and then catches sight of Bryony, staring.

'What's that on your leg?' Bryony asks, indicating the scabby patch on Gigi's calf from where she carved lines into her skin with that wooden splinter a couple of days ago. 'Did you cut yourself?'

'I guess so,' Gigi replies.

'Looks really . . . sore,' Bryony says, her brow furrowed. 'It looks like . . . How did — '

'Is that one the right size?' Adele asks, picking her way through the clothing racks to get to the girls.

'*Ja*. It's fine.'

'Have you tried on the blazer?'

'No,' Gigi says, and picks up the absurd, heavy thing and slides her arms into the sleeves. The lining is cool on her skin, but she can tell that it will warm up pretty fast in the sun. Schoolgirls must get really stinky.

'Super,' says Adele, heading back to the sales assistant. 'We'll take the tunic, the blazer and three of the shirts. Thank goodness it's not winter, hey? I'd be buying up half the shop.'

Gigi looks back at her reflection and sees that she's disappeared even further. She gives a tiny, satisfied smile before realizing that Bryony is still staring at the marks on her leg. Their eyes meet in the mirror.

★   ★   ★

'How about you girls explore on your own a little?' Adele says. 'Get something to eat.' She presses some money into Gigi's hand and points them towards the food court.

'But . . . ' Bryony whines. Sharing a bedroom with Gigi should've made them at least slightly at ease in each other's company, but an awful,

174

solid weirdness persists in the air between them.

'It's half an hour, not the end of the world, Bry. I'll meet you at the bookshop at quarter past; Tyler should be there by then.' Adele has to give both Bryony and Gigi a small shove to get them moving, and then she turns and heads in the direction of a sage-green, raw-silk blouse that she spotted in one of the boutiques on the way in.

The air around the food court is thick with the smell of frying oil, doughnuts and shawarma meat. Bryony glances up at her cousin, and sees that her small, freckled nose is wrinkled in distaste.

'We don't *have* to get something to eat, you know.'

'I know.'

'I'm not even hungry anyway,' Bryony mutters and Gigi says nothing. Bryony's sure that her silly little slice of toast and jam has worn off by now. 'You can get something if you want, though.'

'There's nothing here that I'd touch with a ten-foot pole,' Gigi says. 'It's all just animal products and carcinogens.'

'*Ja*,' Bryony agrees; even if she doesn't know what Gigi is on about, it sounds pretty bad. 'There's a music shop up that way if you want to check it out.'

'OK.' And as one, the girls turn and walk down another iridescent corridor. Bryony notices that even among the jostling crowds, Gigi is very cautious about whom she walks close to. She holds herself especially stiff, with her arms close in to her sides, when any black man walks past. Sometimes she even flinches.

'Are you a racist?' Bryony asks with genuine interest. She's been hearing about racists a lot at school lately because they are studying South Africa's history. As far as she's aware, the only racists now are just a few old people.

'What?'

'A racist, you know. Like apartheid and all that.'

'I know what a racist is, and no, I'm not.'

'The way you looked at that black guy — '

'Jeez, are you like some kind of undercover spy for the government or something?' Gigi snaps, and Bryony's face goes boiling hot. Gigi is the second person to accuse her of spying. This makes her think of Lesedi, and of what she said about darkness moving into their house and her fingers go all numb and cold.

'Simone says that race is just an illusion anyway,' Gigi continues in a softer tone. 'That we're all one.'

'One what?'

'Just one.'

'Oh, I see,' says Bryony, who doesn't. 'So what's this Simone person like then?'

'She's very enlightened.' Gigi stops beside a shop window display full of mannequins in tropical-coloured bathing suits, their plastic feet embedded in artfully arranged sand. 'And beautiful.'

'Like how?'

'She has long, long brown hair and she washes it with rosemary so it's always super shiny and

176

never has any dandruff or anything.'

'Rosemary? Like you use to cook roast lamb with?' Bryony tries to imagine how one would wash your hair with a bunch of spiky little leaves.

'I guess so. Only Simone never cooks lamb. She cares for animals, she doesn't eat them.'

'Like you.'

'*Ja*, like me.' Gigi's cheeks go a pleased pink. 'I'm a lot like Simone in many ways. Some people used to think that she was actually my mom.'

'Not Aunty Sally?'

'No, Mom looked more like you and Adele, same white-blonde hair.'

'I can hardly remember her,' Bryony says. 'Except that she didn't wear any mascara.'

'I'm going inside,' Gigi says sharply, and strides away from Bryony and through the music-shop doors, flinching when the security guard that stands at the entrance to check people's bags and sales slips gives her a friendly grin.

Through the glass and between the promotional stickers advertising the new release of the latest Pixar movie on DVD, Bryony watches her cousin march purposefully towards a shelf of CDs and then stop and stand, staring at nothing, her face hidden in shadow.

★ ★ ★

I stopped wearing mascara the year that Liam kissed me in the parking lot.

A decade later, working on the farm up to my armpits in dust and animal mess and hair and

177

blood, mascara would've been ridiculous, but long before that, in that sticky Johannesburg summer, stopping wearing it had felt like an act of courage.

I didn't stop wearing it the very next day after the drunken kiss; at first I waited, breathless, to see what would happen. Would he tell her? Leave her? Kiss me in secret again? And then, when nothing at all changed and it became clearer and clearer that his decision had been made, and I was not it, I threw that little tube of black tar in the bin. The bin in my bedroom was the same one I'd had since I was about six, and still sported a silly girlish motif of flowers and kittens on one side; the mascara tube clattered very loudly against its metal sides when I dropped it in.

Unlike my sister, who would rather be caught dead than be seen without her make-up on, I was now the brave one who dared to show my true face to the world. When I arrived at varsity the next day, a number of people asked me if I was ill, but I shrugged it off and wore my pale lashes and indistinct eyebrows like some strange war mask in the silent battle that Liam had sparked off between my sister and me.

Of course, Adele had no idea that there was a battle at all. In her opinion, I was still good old Monkey, great for late-night chats and going shopping and helping her study. It was only years later, in her and Liam's glossy kitchen, that she both woke up to the war and vanquished me in one terrible instant.

★　★　★

Gigi, thinking that she is unobserved, has made it out of the Wildings' front gate, and is about to head up the road towards the silent sanctuary of number 22 when Tyler calls out to her.

'Hey,' he says and she turns, flip-flops skidding on the ornamental pebbles beneath the fever tree. He trots up behind her, grinning, squinting eyes almost closed against the glare of the sun. 'Where are you going?'

'Nowhere.' She shrugs and digs her hands into the pockets of her jeans. The heavy fabric is absurd and cloying in this heat, but she needs to hide the wounds on her legs (she's willing them to heal faster before school starts on Monday). She remembers Tyler's knee bumping into her bare leg that night in front of the TV and curls her hands into fists inside her pockets.

'Looks like you're on a mission.'

'Nope. Just getting some air.'

'I'll walk with you,' he says, but she just shrugs again, and leans her spine against the slender trunk of the tree.

'Wasn't going anywhere.'

'Oh.' The shadows of the leaves and thorns make speckled patterns on his cheeks, and in the sunny patches Gigi can see the very beginnings of his soft blond beard starting. Johan had a blond beard. He used to tickle her with it when she was a little girl and make her squeal and laugh. But this year, Gigi had found herself unable to look at Johan's stubble without a strange, melty feeling darting between her belly button and her crotch.

For weeks, Gigi kept herself awake at night,

squirming in her bed as she imagined cupping Johan's jaw between her palms and tipping her head back so that he could lower his lips to hers.

She'd had no one to tell about her sudden crush and the strange heat of it had built up inside her, swirling around her head and colouring all her thoughts until she was giddy with it.

Then, just last month, four days before the incident, they'd been crouching together in the dirt road as he showed her how to identify a duiker spoor they'd found and Gigi had sucked in her breath, turned towards Johan, and reached up to place her finger right in the tanned secret hollow at the base of his throat. Johan had yanked back from her touch, his eyes cloudy, before standing up and brushing the dust from his shorts.

'Let's get back now,' he'd said, turning towards the house. 'Maybe we should give the bush walks a break for a while, hey? Your biology skills are pretty sharp already and I think your ma wants you to spend some more time focusing on some of your other subjects.'

The stinging memory of his rejection is suddenly overshadowed by the more recent one of Johan's sliced-open shin. It had looked as if someone had pulled a zipper down the front of his bare leg to reveal gleaming red and bone.

For a moment, Gigi cannot breathe. Her arms and legs go cold. The blood can no longer circulate through her body properly; all its iron is concentrating on keeping her upright.

'You OK?' Tyler whispers in concern. 'Sometimes when I think what you must've been through . . . I don't know . . . it's amazing that you're still — '

'What? Alive?' she snaps. Her breath comes back in a rush. 'It's harder to die than you think, you know. The human body doesn't just stop because you've had enough; it fights to live.' She scowls down at the pebbles at her feet. There's a tiny beetle crawling slowly across the smooth white bulge of the biggest one.

'Have you seen someone die?' Tyler asks, and then his eyes widen in shock: 'Hey, they said you only arrived on the scene after it all happened — you weren't there like . . . before, were you?'

'Why would you think I'd want to talk about this, Tyler?' she says sharply.

'Sorry.' He swallows. 'I'm an asshole. Forget it.' He feels the blush burning up his neck; it's the first time Gigi has said his name.

The silence between them blooms and swells into something huge and crystalline, and although they both ache to leave, they're rooted to the spot by its weight. A breeze ruffles the leaves above their heads and its breath is followed by engine noise and then the arrival of a silver GTi. The car purrs up to the kerb and idles in front of Tyler and Gigi as its occupants wait for their electronic garage door to open. The man smiles and waves, and the woman with the long braids in the passenger seat turns to smile too, and when she does, Gigi feels as if all the shifting shadows inside her head are on display. She gasps and turns away as gooseflesh rips up and down her arms.

Finally, the Matsunyanes' garage door is open

181

and the GTi moves away.

'Our neighbours,' Tyler says. 'They're pretty cool. About the only people in this place who aren't stuck-up snobs.'

'Uh-huh.' Gigi realizes that he's not going to leave her in peace, and number 22 will have to wait. She starts to move back towards the Wildings' house, but Tyler stops her with a touch on her arm. The feel of his hand is gentle and electric at the same time and sends little sparks of confusion darting over her skin.

'I'm sorry about before, about making you think of all that stuff that happened, Gigi.'

'You didn't *make* me think of it. I'm always thinking about it.' She walks back through the garden gate.

* * *

Adele closes her bedroom door and stands for a moment with her back to it. Her eyes are closed and the lids look tissue-paper thin, their veins very blue. I recognize the large old photo album with its brown cover and bent corners that she hugs to her chest, and remember the argument we had over who should keep it, back when she and Liam had just gotten married. Of course, Adele won.

Adele goes over to the bed and clambers up on to the vast king-size mattress with its dove-grey coverlet and curls her legs beneath her as she used to do when she was a little girl. Slowly, she opens the album, breathing in the familiar scent of the old pages. There's Adele and

182

me at Umhlanga beach in our 1970s crocheted swimming costumes: she is two years old, round-tummied and white-haired, and I am four and sensible, holding her dimpled hand to stop her running off.

Adele touches the clear plastic sheet that covers my face; her fingers are trembling. She turns the page, and then another: family Christmases with wilting tinsel and glass bowls of tinned fruit cocktail; Mom in graphic print dresses and clogs; Dad in an outrageous blue suit that I can't remember him ever wearing; me with two long, white plaits and a grin on my first day of school. The pages turn.

'Addy?' Liam calls out before pushing open the bedroom door. He is pink and damp from the golf course and brings the sharp scent of sweat and grass into the room.

'Hey,' says Adele, but she doesn't look up; she's staring at the picture Dad took of us in the tipuana tree. Adele is perched like a slender bird on the lowest branch, just twelve but already beautifully put together in red shorts and a white T-shirt with round red apples printed on it. I am clinging to the trunk, fourteen and awkward and not quite smiling with a terrible eighties haircut and a big bulky top that hides my rather insignificant breasts.

'Shit . . . ' Liam breathes as he comes up beside his wife. 'Look at that.'

'I look like Bryony, don't I?'

'*Ja*,' he agrees, and turns the page: Adele in a school play as a mermaid, made up with swoops of green glittery eye shadow. Liam gives a little laugh, 'What a cutie.' He sits down on the bed, and Adele says nothing about the dirty streak he leaves on the bedding.

On the second last page is a picture of me and Adele that was taken during the holiday before I went to university and met Liam: we're at the beach again, Cape St Francis this time. Mom took the picture. By that stage, Dad wasn't well enough to do much but sit on the balcony of the sea-view apartment we'd rented for the summer. Even while we were on it, that trip became known as our 'last family holiday'.

Liam stares down at the two girls with their arms around each other in the photograph and feels a terrible tightness in his chest. The sisters are both very tanned, and their hair is almost white from the sun, their heads tilted towards each other so that it's impossible to tell exactly where one head ends and the other begins. They are both so clear-eyed and beautiful that his breath catches in his throat and for the first time ever he knows.

He knows why he chose Adele.

If he'd gone with Sally, Adele would've moved on, found someone else (or many someone elses, more likely), and he would've had only one of the sisters in his life and that wasn't good enough. It was not a conscious decision that he could remember making, but somehow, nineteen-year-old Liam knew that if he chose Adele, he could have the petite, slant-eyed, sexy one, and still be best friends with the tall, loving, funny one. Sally didn't demand to be the centre of attention the way that Adele did. She would stay on the sidelines (doglike and loyal) and, in his way, Liam could keep them both.

He gets off the bed so suddenly that the album bounces against Adele's knees.

'Liam?'

'Fuck.'

'What is it?'

It's impossible to answer. He goes through to the en-suite bathroom and rips off his sweaty shirt, then attacks the buckle of his belt with furious fingers. He jams his fist against the shower to get the water started and plunges beneath the icy spray. He scrubs vigorously at his goosefleshed skin, drags his fingers over his scalp and rubs his face with disgusted, angry jabs.

The water starts to warm up and his shoulders slump and his hands go limp. He drops his head forward to lean against the tiles as the nausea that has been rising up inside his gut finally overwhelms him.

Selfish fucking bastard.

Suddenly, Adele is at the shower door. She wrenches it open and the spray drenches her dress.

'I have to know, Liam,' she says as water splashes around them both and starts to pool on the bathroom floor. 'Because I want to grieve for my sister and I am just so goddamn confused. You and Gigi clearly have . . . a history or something which means . . . ' Adele stops; gulps for breath. 'After I kicked her out and . . . '

Liam looks at his wife with her mascara running and her hair half sodden from the shower water and he begins to weep.

'Liam, did you and Sally have an affair?'

Liam inhales tears and spray. An hour ago he would've answered 'no' without hesitation, and meant it. One drunken smooch in a parking lot as a teenager certainly did not count as an affair, and that was the only time they'd actually ever touched in such a way, but now he can't even manage a shake of the head.

'Liam, damn it, answer me.' Adele steps further into the shower; her sopping dress sticks to his legs and he can feel her hands, curled into small tight fists, trembling between their bodies. 'Did you sleep with my sister?'

'No.' It comes out as a cracked cry, and he collapses against Adele and clutches her to his chest. 'No. I didn't, Addy.'

After a long while, her arms move up around his back, but her hands don't soften. He can feel those little fists knocking into his spine with each shuddering sob.

★ ★ ★

Over the years that Liam had been making his clandestine visits to me and Gigi at the farm, we established a farewell ritual. Every time he left we'd say our goodbyes in the yard, and then Gigi and I would climb into the Mercedes and drive along with him (with Gigi abusing the dials on the stereo system and singing along, more often than not) down the long rutted drive to the gate. We'd then get out and open it for the car to pass through before waving him off until he was nothing but a tendril of dust on the horizon.

186

But it had been months since I'd last seen Liam.

The afternoon was too quiet, and the heat too cloying, and my new charge, a young female baboon with a broken back leg, had been screeching like a banshee all morning as I'd tried to minister to her wounds.

My ears were ringing by the time I allowed my restless feet to take me away from her enclosure, out of the yard and along the driveway, all the way to the gate. I stood in the spot where I'd last touched him; it had been a small flick of my fingers against his shoulder through the open car window. From here, even the baboon's tantrum was muffled by the silence and the solid heat. Beyond the gate, I could see the dirt road curving off into the distance: orange powdery dust and lumps of gravel and stillness. In the distance, the solitary baobab reached its sculptural branches towards the sky. I leant my body against the mesh of the gate and pressed myself against it, feeling each little wire diamond cut into my skin.

For a childish moment, I let myself imagine a distant puff of dust that would soon materialize into the familiar bulk of Liam's white Mercedes. I closed my eyes for a moment to see it more vividly: Liam arriving unannounced, climbing out of his car, taking me into his arms . . .

'You're an idiot, Sally.' The voice seemed to come from nowhere, and I gave a startled little cry before realizing that Johan had been tightening a wire on the electric fence only a few metres away from me the entire time.

187

I whirled around and stomped towards him. 'What the hell's that supposed to mean?' I demanded. Johan's face was beaded with moisture beneath his wide-brimmed hat, and there was a large damp V of sweat down the front of his khaki shirt. I could smell the warm, glazed-pastry smell that his skin gave off in the sun.

'I meant . . . ' He trailed off. His eyes locked on to mine and then slid away again. 'Nothing.' He turned his attention back to the fence.

'Rubbish. You meant *something*, Johan.'

He gave the wire a vicious yank with his pliers and the thick rope of muscle on his tanned forearm twitched.

'Why are you so mad at me?'

'Why are you so mad at *me?*' he muttered.

'Because you gave me a fright, because you were spying on me, and because you called me an idiot and now won't tell me why.'

'I wasn't spying on you, and . . . Ag, you *know* why, Sal,' he said in a softer tone, still not looking at me. 'You know.'

'What?'

'Liam,' he said in a flat voice.

I felt utterly naked, as if he'd climbed right inside my head and seen my childish fantasies. It was mortifying.

'You're like a schoolkid with a crush, only you're not a schoolkid, and he's never going to leave his wife and choose you, and you're wasting your whole goddamn life lusting after something that you can't have and don't even need.'

I was too shocked to speak. In the ensuing silence, Johan crouched down to work on a lower

188

wire. A slight breeze picked up and ruffled the grass around us. It blew soft cool kisses on the back of my boiling neck.

'Wow, that's a long sentence from you,' I finally sneered. 'Thanks for sharing.'

'I didn't mean to upset you, Sal — '

'Really? That's funny, because it feels like that's exactly what you were trying to do.' I battled to keep the rising tears out of my voice, but it wasn't working.

Johan dropped the pliers into a patch of sand and stood up, turning to face me. 'Sorry, man,' he whispered. 'That's not what I really wanted to say.'

'Then what did you want to say, Johan?' I snapped, dragging my hands over my wet cheeks.

'That I'm right here.' It came out so softly that, for a moment, I wasn't sure I'd heard correctly. The look on his face told me that I had.

'Johan . . . ' I took a small step backwards. 'I didn't know.'

'No, of course you didn't. You've been too 'busy'.'

'You don't understand about Liam, it's very — '

'I know how it feels to be in love with someone who doesn't see you the same way, if that's what you mean,' he said, and bent down to pick up his pliers again, hiding his face from me.

'Johan, it's not that I don't . . . I just . . . I didn't know you felt . . . '

'Of course you didn't.' His voice lost its softness. The unfortunate wire got a brutal yank.

'Even your kid is more aware of me than you are.'

'Gigi? What do you mean?'

'She's got a crush, that's all.' He grunted as he tested the tautness of the wire. 'She's a teenager now, or hadn't you noticed that either?'

'Of course I had, but . . . ' I trailed off, wiping my sweaty hands on my shorts.

'Perhaps it's time she hung out with some kids her own age, Sally.'

'Yeah,' I said, the wind knocked out of me. 'You're probably right.' Something made me look up and over at the clump of acacia trees to our left. For a moment, I was certain I saw movement and a flash of white amongst the leaves. I stared hard, but nothing moved except the breeze and the bugs in the swaying green grass. If someone or something had been there, they weren't any more. 'I'm sorry, Johan,' I whispered.

'Don't. Just . . . '

I waited for a very long time, listening to the shrill cicadas and the squeak of his pliers against the wire, but he didn't say another word.

16

Bryony has chosen to walk the long way round the townhouse complex to get to Dommie's because, even though it will take a lot more time, at least she won't have to cross the Matsunyanes' driveway and risk running into any witches. She balances on the kerb stones that line the road, stepping from one to the next with straight legs and pointed toes like the Olympic gymnasts on those skinny balance beams that she's seen on TV. She raises her arms above her head and imagines leaping into a graceful forward flip, spinning through the air and coming down to land with feet perfectly placed, one in front of the other. Ta-da!

Then, suddenly, she gets a funny cold feeling right between her shoulder blades. She jiggles them to release it, but the cold spot only grows bigger, spreading down her arms and into her fingers. *Lesedi's behind me*, Bryony thinks, and then shakes her head to force the silly idea back to where it came from. She tries to walk like a gymnast again, but her movements are clumsy now, and she stubs her smile-toe on the edge of a kerb stone. She bends down to inspect the painful damage: a tiny flap of transparent skin with a seam of fresh red blood seeping out from under it. She blinks back tears. She's going to need a plaster when she gets to Dommie's.

And then the cold spot is back.

She made it happen.

Bryony looks around, heart pounding. Instead of Lesedi, wrapped in worms with a white-painted face ready to curse her, there are two small boys playing with a frisbee on the grass a little way off. *You're being an idiot, Bryony.* She gets back to her feet and starts to jog towards Dommie's. She can feel the flap of skin moving loose on her toe, but she goes even faster, trying to control the mounting panic that has colonized her chest.

She turns the corner and skids to a stop. There's a large black dog standing on the herringbone paving in the centre of the road. The dog has a rough coat and sticking-up ears and it stares right at her.

'Hi, boy.' She tries to sound friendly. The dog remains motionless. 'Go home,' she commands, but there's not enough air in her lungs to make it forceful enough.

The dog doesn't move.

It's against the Body Corporate rules to let a dog run around the communal areas without being on a leash, but there's no one here to enforce the rule. In fact, Bryony feels entirely alone, as if everyone in the whole complex has just suddenly packed up and left without telling her. Bryony stares at the black dog and the dog stares back. A sudden gust of wind howls up the road and forces her to close her eyes against the swirling dust. When she opens them again, the animal is gone.

The ice-cold spot in the centre of Bryony's spine is now an all-encompassing paralysis and she can only manage tiny little sips of breath. There is no sign of the dog. The wind has stopped completely and the afternoon air hangs still and heavy, hot against her icy skin.

Finally, she runs again, throbbing toe thumping down on the bricks as she pounds towards Dommie's house. She crashes through the Silvermans' garden gate, hurtles up the path and collapses against the front door, sobbing.

'Good grief, Bryony!' Mrs Silverman says when she finds the white-faced wreck on her doorstep. 'What on earth has happened? Are you all right?'

'There's a . . . She's put a curse on me . . . ' Bryony splutters through her sobs.

'Now now, come inside and sit down,' Mrs Silverman says, ushering Bryony into the front hall where the rest of the Silverman family has now congregated, drawn by the commotion.

'Her foot's bleeding,' Dommie whispers.

'So it is. Looks like you've had a bit of a journey getting here, Bry.' Mrs Silverman guides the girl into the kitchen and helps her into a chair. 'Craig, get the Dettol and some cotton wool from the upstairs bathroom, will you?'

'OK,' Dommie's brother says and dashes off.

Without needing to be asked, Mr Silverman goes to the fridge and pours a small glass of guava juice. As Bryony sips the soothing pink liquid, her tears begin to dry on her cheeks.

'Now tell us what happened, darling,' Mrs Silverman says, dabbing Dettol on to Bryony's injured toe.

'It's our neighbour, Mrs Matsunyane,' she manages between heaving breaths. 'The one who

193

lives in number thirty-seven. I didn't mean to spy on her, but she seemed so interesting and different and I wanted to be her friend actually and then I saw the mask.'

'Mask?' Mrs Silverman exchanges a baffled look with her husband.

'And then I saw all the people coming to her house and she told me about her business and I said I wouldn't tell on her but still she said that the darkness was coming to get me and that there were monsters under the bed.'

'Mrs Matsunyane is running a business?'

'Yes. She's a sangoma and people come to her for *muti* and spells and I don't know what else.'

'Gracious.'

'And now she's put a curse on me and I can feel her watching me even when she's not there, and then the dog was there and then it was gone and I was all cold.'

'Well, darling, it sounds like you've had a hell of a day.' Mrs Silverman gives the plaster she's just put on Bryony's toe an extra smooth-down. 'But in my expert opinion, you're going to be just fine.'

'But what about Lesedi?' Bryony sniffles. The sobs are gone now, and the guava juice is almost finished.

'Well, Geoff and I are on the board, and we're going to have to look into this whole 'running a business' thing. It's strictly against Body Corporate rules to do that on these grounds. We had another woman once who started selling imported handbags from her front room, can you believe it? We'll put a stop to it, trust me. A practising sangoma . . . Who knows what sort of people must be coming in and out of here all day. It's not at all good for security.'

'No,' agrees Bryony vociferously. 'It isn't.'

'Thanks for letting us know about this, Bryony,' says Mr Silverman. 'If this woman is running a consulting practice here in Cortona Villas, we'll put a stop to it, don't you worry about that. That sort of behaviour just isn't on.'

'Please don't tell her I told you,' Bryony pleads, her eyes welling up again. 'She scares me and she comes to me in my nightmares.'

'Good heavens, Geoff, we can't have someone terrorizing the kids like this . . . ' Mrs Silverman begins, guiding her husband out of the room so that they can continue their discussion in private. Dommie looks at Bryony and Bryony looks at the new beige plaster on her toe. The kitchen is quiet except for the ticking of the large clock on the wall beside the fridge.

'Are you OK?' Dommie asks at last.

'*Ja*.'

'You should've told me that all of this sangoma stuff was going on.'

'I know. Sorry.'

'Did that lady really curse you?'

Bryony takes a big, shuddery breath and nods her head.

'What a bitch.'

* * *

Bryony is not sure why she feels so nervous. It is Gigi's brand-new school uniform that's hanging on the cupboard door, not her own, but she's all squirmy and jittery as if she is the one who has to start at a new school in the morning.

'I hate first days,' she whispers and, across the dark bedroom, Gigi's bedding rustles.

'I'm not scared.'

'That's good, then,' Bryony says. 'I guess you've had scarier stuff happen lately than a stupid first day at a new school.'

'*Ja*.' They lie in silence for a while. 'I am kind of nervous, I suppose,' Gigi says and Bryony stares hard into the gloom, trying to make out Gigi's features in the dark. At any moment, Gigi might remember that she's a zombie, and Bryony doesn't want that to happen. It's nice having someone to talk to in the dark.

'It sucks not knowing anyone,' Bryony says.

'*Ja*. But it's just for a little while, until Simone comes back.'

'Well, if the people at the school are horrible to you, you can just think of that.'

'Yeah.'

'When's she coming, again?'

'Tonight on the phone she said she's going in to the travel agent tomorrow to book her flight. So it might be this week, even.'

'Does Mom know you're going to go back and live with Simone, then?' Bryony asks, thinking of the brand-new uniform and school shoes that Adele just bought for Gigi. They will probably just hang in the cupboard for ages until she's ready to start high school herself. *Hopefully the tunic won't be quite so loose over the top when I wear it.*

196

'Don't know. It's kind of obvious, though, isn't it? I mean Simone is sort of like my other mother.'

Bryony is so thrilled to have zombie Gigi responding like a normal person that she finally has the courage to ask the question that's been plaguing her for weeks: 'Hey, do you remember me from under the table that time at Granny's place?'

'Of course. The tablecloth was like a tent.'

'Exactly.'

'And I had that jar of peanut butter,' Gigi says, and Bryony giggles.

'You ate the whole thing; I can't believe you weren't sick.'

'I was. That night I puked up a whole load of disgusting nutty puke.'

'Gross!' Bryony says and Gigi laughs. Bryony begins to drift towards sleep. 'Goodnight, Gigi.'

' 'Night.'

* * *

The first night I went to Johan, the moon was full, and the patch of earth between the main house and the cabin where he slept on the far side of the lucky bean tree seemed to be lit up like a football pitch. It illuminated the baggy sleep shirt and hiking boots I was wearing (in case of scorpion and snake encounters) and leached the colour from my skin. I knew that I looked nothing like a sultry enchantress, but I continued on, pulse beating hard in my throat.

I didn't really know what had finally propelled

me from my sleepless bed, but ever since Johan had confronted me by the fence the previous day, I'd felt as if a door had opened inside me and a draught of cool fresh air had rushed in, displacing stale old stuff that had been sitting there for years. Earlier that evening, as Simone and Gigi had fussed around the kitchen laughing over the ludicrousness of trying to create an egg-free, dairy-free lasagne, I'd kept glancing over to where Johan and Seb had been standing by the open door, deep in discussion about the gang of vervet monkeys who'd started stealing food from some of the rescues. At first, when he'd caught me looking, Johan had gone pink and looked away, and I'd quickly returned my attention to the carrots I was peeling, but then I looked again, and he looked back and each time our eyes met, we grew bolder, held the gaze longer. My heart was thundering. I felt silly and young and just a little bit drunk.

'Come on, Mom, hurry up with those carrots,' Gigi had barked from her post at a pot of simmering lentils.

'Hey, who's the kid here, and who's the mom?' I grinned back, but my daughter had just glowered at me before turning to ask Simone's advice on something lentil-related.

I knocked on the wooden door of Johan's cabin. Despite the chorus of crickets and cicadas, it sounded too loud.

'Yes?'

'It's Sally.' I heard shuffling noises and then the door opened. Johan stood before me in a pair of boxer shorts. Wide-shouldered and lean and silver-skinned in the moonlight. He rubbed his eyes; blinked.

'Is something wrong?'

'No.' A long pause. 'I wanted to . . . ' Behind him, I saw the messed-up bedding of his single bed through the gauze of the mosquito net. He saw me looking. He looked back at me. His eyes widened.

'Sally?'

'I wanted to say sorry. For the other day. For being . . . ' I trailed off. We stared at each other. I felt something loosen deep in my abdomen. My face was on fire. 'I would like to — ' He reached out and touched my jaw, just below my ear. I closed my eyes; swallowed. 'I would like to try.'

His hand, large and very warm, cupped my chin. My traitorous skin remembered Liam's hands on my face, so many years ago. I forced the memory back by stepping forward, into the cabin. Johan took my hands and pulled me towards his body. The cabin door closed behind me, but I couldn't be sure I'd truly left Liam outside.

The next night, I crept across the yard once again, and then later, as Johan fell asleep beside me on his narrow bed, I lay and watched the shadows of the flying ants crawl on the outside of the mosquito net. My body hummed with release, but my head? I couldn't shake the feeling that I was betraying someone.

'You OK?'

'I thought you were asleep.'

'With a naked goddess in my bed? Are you kidding?'

'Oh, please!' But I smiled and turned towards him.

'I know I'm very likely about to blow this by asking, but I need to know . . . Are you here to scratch an itch, Sal, or do I have permission to hope?'

I sat up and wrapped my arms around my legs. The bed suddenly felt too small. 'I don't know.' I rested my forehead against my knees. It was close and hot inside the mosquito net. Sweat coated my skin.

Neither of us said the name *Liam*, but both of us were thinking it.

Simone had once said to me: 'You're scared that if you let go of Liam, if you stop seeing him, you'll lose the only remaining connection you've got with your sister.' I'd thought she was crazy at the time, but Adele's absence was still a vast hollow cavern in the centre of me. I thought of her swinging on that damn garden gate, looking out into the road, always beside me as we waited for Dad to come home from work.

'Well, whichever way the cookie crumbles . . . ' Johan said. I waited. He raised himself up on his elbows and kissed my shoulder before flopping back down again. 'I'm here now.'

I turned and slid my hands along the moonlight-coloured skin of his belly. 'Me too.'

17

The school grounds look as though they're covered with immaculately ironed, tightly tucked-in green blankets, and Gigi has to step on it to check that the grass is real.

'Stay on the path.' An older girl with a prefect badge pinned to the centre of her blazer lapel barks as she strides past, and Gigi is so surprised at the authority of the command that she does a daft little skip from the lawn to the paving.

No wonder the grass is so perfect if no one is allowed to walk on it, she thinks as she rejoins the brown-blazered, faceless throng that surges towards the white school buildings.

To avoid turning round and running in the opposite direction, Gigi forces herself to imagine describing every moment of today's experience to Simone. *The girls look like a herd of impalas,* she silently explains, *all brown coats and slender ankles with long hair to flick instead of tails. They know that I am not one of the herd and look at me with little sideways movements of their eyes like my coat is not quite the right brown, or my ponytail is tied up wrong. Maybe they think I am a jackal in disguise or something. Up close, they stink of ten different kinds of deodorant and shampoo and sweat all mixed into a horrible stew.*

Gigi breathes through her mouth as the press of girls increases at the entrance to the school building. She now wishes that she hadn't told Adele, who had offered to accompany her, that she could find the school office on her own.

'All right. If that's what you prefer. Just go the office and tell them who you are. They're expecting you, and they'll have someone to show you to your class and everything,' Adele had said with a worried smile. 'I'm sure they'll look after you very well.' She'd glanced up to the school insignia welded on to the iron gates, and then slid her sunglasses back down over her eyes. 'It's a very good school.'

'I'll be fine,' Gigi had lied, desperate to be left on her own so that she could take a moment to absorb all the strangeness and get her breath.

But now, in amongst the perfumed herd, with white walls and corridors and chattering noise in every direction, she's starting to feel faint. She slips round a corner, away from the crowd, and finds herself alone in a little dead-end passage that just seems to be used for storing extra desks. It's gloomy and smells of dust. Gigi's head swims. She drops down to her haunches, the uncomfortable hard shoes digging into the tops of her feet as she does so, and cradles her head in her hands. Maybe if she just stays here until home time, no one will notice.

'What are you doing?' says a stern voice. 'Everyone's going into assembly.' Gigi glances up to see that the voice belongs to another impala with a prefect badge; how many of them are there? The prefect frowns and takes a step closer. 'Are you feeling all right? You look a little sick.'

Gigi shakes her head, unsure if she can speak

without throwing up. 'Come with me to the office,' the prefect says, and holds out her hand as if Gigi is a small child.

Gigi slowly gets to her feet, holding on to the wall to help herself up.

'I don't think I've seen you before. Are you new?' the girl asks and Gigi nods. 'Oh, no wonder you're feeling faint,' she says, marching purposefully towards the office. 'It gets better, don't worry. First days are always hell.'

★ ★ ★

Gigi sits motionless and silent in her stiff school uniform. Bryony glances across the back seat of the car and is pretty sure that her cousin has not moved a millimetre since they picked her up from outside the high-school gates. Bryony notices that Gigi's fingernails are bitten down worse than they were that morning. There is a thin tracing of red around a few of them from where hangnails have pulled and bled.

'How was it?' Bryony asks, but Gigi just lifts her shoulders in a single shrug.

'Were the peanut butter sandwiches I made you enough for lunch?' Adele asks from the front seat, but Gigi doesn't even bother to offer a shrug to that one.

Zombie Schoolgirl, thinks Bryony, making a mental note to tell Dommie: *You'd better hope she's packed a lunch, or she'll spread your brains on bread.* The thought makes Bryony feel queasy, and it's not because Dommie's Gigi-inspired movie title inventions are somehow always funnier than her own; she's remembering how nice it was to chat to her cousin while they were in bed last night. *Maybe the zombie only comes to life in the dark.* She shudders and turns away from the motionless Gigi to look out of the car window.

The black dog! It can't possibly be the same one because they're still streets away from Cortona Villas, but Bryony is suddenly icy. The dog is standing on the pavement by the side of the road; its pelt is coal-dark and polished-looking and it has the same kind of sticking-up ears as the one she saw yesterday. It turns its head to watch the car pass and Bryony's stomach heaves. Have the Silvermans told anyone on the Body Corporate board about Lesedi yet? Does the sangoma know she's been betrayed? Is she planning some terrible revenge? Bryony shuts her eyes, leans back into her seat and clutches her frozen fingers in her lap.

The role of Zombie Schoolgirl will now be played by Bryony Wilding, she thinks. But it's not funny at all.

* * *

I rise up until Adele's car becomes just one of many bright spots of metal moving along the grey ribbons of the suburban streets below me. From up here, I can see succulent, purple storm clouds gathering on the southern horizon as they prepare themselves to move in for the evening rains.

I can smell the lightning, and tiny static charges feel as if they're sparking beneath my

204

non-existent skin. I am ozone breath and rustling movement in the blond grass as small creatures prepare for the impending storm.

I am also not alone.

Ancestor. Lesedi's greeting comes to me as a feeling. It seems to emanate from everywhere at once. The hot wind sighs, and strange grey shadows shift around me. *The black dog is a warning.*

What? My response shakes the sky. I was enjoying the absence of sticky Bryony threads and the respite from constant cloying humanness.

Black dog symbols can sometimes appear when something bad is about to happen. Lesedi's answer brings the first rumble of distant thunder. *Bryony could be in danger.*

It's YOU Bryony's scared of, Lesedi. White lightning heat burns the sky.

I know.

I suddenly see a new story thread twisting in the storm ahead of me. Unlike the others I've encountered, this one is made up of two strands: one is sky blue, the other a searing white, like the lightning itself. At some points, the colours almost blend as the thread twists into complex patterns, and in others, the two strands strain to separate, tearing at one another with shocking violence, whipping back and forth.

I never planned to be someone that frightened children. I never planned for any of this at all. I can see where Lesedi's blue-white story thread burrows backwards into the past.

Come back into my memory with me, Ancestor, and see for yourself.

I follow.

Suddenly I smell Dawn body lotion and something meaty with onions cooking on a stove. I see Lesedi at fifteen. Her hair was short and fuzzy, no braids yet. She wore little gold studs in her ears and her face was moon-shaped, open.

Fifteen-year-old Lesedi walked into her grandmother's lounge and the radio jumped from station to station without anyone touching the dials. The third time this happened during Lesedi's afternoon visit, Gogo gave her a long look, and then proceeded to tell her about *the calling:* 'It can sometimes run in families. Your great-great-grandfather had the calling. He became a very powerful sangoma, the cornerstone of his community.'

'Nobody really believes that old-fashioned traditional healing stuff any more, Gogo.'

'Is that so, child?' Gogo shook her head. 'Easy to think that if you live in the city and have so little connection to your people.' This was an old gripe of her grandmother's, who thought that Lesedi's parents had abandoned rich tradition in favour of an empty western culture of *buying more things*. Lesedi was relieved when Gogo didn't launch into her usual diatribe. Instead she smiled and patted Lesedi's leg.

'Well, your great-great-grandfather was miserable, miserable and in constant pain, until he listened. He followed his dream signs to go and find his teacher, and the pain stopped and the strange things' — Gogo gave a pointed nod towards the radio — 'stopped too. And then everything was fine.'

The cooking-onion smell vanishes. I am wrenched out of Lesedi's grandmother's small, dim house and sent whirling through darkness. The blue and white story thread unwinds before me. It's all I can see.

★   ★   ★

I stop. I'm in Lesedi's cheery bedroom in her parents' large home. An unmade bed, a patterned rug, a desk with piles of university notes and Marketing textbooks on the top of it. Less than a year to go and she'd have her degree. Lesedi at twenty, staring at herself in the mirror. I watch over her shoulder and, as I do so, I can sense all her turbulent thoughts.

Lesedi knew she'd lost more weight. Her cheeks were those of an old stranger, sunken in and losing their colour. There was something else in the mirror, too, something worse. Out of the corner of her eye she could sense indistinct shapes, hundreds upon hundreds of them pressing up against her from every direction, all of them impatient, all of them waiting for her to see, to accept.

Lesedi hadn't told anyone about the ghostly shapes. She didn't want to. She hadn't even told her mother about the headaches she'd been having. They'd been getting steadily worse for years, and now they were all brain-shattering, eyeball-smearing madness and she was nauseous and exhausted and struggling to hide them.

If she told someone, it would be really happening. She would have to give up her dreams to go and live in a hut somewhere and dance around to drums and go all weird and scary and talk to dead people. The moment the words left her lips, she'd have to face up to what she knew to be the non-negotiable truth: her life was over.

What about her degree, her friends, her Thabo? She fingered the modest stone on her ring finger. What about her wedding, planned for September next year? What about her life?

Only in the mornings, after waking from a dream in which she'd seen *the woman's* face, was she calm and pain-free. The woman in Lesedi's dream wasn't someone she knew, or had ever glimpsed in real life, but her lined face always brought relief. Lesedi knew what this was supposed to mean. The woman was a sangoma somewhere, and she was supposed to seek her out and get her to teach her how to be one too. She closed her eyes and saw green mountains with sloping sides and pointed tops. Was that Swaziland?

No. I won't do it.

The smell of burnt grass filled her nostrils and her temples felt as if they'd been set alight. She dragged herself out of the house to go to class.

★   ★   ★

The bright story thread tugs forward, and I follow. I smell bus fumes and old dust. I can hear the soft mechanical hum of air conditioning and the chatter of distant voices.

Lesedi in an empty lecture hall, hours later.

208

Everyone else had already left, but Lesedi was in too much pain to stand, let alone leave the room. She hadn't heard a word of the class, and could barely even breathe without wanting to vomit. She sat rigid like a frozen doll. Suddenly, all the lights went out. There were close to a hundred little pot lights embedded into the ceiling of the lecture hall, and they all went dark except the one right above Lesedi's head.

The story thread writhes in my grip as if trying to tear itself to pieces. I wait for the wrench and the darkness, but it seems that this memory is not over. I am still there when Thabo walks in.

His expression of relief turned to concern when he saw the girl in too-loose jeans and a crumpled T-shirt in her own tiny spotlight within the vast black space. He made his way through the lecture hall, bumping his knees on chairs, and sat down beside her.

'Hey, my babe.'

'Thabo.' Her temples pulsed. Tears leaked from the corners of her eyes. 'I can't do this any more.'

'Tell me, Lesedi.'

And so she did. She told him about the pain and the dreams and her terrible, nagging suspicion that she had a calling to be a sangoma, and Thabo listened, and held her hand.

Afterwards, they sat in silence for a long time.

'Maybe you should stop trying to resist this,' Thabo said at last.

'What do you mean?'

'Do an experiment. See if you can find this dream woman and see what happens. You can't carry on like this, baby, it's no life at all.'

'But what about the wedding?'

'We'll move it.'

'What about my degree?'

'Maybe you can come back to it.'

'Will you still want me when I come back?'

'Will you still want *me*, is more to the point.' Thabo rubbed a hand across his face. 'A powerful healer who talks to the ancestors might have more on her mind than marrying a boring old business student like me.'

They looked at each other in the strange, dim light. There was so much to lose, either way.

'I'm scared, Thabo.'

'I know, my babe. Me too.' He smiled, and Lesedi nodded. She would do the experiment. She would try. As if someone had just pierced a hole in her head somewhere, all of the migraine agony was now draining out of her like water down a plughole.

★　★　★

For a moment, I'm surrounded by nothing but weightless black with the story thread spooling through it, but when the darkness clears this time, I smell wild grass and unpolluted air. Green-shouldered mountains with their rocky innards exposed in cracks and outcrops rise up around me. I can feel Lesedi's reluctance, and her hope.

Lesedi was in rural Swaziland, walking from the dirt road towards a spare collection of rudimentary buildings. Standing in the yard between them, wearing a red and black woven blanket around her shoulders, was the woman from her dreams.

Lesedi's shoulders were rigid with nerves as she walked towards the stranger to whom she knew she must be apprenticed. Her name was Ma Retabile, and she'd been dreaming of Lesedi too, but the moment she spotted the real flesh-and-blood girl in her city clothes with her lip curled at the rural smells, high-stepping through the yard to avoid the goat droppings, she'd thrown her head back and laughed.

'Oohee!' Ma Retabile yelped in Siswati between gales of mirth. 'This is going to be interesting.'

In a rush, I sense all of the confusion Lesedi felt during her first weeks in Swaziland. Her raw shock envelops me until I feel every sharp needle of horror that she experienced at the unfamiliar language, the earthy, pungent smells, the outhouse, the slaughter of chickens in the yard outside, having to go without her western underwear or familiar clothes and the strange garments she was instructed to wear instead. Her stomach was upset for days as her city-bred digestive system battled to cope with the strange, unseasoned food and the dubious water, and she sobbed herself to sleep at night in a rough blanket on the hard floor in the corner of a small room with bare grey cinder-block walls.

But the living conditions were just the start. The indistinct shapes she'd sensed in the mirror since she was a girl suddenly solidified and followed her around, everywhere. In the ink-dark hut in the middle of the night, she could feel them all pressing down on her, pinching her mud-daubed skin to get her attention, whispering consonants in her ear like the rattle of riverbed stones.

★ ★ ★

I am pulled forward again. I smell hot dust. I hear the incessant singing of cicadas that seem to solidify in the thin mountain air. Lesedi beside her teacher on a rock in the middle of a vast landscape of waving grass. I can feel the hot sun that burnt her scalp and the sweat that coated the backs of her legs.

'You are not a natural herbalist,' Ma Retabile said matter-of-factly. 'I will teach you the *muti*, but it's not going to be your strength, you don't have the nose for it.' She crumbled a fragment of dried bracken fern root between her hard brown fingers and tossed it over Lesedi's shoulder. 'You have the spirit connection very strong, though. They are talking to you, talking to you all the time and we must teach you to listen.'

Lesedi's skin erupted into goosebumps despite the heat of the morning. Her mouth tasted bitter. She longed for a cup of hot, sweet tea, but luxuries like sugar and milk were forbidden for the duration of her training.

'And you need to learn to see the pictures that are all around you, screaming for you to notice them,' Ma Retabile went on.

'Pictures?'

'Symbols. Patterns. We read them in the fallen bones, but they are also in the way *life* falls. All around us. There. What do you see?' Ma Retabile pointed across the yard at the top of the closest hill. It was low and rounded and, unlike its large, inhospitable sisters with their sharp peaks stabbing the sky beyond it, temperate enough to sport a small collection of twisted trees on its crown. The trees. A pattern.

Lesedi breathed in and out. The air was suddenly sweet. The trees were women, dancing together, one larger and thicker, its limbs enclosing the smaller slender one, guiding it, holding back the sky from crushing it.

'You and me,' Lesedi whispered, and then blanched when a sudden mist billowed up from behind the hill and flowed between the branches, surrounding the trees in a cloying blanket of dense white. 'It is going to be hard. It will put my life in danger.'

'Yes,' Ma Retabile said and, for the first time, covered Lesedi's trembling hand with her own. 'The *thwasa* is always hard. But I will be beside you, even though you can't always see.'

★ ★ ★

Hot dust and mountain sun is gone. I smell rain. I can hear it thundering on to a tin roof. It's one year later. I feel the scratch of the woollen blanket that Lesedi wore around her shoulders. She was in a large room crowded with people in tribal dress, and beyond that, a crowd of another kind waited unseen. Wild drumming competed with the rain, encouraging the drops to fall faster and faster. Lesedi could smell sweat and frankincense, musk and the now familiar sour yeastiness

213

of brewed beer. She'd been preparing for this. As Ma Retabile had often told her: 'Sometimes, reading the bones will not be enough. Sometimes the Ancestors will not want to talk in this way to you. Sometimes, you will have to go to them.'

She was ready to go, ready for the trance, but when the people and singing and the room finally receded behind a veil of charred shadow, she was not prepared for the moths.

They came from everywhere at once, zipping towards her on furred wings. An onslaught of grey, fawn, tan, white, chocolate and pitch. Moths on every side, tickling every crevice of her body and her mind. Insects, trying to get in, right inside of her!

'Breathe, Lesedi!' She heard Ma Retabile's voice as if from a huge distance away. 'You are not theirs to control.' Lesedi was dimly aware that back in the crowded room she was just a woman lying on a dirt floor, there was nothing trying to get inside her, but on this shadowed side, her mouth was full of fur and tiny legs and her throat was closing up. 'You need to take charge.'

'*Hamba.*' It was a feeble whisper. 'Listen to me.' But they had already fluttered into the chambers of her heart and the marrow of her bones.

When a grey mist swims in and swallows the rest of the scene, I realize that Lesedi had then blacked out.

I reach for her story thread lest I become adrift in the featureless void myself. It pulls me forward once again, and I smell wet soil and burning wax, and can sense Lesedi's disorientation as her consciousness returned.

It was dark. Ma Retabile was seated at her head, wiping her forehead with a damp cloth that smelt of cooked leaves. Lesedi could see a flickering candle jammed into the neck of a bottle in the corner of the room. Ma Retabile seldom wasted precious candles. There was one tiny moth circling the flame.

'I'm failing, aren't I, Ma? I'm not going to be able to become a sangoma, am I?'

'Perhaps you stand too lightly on this side of the world, Lesedi, I do not know. But I do know that it is this very connection to the other side that will make you a *great* sangoma,' Ma Retabile whispered in time with the swish of the cloth. 'But you will have to be very careful. The ones that have passed often have messages and stories they are desperate to share. Even if you wanted to, you could not keep them away.'

The dead, drawn to the living, like moths to light.

★   ★   ★

Quite suddenly, without any whooshing or parting of shadows, I am in the Matunyanes' living room in Cortona Villas. The story thread of white and blue that led me back into Lesedi's past is nowhere to be seen. The lounge suite is expensive dark brown leather and there's a woven kind of kelim rug on the floor. Lesedi sits across from me on the couch as if I am just another normal guest. She blinks. There is no story noise. I feel almost . . . solid. For a moment, I crave hot tea, and I realize that I haven't once thought of such a thing since I stopped being in Sally's skin. I swear I can almost feel the cool leather of the sofa seat as if I have nerves and blood again.

My mother still refuses to accept what I am, what I do. Lesedi looks down at her hands. *Since I returned from Swaziland with my amulets and my new wisdom, and a huge hunger to help those who needed me, she's insisted I'm just a foolish woman who dropped out of varsity, got married, and hasn't yet had the decency to produce a single grandchild. I pretend. I hide. It is not easy to be in two worlds, but you would understand that, wouldn't you, Ancestor?*

Why are you telling me all of this?

Bryony. The lounge fades behind the image of the black dog-cloud that Lesedi saw the other day. *There's something . . . dark following that child. I tried to warn her, but she'd made up her mind that I was not to be trusted; and now they are coming for me.*

Who is coming for you? My question coincides with the harsh, insistent buzz of the Matsunyanes' doorbell. The dog-cloud vaporizes. Lesedi smooths her hands over her jeans and stands up. Her brown face is expressionless.

Thank you for joining me in my memories, Ancestor. Forgive my rudeness, I must go now. Lesedi makes her way out of the living room. I hear her bare feet on the tiles, and then the sound of her opening the front door.

'I hope you don't mind me dropping in like this, Mrs Matsunyane.' I recognize Mrs Silverman's voice. 'We're here on behalf of the Body Corporate. Would it be all right if we came inside

216

for a moment to have a little chat? You're not busy, are you?'

'I just had a guest, but they're on their way now,' Lesedi says, and as she does so, I am released from the living room and the craving for tea and the almost-feel of cool leather, and am back in the sky with the story noise and the gathering storm.

*   *   *

Liam arrives home from work just as the first, fat drops of rain begin to fall. They splatter on the path leading up from the garage to the front door, sending up little puffs of dust. He pauses and then bends down to remove his shoes and socks, clutching them in one hand and his briefcase in the other as he walks towards the house. Droplets burst against the newly freed skin of his toes and the bricks of the path are warm beneath the soles of his feet.

When he gets to the front door, it swings open before his key can make contact with the lock and there stands Adele with her hand on the brass doorknob.

She crosses her arms over her cream cardigan with the shell buttons, and then uncrosses them almost immediately. Adele stands aside to let Liam in. He steps on to the Persian rug with his damp bare feet and turns to see the charcoal sky break behind him and the rain pelt down.

*   *   *

Bryony and Gigi watch the storm from the window in their bedroom. They have kept the light switched off so that their reflections cannot obscure the drama unfolding beyond the glass. Bryony moves her face as close to the open window as she can.

'Do you think this is what clouds smell like?' she asks, breathing in huge nosefuls of ozone, but Gigi is still in zombie mode after her first day of school and doesn't answer.

'What the hell are you guys doing in the dark?' Tyler asks as he pushes open the door and peers into the room. For a moment, as he stands silhouetted against the passage light, Bryony thinks that with his wide shoulders and loose-hanging arms he could be her father.

'Don't switch the light on,' she orders. 'You'll ruin the storm watch.'

Tyler, astonishingly, obeys, and then closes the door behind him and walks over to join them at the window.

'Jeez, check it out,' he says at the sight of the black trees waving wildly at the choking sky. 'It's really cooking it up out there.'

'I know.' Suddenly, a squall of rain batters against Bryony's face and she tastes icy, metallic-flavoured water before the wind changes direction again.

'Holy shit!' Tyler mutters as a flash of lightning strobes across the sky, turning the garden into flat white and blue cutouts that burn on to the inside of their eyelids. Bryony silently counts the seconds before the thunder crash, one for each kilometre.

'That's pretty close,' Tyler says. Clearly he was

counting too. That strike was only about three Ks away.'

'How far is that?'

'About as far as the Spar, I think.'

'That's close!'

'It's hailing.' It is the first thing Gigi has said all day. Tyler and Bryony stare at her for a second before following her gaze out of the window once more. She's right. Intermittent at first, plopping down in between the slashes of rain, white bullets of ice have begun to fall. They slam against the glass and ping down on to the windowsill.

'Ouch.' Bryony jumps back, giggling, as a hailstone smacks into her forehead.

'See if you can catch one in your mouth,' Tyler laughingly instructs her, and she opens her jaw wide against the wind, waiting for ice to bounce in.

'Hey,' Gigi says, as if the storm has woken her from her miserable trance, 'they're tasty.' She picks a hailstone off the sill and pops it into her mouth. She chews, grins at Bryony, and reaches for another. Bryony follows suit, crunching the frozen rain between her teeth. It tastes so fresh that it's almost fizzy.

'Mmm, vegan treats,' Gigi says, and holds out her hand to catch a handful of falling stones. She's laughing so much as she pops them into her mouth that some of them bounce right out again and fly back outside to join their uncaptured brothers.

Tyler laughs. 'You girls are nuts.'

'You should try them, they're yummy,' Bryony

says, crushing a large one between her molars. Her whole mouth is numb from the cold.

'*Ja*. Try one, Tyler,' Gigi says and, as she speaks, she turns from the window and pushes a hailstone right into the pink heat of his mouth.

Tyler's eyes go very wide at the shock of her cold fingers on the intimate inside of his lips, and he almost chokes on the little hailstone that now melts on his tongue. Gigi turns back to the storm with a toss of her head, and he can smell her hair: traces of the familiar shampoo that Adele buys for all of them to use, and something else — something warm and almost animal.

Drunk from the thrill of her slippery fingers inside his mouth, Tyler lets himself lean forward till the length of his body is almost touching Gigi's slender back. He bends to breathe in more of her hair, only jerking back, confused, when he realizes that Gigi is suddenly holding herself rigid, like a statue.

Lightning once more flashes into the room, and in the electric purple-white, Tyler glances sideways to see his sister watching them both. Her pupils are very black and large and her mouth is open in a little 'o'.

★   ★   ★

Next door to the Wildings, in the kitchen of the Matsunyane household, Thabo stretches across the granite countertop and curls his fingers around one of his wife's braids. He resists the urge to give it a hard downward tug like a bell-pull, but from the way she looks up at him it's clear that she knows he wants to. Thabo sighs and lets the braid slip out of his fingers.

Outside, the storm is building, and the wind chucks furious handfuls of rain against the kitchen window.

'You've every right to be angry, Thabo.' Lesedi wraps the same braid around her own finger. 'I'm pretty pissed off myself.'

'You sure you want to do this, Sedi? Can't you just stop consulting here at home? I'm sure this whole thing would blow over soon.'

'Ag, babe, you didn't see how they looked at me,' Lesedi says. The kettle clicks and she lifts it to pour hot water into the instant coffee and sugar mixture waiting in the bottom of two mugs. The coffee foams up, brown and creamy. 'I know the score by now. They're never ever going to forget that there's a sangoma living right beside them in their safe little gated village, trust me on this.'

'Can't you just explain to them that it's not what they think? It's not all crazy juju, but common-sense counselling for the most part?'

'With a spot of bone-throwing here and there.'

'Sure, but half these housewives go to fortune tellers and crystal healers and what not. It's the same damn thing.'

'That doesn't change the fact that I scare them, Thabs. Sure, it's against the rules to run a business here, but when Mrs Pieterson was operating her interior-design thingy from her dining room, no one even raised an eyebrow. South Africa may have come a long way from the dark days, babe, but sangomas sanctioned in

Cortona Villas? Even I know that's pushing it.'

'Shit,' Thabo mutters as he goes over to the fridge to get the milk. 'I've worked hard to get us into a place like this, Sedi. Somewhere safe and nice with good resale value and everything.'

'And I've messed it up. I know. I am sorry, Thabs.'

'I thought you were going to lie low this time.'

'I did lie low. I never did anything that would cast the slightest suspicion. But these things have a way of coming out, babe, they always do.'

Her husband is still standing at the fridge with his back to her. She stares at the creases on the bottom of his mauve Hilton Weiner work shirt from where it was tucked inside his trousers all day and bites her lip.

'I'm going to leave for Swaziland in the morning,' she says.

'What?' He freezes, and then closes the fridge door very slowly and deliberately. 'Why?'

'Well, for one thing, I need to get away from here as fast as possible so that the Body Corporate board can simmer down.'

'So go to a hotel or something close by. Your sister's place in Parkview, even? You don't need to go trudging off to the bloody middle of nowhere just because a bunch of scared whiteys are on the warpath.'

'No, it needs to be Swaziland.' Lesedi sips on her coffee and pictures the tufted green of the triangular mountains rising up towards the blue. 'I need to speak to Ma Retabile and get some advice on how to do this, Thabs.'

'How to do what?'

'Live in two worlds.'

'For God's sake, Lesedi.' He huffs out a breath and the large metal buckle on his belt clinks into the countertop as he leans heavily against it. 'What does she know? Out there everything is still one way, babe. *Sangomas* still wear beads and animal gunk and everyone hangs on their every word — what advice can she possibly give you about trying to follow your calling here in Jozi.'

'I don't know, but I do know that somehow there's an answer for me out there where she is.' Lesedi stirs milk into their coffee. Thabo likes his pale brown and very sweet, like a child. 'I'm sorry.'

'How long for? You were in Swaziland for nearly two years the last time. Three if you count the back-and-forth with apprenticing and ceremonies and stuff.'

'That was for my *thwasa*. Not that long this time.' Lesedi takes a sip of her drink. Despite the sugar, it still tastes bitter. 'But I really don't know.'

'When are we going to be able to start building up a life, have kids and . . . ?'

Lesedi puts her mug down and folds forward, sinking her head down to rest on the cool stone of the counter. She smells rain and ice. 'Oh God, I don't know. That's what I need my teacher for. Ma Retabile is about a million times wiser than I could ever be, babe, she can help me find the answers.'

'Just tell me this, Sedi,' Thabo says, and then waits for the loud rumble of thunder to pass. 'Do

223

you still want to have a family and a life with me and everything? I mean, does it fit in with your . . . other plans?'

'Yes,' Lesedi says, and means it. 'I do. I am just not sure how, and this whole Body Corporate drama has made me see that I can't just go along pretending that I'm doing OK when I'm messing up.' Her voice rises, and she clenches her fingers into fists on the cool granite. 'I'm a lousy sangoma and a lousy Joburg wife and I miss marketing and sometimes I just want to forget all of this and go back and get my degree but I know that I can't because *the calling* won't let me.'

'Hey hey, Sedi, come now,' Thabo says, finally walking around the counter that seems to have ballooned into a cliff face between them. He takes his wife into his arms. 'Don't start beating yourself up about all this again, OK?'

'I didn't choose this, Thabo. You know it.'

'I know.'

'I didn't plan for all of this sangoma stuff to come and unstick our lives,' she says into the warmth of his neck. 'There must be a way for me to be able to do it, to have us and a family and to stay true to the calling.'

'I don't know, Sedi. I sure as hell hope there is.'

'Which is why I must go to Swaziland,' she says. 'To find out.'

'I guess.' Their reflection in the blank face of the kitchen window is made wild and blurry by the thrumming rain outside, and to Thabo it looks as though the kitchen is dissolving. He shuts his eyes and makes a few mental calculations: how much could he sell the house for? The

224

market is lousy. Maybe he should keep it and rent it out: the rents in Cortona Villas are high, maybe even enough to cover the bond. With the market the way it is, he can probably pick up a new property at a really good deal.

'Thabs?' Lesedi says.

'Uh-huh?'

'Don't get another place in a townhouse complex. Just a regular house, OK? A place where we won't be spied on every minute of every day.'

'Somewhere with no Body Corporate?'

'Exactly.' She smiles. 'Now I'd better get upstairs and start packing.'

'And we've got some serious 'going away' sex to get covered too,' he says, and her laugh is drowned out by another peel of thunder.

I leave the Matsunyanes. I rise up out of the house, through the madness of the storm and into the calm above. The sky here is inky and studded with stars, and below me the carpet of clouds heaves and roils, lit up from within by electric flashes that smell like burnt rain.

18

Bryony, Tyler and Gigi step out of the front door into the unseasonably cool morning to find that the garden is a wreck: all the flowers have been pulverized by the hail, and the once colourful flowerbeds are a mulch of bruised browning petals and broken stalks.

'Oh, for heaven's sake,' Adele mutters when she comes out behind them and spots her potted lavender. Half the grey-green stalks have been broken. Their damage perfumes the air and the tips of Adele's fingers as she brushes the plants on her way past.

The lawn is dotted with shredded leaves and small branches that have been ripped from the surrounding trees, and Bryony kicks bits of it aside as she follows her mother and brother down the path towards the garage.

Gigi stops to inspect the remains of a tattered nest that must have been blown from a nearby tree and is now lying on the ground beside the path. There are two little broken eggs in it. She touches the edge of one translucent, speckled shell and looks up to see if she can spot the bereaved parents. The sky, wiped clean and brilliant blue by last night's rains, is empty.

'Come on, Gigi. You don't want to be late on your second day of school,' Adele calls from the garage and climbs into the driver's seat. 'You too, Tyler, get a move on.'

'You can have the front for a change, Bryony,' Tyler mutters to his surprised sister, nudging her out of the way so that he can slide into the back beside Gigi.

Gigi's shift away from him is almost imperceptible, but it is enough to make his face pink with confusion. For the hundredth time since it happened, he remembers her fingers flicking along the inside of his lip. He turns to glare out of the window. Why won't she even *look* at him now?

Bryony stretches out in the luxury of the big front seat and clips in her seat belt as Adele reverses out of the garage.

'Oh no!' Bryony gasps.

'What?'

'The fever tree. Look.' The slender, powdery green trunk of the little tree that stands between their driveway and the Matsunyanes' has bent and split in last night's storm, and half of the branches hang from shreds of bark, their small leaves and broken thorns crushed into the white pebbles.

'Oh damn,' Adele says, braking beside it to get a better look. 'Those trees take ages to grow.'

'Is it going to have to be cut down?'

'Hmm, maybe some of it can be saved if they saw off the broken parts.'

'Shame.' Bryony stares at the raw, pale innards of the tree that are now exposed. 'It looks sore.'

'Since when are you so worried about trees?' Tyler sneers from the back seat.

Bryony doesn't answer. Adele's slow reversing has now revealed that Matsunyanes' garage door

227

is open, and she can see Mr Matsunyane loading what looks like a suitcase into Lesedi's car boot.

'Looks like someone's going on a trip,' Adele says, and waves to Mr Matsunyane as she accelerates past.

* * *

Gigi squats on top of the closed toilet lid, not daring to touch the surface of it with anything other than the soles of her school shoes. It is quiet in the bathroom. She is the only one in here, crouching on her loo seat in a stall at the far end of the row. The bathrooms are gloomy, but this particular stall glows a strange green from the light filtering through the leaves of the creeper whose verdant growth has covered the small, high window.

The smell in here is horrible, but at least she is alone. At least she doesn't have to try and pretend that she understands what on earth is going on in algebra. The teacher seems to be talking in another language. Although she seems to be up to speed with English, History and Biology, Gigi has quickly realized just how sorely her home schooling was lacking in the Maths and other Science departments.

The impala herd appears to communicate in another language too, full of references she has no clue about, like TV shows on DSTV, something called Mxit, and people she thinks must be pop stars, but she's not quite sure. No one talks about the Four Noble Truths, or how to give subcutaneous rabies injections to small

228

mammals, or what best to do to get a terrified mongoose to start eating. It is becoming clearer and clearer that Gigi is another species altogether.

She digs in her blazer pocket and pulls out the badge that she found lying on the school lawn during first break. It is blue and shiny and says something in Latin, and she thinks that it's probably indicative of some kind of academic achievement; she's seen others like it pinned on to some of the less sporty-looking impalas' blazers. This one must've fallen off. Gigi runs her fingertips along the glassy top, and then turns it over and releases the pin. It's very sharp, made to stab through the thick fabric of a blazer lapel with no trouble at all.

She rolls down her left sock and touches the badge pin to the soft hollow beneath the pointed pale triangle of her ankle bone. It tickles. Then she presses, hard, shutting her eyes and focusing on the feeling of the metal sliding into her skin. Tears spring out from under her eyelids and she bites her lip. Her sweating fingers slip on the slick badge, but she readjusts her grip and stabs once more before ripping the pin out of her flesh, clipping it closed and shoving it back into her pocket.

Gigi has a handful of crumpled toilet paper ready to sop up the blood, and as she sits with it pressed against the tiny wound, she stares at the blooming red flower seeping and growing across the white paper. When it is almost saturated, she replaces it with another before lifting the wet, red piece up to her face and breathing in the smell of meat and metal. Her stomach heaves, but she forces herself to inhale it again.

* * *

'Hey, did you hear?' Dommie whispers to Bryony across the art-room desk. 'Your sangoma left this morning.'

'Left?' Bryony pauses in her drawing. She has abandoned the mask idea for her 'What South Africa Means to Me' picture and is now happily drawing a dung beetle with different designs in each stripe on its shell to represent each of the eleven national languages. 'Like how do you mean?'

'I mean gone, vamoosed, left the building. My mom and some other board members went round to visit her yesterday to tell her off about the running a business thing and she told them not to worry, she was going away. And then this morning, she went.'

'Oh.' Bryony feels strange, as though her head is suddenly very light and is going to go floating up towards the ceiling. She clenches her jaw as hard as she can to stop it from doing any such thing.

'I thought you'd be thrilled.'

'I am.'

'Then why do you look so weird?'

'Just got a little dizzy, that's all.'

'Your nightmares will probably stop now that there's no longer a witch doctor living next door.'

'*Ja*,' Bryony agrees.

'Girls, let's have less whispering and more drawing, please,' Miss McCrae says in a firm voice as she stops beside their desk to take note of their progress. 'Nice, Dommie, you've got a real sense of movement there.'

Bryony glances up at her teacher and gasps.

'Goodness, what is it, Bryony?'

'Your earrings.'

'I know, aren't they adorable?' Miss McCrae smiles and touches one of her dangly earrings with a finger. 'They're Scotties. My favourite of the terrier family.' A little carved black dog glitters as it swings on the end of its silver chain, back and forth, back and forth beside Miss McCrae's tanned neck.

'Lovely,' croaks Bryony, and bends her head down over her work. She has to concentrate hard to keep from throwing up.

★　★　★

Lesedi winds down the car window and breathes in the rich scent of earth and low cloud. A woman selling small, hard-looking mangos from a plastic bowl at a rickety table by the side of the rutted road shares a luminous smile, and a small boy with a herd of floppy-eared goats waves as Lesedi drives past.

Hello, Swaziland.

Ahead, the road swoops upwards and then curves left behind the aloe-spotted, green skirts of an approaching mountain. *It's good to be back.*

231

* * *

Bryony walks up to the fever tree and inspects the places where the Cortona Villas gardeners have neatly amputated its broken limbs. They have also swept up the fallen leaves, but Bryony can see one papery thorn still jammed in between two pebbles. She steps closer, avoiding the thorn, and places her palm on the raw blond patch of torn trunk. She is surprised to find that it is slightly damp, as if the tree has been sweating.

'Sorry, tree,' she whispers under her breath. 'You look too skinny now; like a certain cousin of mine.'

Bryony glances around to make sure that she's alone, although there's seldom anyone about this early in the afternoon, and the absence of Lesedi and her tapeworms from Cortona Villas is almost tangible, like a seasonal shift in the air. Then she carefully puts her arms around the fever tree's wounded, lop-sided trunk and rests her head against the warm green bark.

'You'll be OK,' she whispers, and shuts her eyes and feels the tree beneath one cheek and the soft breeze on the other and for a moment forgets about her nightmares and the Gigi-zombie and her mother's permanent tension and her dad's strange sadness and just breathes in time with the movement of the remaining branches above her head.

The sound of an approaching car engine startles her out of her reverie. Her first horrible thought is that Lesedi has come back, but the car

232

is neither Mr Matsunyane's silver GTi, nor Lesedi's dark blue Polo. It is a small maroon Kia with car-hire stickers on its windows, and when it pulls up in the guest parking bay opposite the house, a slender woman with shiny long brown hair gets out and then carefully locks the car door behind her.

The woman is wearing floaty caramel-coloured pants and flat leather sandals and has a chunky string of reddish wooden beads wrapped around one delicate wrist. As she crosses the road towards Bryony, the breeze carries the scent of herbs and flowers ahead of her. Bryony's heart begins to thump.

'Are you Simone?' she blurts out, and the woman pauses, startled.

'Why, yes I am,' she says with an uncertain smile.

'I'm Bryony. Have you come for Gigi?'

'Gosh, aren't you an intuitive one?'

'She's inside. Come, I'll take you.'

★   ★   ★

'She's upstairs in my bedroom.'

Gigi, lying on her side on top of the racing-car duvet with her knees held in close, can't hear the words, but is alert to the excited tone in Bryony's voice and the sing-song syllables of her own name floating up from the garden below.

The front door opens and shuts, and Gigi, who has been staring across the room at the cherries on Bryony's bedding for so long that her vision is now all patchy with bright fruit shapes, slowly sits up and swings her legs off the bed. Her wounded ankle throbs, but she doesn't allow herself to rub it.

Footsteps pound on the carpeted stairs, and then the bedroom door flies open and Bryony bursts in, pink-faced and out of breath. 'She's here,' she says.

'What?' Gigi's mouth is stiff from another day of silence. 'Who?'

'Simone.'

Gigi blinks; then she almost levitates off the bed, jams on her flip-flops and hurtles past Bryony and out of the room. She barely sees the stairs beneath her feet and then the Persian rug of the hall as she races towards the lounge. There, finally, standing beside the sofa in the lounge, deep in serious-looking conversation with Adele, is Simone.

Gigi stops. There's an avalanche of sobs fighting to get out of her aching throat but her lips are pressed tight. Something is different about Simone. The set of her shoulders and the hard little points of her bare elbows prevent Gigi from running towards her.

'Simone?' she whispers, and the woman turns and smiles despite the tears that spring at once from her eyes. Gigi goes to her then, and inhales the Turkish-Delight-sweet smell of geranium as she curls into her arms.

'I'd better get that kettle on, hadn't I?' Adele mutters. 'Come on, Bryony.'

'But — '

'No buts. Off we go.'

Bryony trots out of the room behind her

mother, who is pulling her ever-faithful sun-glasses down from their spot on the top of her head (where she always seems to keep them now) and over her raw eyes.

Simone pulls away from the embrace too soon and wipes her cheeks. 'Well, who knew there were any more tears inside this old girl, hey?'

Gigi stumbles to regain her balance as cool air rushes in to take the place of Simone's scented warmth.

'You're here,' she says. Unlike Simone, Gigi's tears aren't anywhere near done. She can feel them all throbbing and swelling behind her eyes, but she forces them back in, trying to mirror Simone's decorum. 'When did you get back from Scotland?'

'This morning.' Simone sits on the edge of the sofa with the floral cushions on it, and the fabric of her loose pants hangs down so that Gigi can see how thin her thighs have gotten. Her eyes look as though they've lost something too, as if some of the light that was in them before has been left behind in Scotland. 'It was a ghastly flight,' Simone says in a bright, chatty voice as Gigi sits down on the sofa beside her. 'I think that if Dante had lived today and spent twelve hours in a tiny aeroplane seat, his circles of hell would've been somewhat different.'

It feels like decades since Gigi's heard some-one talking about things like Dante and hell circles. Simone and her mom often made literary references: *I have to do something with my English degree, darling.* At the memory of her mother, Gigi dips her head and stares at her knees poking

235

out from beneath the ugly brown school tunic; they look pale with mottled bits of mauve in them. She pulls down the hem of the skirt as far as it will go.

'Isn't this a lovely house? You've landed with your bum in the butter, haven't you, Gi?'

'It's all right. I miss home, though.'

'Me too.' Simone's voice drops to a taut whisper, all forced cheeriness gone. Her hands clench in her lap as if she's trying to squeeze the blood right out of them. 'I still can't believe that those men just marched in there and did those terrible things . . . '

'It's going to be all right,' Gigi says, placing a hand on top of Simone's clutching ones. 'You'll make it better again. You're good at healing broken things.'

'Oh, Gi.' Simone flicks her head back hard, as if trying to shake the imagined images of the massacre out of it. 'There's no way I can ever go back to that place. Not after what happened.'

Gigi's stomach swoops. 'Of course you can. You know, get back on the horse like you always say.'

Simone remains motionless. Gigi can hear the hiss of the kettle boiling in the kitchen and the sound of Bryony's voice somewhere in the house.

'I've sold the farm, Gigi.'

Gigi looks down at her knees again. She can feel the thumping of her heart all through her body, but especially in the wounded hollow of her ankle. There's a strange buzzing sound in her ears.

236

'How . . . What do you mean, sold it?'

'A friend of my father's has been wanting to buy the land for years, and so I contacted him from Scotland and we made a deal. He's been very kind. He even packed up all our things and organized for them to be transported down to my brother's place here in Joburg.'

'Oh.' Gigi takes her hand off Simone's.

'Seb's folks had already collected anything they wanted after the funeral, to remember their boy by.' Simone's voice trembles as she tries to keep it steady. 'And Johan's sister came by and did the same.'

At the mention of Johan's name, Gigi opens her eyes very wide, forcing away the memory of his body as it lay crumpled up against the grimy kitchen skirting board. There'd been a gash across his wide lovely chest, with the stuff in it congealing and clotted, reminding her of Simone's homemade blackcurrant jam. There had been flies.

'I told you over the phone that the animals have all found new caring homes, didn't I?' Simone says.

'But where are we going to live?'

A plane flying overhead slices through the thick afternoon air and fills the room with engine noise.

'You live *here*, Gigi.'

'No I don't. I've just been *staying* here until you get back.'

'But, sweetie, I'm not coming back.'

There is a very long pause as Gigi tries to get enough breath into her lungs to speak.

'What? I don't . . . ' Her suddenly numb

mouth isn't capable of forming any more words.

'I can't live in a country where people can just march into your home and violate everything you've built and slice you and your family to pieces for no goddamn reason whatsoever.' Simone's voice has a ragged edge to it.

'But you always said that the farm was where you felt the most free.'

'I know. I used to feel that way, Gigi, but everything's changed now.' Simone's face crumples, and she lets out a small sob. 'I'm so sorry, hon, I'm just not nearly as strong as I thought I was.'

Gigi pinches the skin above her knees.

'I have decided to emigrate to the UK,' Simone whispers. 'Thank goodness for my British passport. I just came back here to see you and my family and to tie up all the loose ends.'

'But you hate the cold.'

Simone says nothing. The sound of her breath is loud in the still room.

'You hate it.'

'Gigi — '

'You always said you hated it.'

'I know.'

★   ★   ★

Gigi stands by the torn fever tree and watches as Simone crosses the road, opens the boot of her hired car, and pulls out a large, faded blue suitcase. The case thumps on to the pavement, sending up puffs of dust around its little wheels, and then rattles and swerves as Simone steers it back towards the Wildings' garden gate.

238

'I wasn't sure how many things of your mom's you wanted to keep, Gi, so this is a bit of a hodgepodge of your stuff and hers that were sent to my brother from the farm. Your kudu horn is in here. I know how fond you were of that.'

Gigi doesn't answer. She rubs the back of her wrist across her eyes and blinks to try and clear her vision. The sun is low on the horizon, and the light it sheds is gold and thick and buttery, making Cortona Villas look like a movie set: flat, newly erected and painted to look almost too real. Simone herself looks no more convincing, as if she's nothing but a slender animated figure constructed from pixels.

'Tell your aunt thanks so much for the offer of dinner, darling, but they're expecting me at my brother's house before it gets dark. We're all a little highly strung about safety at the moment — as you can imagine.' Simone tilts her head to one side and tries a smile. 'Don't be cross with me, Gi; I'll see you before I go back to the UK, I promise.'

Gigi looks away and focuses intently on wrapping her fingers around the handle of the suitcase.

'It's such a relief to see you so well settled in here. What a lovely family, hey? They really deserve to have a super girl like you join the ranks.'

Super girl. Gigi doesn't recall Simone ever saying such inane things before. She used to talk about healing energy and the preciousness of life and could quote all sorts of things from the Bhagavad Gita and Patanjali's Sutras.

Simone leans across the bulk of the suitcase to give Gigi a geranium- and lemongrass-oil-scented hug. Through the fine fabric of her top, Simone's spine is like a warm string of beads and Gigi imagines digging her fingers through her thin flesh, gripping one of the bones and then ripping the whole thing out in one swift movement. For a second, her arms tighten. *I could beg. Maybe if I beg her, she'll change her mind.*

But then Simone kisses her cheek and steps away, and Gigi's arms flop back down to her sides.

'I'm amazed at how strong you are, Gi. After all you've been through. Your mom would be so proud.'

Gigi shrugs, turns and, dragging the clattering suitcase behind her, walks towards the house.

★　★　★

I follow Simone for a while, hovering above the little maroon bonnet of her hire car as she drives (badly, as it happens, she's clearly unused to the clutch) through Johannesburg's evening rush hour traffic. She is weeping behind her steering wheel and taking in oxygen in big, sobbing gasps. Her nose is running but she doesn't bother to wipe it, and her beautiful face looks as if it is disintegrating beneath tears and snot.

Simone was never a big cryer, even when we were at primary school together in our blue uniforms, white socks, black shoes and uncomfortable regulation royal-blue panties. As I remember it, there always seemed to be *something* to cry

240

about in those years, and I often felt as if my tears were hovering just below the tissue-fine surface of me, waiting for an opportunity to spring free. But my small-boned, fragile-looking best friend Simone hardly ever cried.

As an adult, Simone seemed to continue to motor on through life in just as dry-eyed a fashion; but there was one occasion when I saw her fall apart . . .

Gigi and I were just approaching our fourth anniversary on the farm in Limpopo, and had become as much a part of the scenery as Seb's old ploddy Polonius and the saggy-bottomed sofa that lived on the stoep and sent up clouds of dust and animal hair every time someone flopped down into it.

One night, Simone and Seb were driving back from the successful release of a steenbok on a nearby game farm, when they swerved to miss a pothole on the dark gravel road. They felt the jolt of an impact and heard a squeal, and in the spill of the headlights could just make out an animal scrambling to its feet and running off into the night. Seb got out of the bakkie and crouched down to inspect the tracks the wounded creature had left: in the moth-flecked light of his torch he could see that the prints were those of a jackal, small, most likely a female. They drove back to the farm in shocked silence.

At daybreak the following morning, Seb and Simone got into the bakkie and drove back along the same road, found the spot of the accident, and then proceeded to track the jackal's bloody and stumbling journey back to her den. By the time they finally found her, she was close to death, her ribs broken and body clearly racked by internal bleeding. Snuggled into her heaving belly were two tiny, flop-eared offspring, trying to suckle. The pups were a few days old at most, eyes still shut and unable to use their fuzzy new legs for anything more than dragging themselves to a teat. Simone pulled off her T-shirt and wrapped them inside it as Seb hoisted the wounded mother into his arms, and they trekked in this fashion for over an hour through the singing, fragrant bush and back to the bakkie.

By the time they reached the farm, red-shouldered, white-faced and silent, the mother jackal was dead, and the babies, little scraps of tan and grey fur nestled inside Simone's lilac 'Save the Whales' T-shirt, were squealing for their missed meals.

She tried that entire day to get them to drink from a tiny bottle, and then a syringe, using every trick she could think of, but the two little jackal pups wanted their mom and were having none of it; no more than a few, meagre drops got past their whiskery snouts and on to their quivering pink tongues.

Simone refused to give up; she stayed with those pups the entire day and all through the next night, refusing to let any of us take over to give her a break, trying to get them to take drops of warm milk from her shaking fingers, talking to them, hugging them against her skin to try and keep them warm, and eventually whimpering along with them in desperation as they grew weaker and weaker.

Finally, in the grey dawn hours, before the birds began their morning racket, she got one of the little guys to open its mouth and accept the bottle teat, but it seemed to have forgotten how to suck, and streams of pale milk just dribbled out of its jaw and soaked into the baby blanket it was wrapped in.

I found Simone a few hours later, holding the tiny, limp puppy corpses to her heart and staring out into the garden with hollow, grey-ringed eyes. Later that day, she and Seb buried the pups beside their mother in the little piece of land behind the old farm-equipment shed that we reserved for the graves of the creatures who hadn't made it. Gigi stood at Simone's side and sang a goodbye song for the dead family in her high, lilting little-girl voice. The words were meaningless sounds, and the tune something she made up on the spot, but the sincerity behind it was naked and beautiful.

I watched, fascinated, as the tears streamed down Simone's sunburnt cheeks, collected beneath her neat little chin and plopped down on to the vivid, freshly turned soil at her feet.

That afternoon, I returned to the gravesite, but her tears, of course, were gone; long soaked down into the red earth to join the little jackals beneath.

*   *   *

Adele had been expecting Simone to stay for supper and had instructed Dora to conjure up a rather peculiar collection of meat-free dishes and lay the table, but at the sight of her niece trudging up the stairs alone with that terrible dusty old suitcase, she'd quickly whipped off place setting number six and rearranged the remaining five to hide the gap. She needn't have bothered, for, once again, just as when she first arrived at the Wildings', Gigi has not come down for dinner.

'It's like eating something that's been scraped out the bottom of a pond,' Tyler mutters after a mouthful of lentil biryani.

'Rubbish. It's surprisingly tasty,' Liam says, clearly in no mood to indulge the *angry young man* tonight. Bryony has to agree with her dad; she rather likes it, even though the texture is a little gluey.

'You sure you told Gigi we were about to eat?' Adele asks, and Bryony rolls her eyes.

'Yes, Mom. I've already told you.'

'What did she say?'

'Nothing, of course. She just lay there under the duvet with her flip-flops on.'

'She's just upset that Simone isn't staying for dinner, that's all,' says Adele.

'Oh, Sim-o-ne,' Liam says, scooping up another forkful. 'I remember Simone. I know she was really kind to your sister and gave her a new life and everything, but boy, what a tree-hugging nutcase.'

'Well, she's kind of hot for an old lady,' Tyler grins, shovelling in another mouthful of pond scrapings.

'Oh honestly, Tyler.'

'Well, she is, Ma. Nice bod.'

'Not at the table, please,' Adele snaps and Tyler pulls a face. Bryony doesn't giggle; she's remembering the way Gigi's face had looked when she stumbled into the bedroom with that weird suitcase after Simone had driven away.

'So what did nutty, hot Simone have to say for herself, then?' Liam asks.

'She told me that she's emigrating. The poor thing can't stand the thought of coming back to live in South Africa after what happened,' Adele says.

'Emigrating? Like leaving the country?' Bryony gasps.

'Duh, what else do you think it means, Bry?'

'What about the farm?' There's a headachy tightness at the base of Bryony's jaw.

'She's sold it, apparently,' Adele says. 'Best choice she could've made, if you ask me.'

Bryony stares down at her strange food. She thinks of Gigi going on about how wonderful everything is going to be when she moves back with Simone and blinks hard to try and chase away the sudden shadows that seem to swim in from the corners of the bright kitchen. 'Oh, shame,' she whispers.

'What was that, Bry?' Adele asks.

'Nothing.'

'Well, Gigi's obviously taking this news rather badly. I think I'd better go up and talk to her,' Liam says, pushing his chair back from the table. 'We really can't have all this staying-in-bed nonsense again.'

Adele gives her husband a brief, sharp look, and then shrugs. 'Be my guest.'

'She's going to be staying with us forever now, isn't she?' Bryony asks as her father makes his way round the table.

'Well, of course she is, Bry, we're her legal guardians,' Liam says as he passes her chair, and gives her hair a quick ruffle. 'She was never going to be going anywhere else. Nothing's changed.'

★ ★ ★

'Gigi?' Liam walks into the bedroom and switches on the light. 'Honey, you're missing dinner.'

The racing-car-patterned lump remains motionless. Liam hovers at the foot of her bed and rubs the back of his neck.

'Seeing Simone again must've brought back a lot of memories, hey?' Still the bedding does not move. Liam notices the red, rubbery edge of one dirty flip-flop sticking out from beneath the duvet cover. 'I know you're feeling pretty upset right now, but just imagine what a wacky world it would be if everyone just dived into bed with their shoes on every time something went wrong?' He gives a soft laugh. 'My law firm would be a very different place, I'll tell you that!'

A mosquito, drawn by the light in the room, hums out of hiding and whines close to Liam's ear. He tries to swat it, misses, tries again, and slaps himself unexpectedly hard on his right cheek. At the sound of the slap the bedding lump twitches.

'Ah, so you are awake, then?' Liam says, leaning over the spot where he thinks Gigi's head must be. 'Come on out, Gigisaurus. We're all waiting for you at the table.' His no-nonsense tone has no effect. Gigi remains hidden, still and silent. 'Right, I think it's time to shed a little light on the situation, hey? What do you think, Gi? No means no, and no answer means yes.' He pauses, waiting. Nothing.

'Okey-dokey!' he says in a too loud, jocular voice. 'The time has come.' With that, Liam lunges forward and whips the bedding off the bed. Gigi is curled up on one side with her knees pulled up and her school tunic riding high on her thighs, barely covering her panties. Her hands fly to the hem of the dress to try and yank it down, and then she rises off the bed like a fury, her face very white.

'How dare you?' she screams at Liam, who leaps back, startled and horrified. 'What kind of pervy old asshole are you?'

'I didn't mean . . . you know I was just trying to get you to come down to sup — '

'You had no right to do that! Get out!' Gigi sobs and spits at him; her whole body is vibrating with indignant rage.

'Come on, Gigi, you know that I — '

'GET OUT, GET OUT, GET OUT!' she howls like an animal, and the sound is so electrifying that Liam cannot move at all. He just stands and gapes at the unrecognizable girl with her distorted mouth, wild hair and now bright-red face.

'What is going on up here?' Tyler bursts through the door, breathless from his sprint up the stairs. 'Dad, is — '

'You!' Gigi whirls around to face Tyler. 'Why

the fuck won't you leave me alone?'

'Tyler?' Adele calls up the stairs in a high-pitched, frightened voice.

'Are you people DEAF?' Gigi screams, her voice now hoarse and breaking. 'GET OUT!'

Tyler, white-lipped, reverses back the way he came, bumping into Bryony who has just arrived to see what's going on, and hustling her away from the doorway to make way for Liam. Liam hesitates, staring at his raging niece for a moment before striding out of the room in such a way that it looks like his idea all along. As soon as he's on the landing with the rest of the gathered Wildings, Gigi slams the bedroom door shut.

They all gape at the blank white wood. Nobody moves. From the other side of the door they can still hear helpless, furious sobbing.

'Come on, everyone,' Adele whispers at last. 'Let's give her some space.'

'We haven't finished supper,' Liam adds, as if this is suddenly very important.

They all back away from the door and start trooping down the stairs. Bryony, walking behind her father, notices that his ears are pink and his hand on the banister is shaking.

'What happened?' Adele mouths to Liam, but he just shakes his head.

★ ★ ★

Bryony pauses on the threshold of her bedroom. She's tingly from her bath, and her head, which feels light and empty and strange, seems to be missing out on some of its regular supply of blood. She grips the doorframe to steady herself as she peers into the darkness. Gigi has returned to her bed, and the room is stuffy and silent.

I really don't want to go in. But Bryony's eyelids are heavy and her limbs feel all achy as if she's been playing hockey all day. Her need to lie down overwhelms her trepidation, and she stumbles into the bedroom and clambers into her bed, tucking the cherry duvet high up under her chin and facing the wall away from Gigi.

Demon Zombies with PMS. *That's a good one. I must remember to tell Dommie tomorrow . . .*

★ ★ ★

Bryony dreams. She's at school. The bell rings and everyone is grabbing their bags and rushing off, chattering. It seems to take Bryony ages and ages to get her things together and by the time she's ready to leave, the corridors are empty and full of echoes. She hears someone laugh, and the patter of school shoes on the shiny concrete around the corner, but then, nothing.

It is late. Why is she at school so late? She begins to run towards the gate, praying that her mother is still waiting for her in her big silver car. The street is empty. No Mercedes. There's no one around at all.

But the black dog is back.

It is waiting at the bottom of the school steps. It cocks its head to one side and opens its jaws, wider and wider, impossibly wide. Darkness, like putrid vomit, streams from its throat and coats the road, the steps, Bryony's shoes. It billows up around her legs, blankets the buildings across the street and clots the sky. She can no longer tell what is dog and what is darkness.

And then she is swallowing the darkness down into her; she can feel it ripping her throat up and sinking into her belly.

Bryony screams and screams till her throat is raw, but her voice is nothing but night.

* * *

Bryony wakes up drenched in sweat. Her mouth is jammed open and has glued the side of her face to the pillow with drool. Her throat feels as if it is on fire. She opens her eyes, but the room is inky black, and she cannot even make out the lump of Gigi in the bed on the other side of it.

'Mom,' she croaks, but everything is dried up, and no sound comes out. She drags herself, shivering, from beneath the covers, and flinches when her feet touch the carpet. The soft pile feels like hairbrush bristles on her tender soles. She braves the pain, and forces herself to stand up, but her head swims, and she collapses down to a half-crouch, hurting the back of her thighs on the wooden edge of the bed as she goes down.

One breath.

Another breath.

She manages to stand properly this time and, clutching the wall for support, even though it is icy cold beneath her fingers, she makes her way to the door and out on to the landing. It's lighter out here thanks to the spill of moonlight coming in through the curtainless window in the bathroom.

'Mom.' Her voice is a harsh rasp that slices through her aching throat. 'Mom, I think I'm sick.' She grabs for the door handle of her parents' room and falls against it.

'Bryony? Good heavens, what is it?' Adele sits up in alarm when her daughter stumbles into the room.

'I had a really bad nightmare and I think I'm sick.'

'Oh dear, sweetie, come on, let me feel your forehead,' Adele whispers. Beside her, Liam grunts in his sleep and turns over. 'Good Lord, you're burning up. How's your throat?'

'Sore,' Bryony says and begins to cry.

'I bet it's those nasty tonsils again, isn't it? We haven't heard a peep from them in ages, have we?' Adele gets out of bed and pulls on her dressing gown. 'Come on, let's dose you up so you can get some decent sleep and we'll see how you're doing in the morning.'

'I don't want to sleep,' Bryony whimpers as her mother leads her out of the room and deposits her on the closed lid of the toilet in the family bathroom down the hall.

'I know, sweetie. You must feel awful.' Adele's skin looks pale and slack in the harsh neon light, but she smiles a reassurance to her daughter before rooting through the medicine cupboard. 'But the medicine will help.'

'The nightmare . . . '

'It was just a dream, Bry, probably a result of your nasty fever.'

'Well, I don't want to go back to the bedroom.'

'Don't be silly, angel, you need some proper sleep to get better. Open wide.'

'But I don't want to.' Bryony sniffs, but then opens her mouth to receive the brimming plastic medicine spoon. The sugar in the mixture both burns and soothes her raging throat.

'That should make you feel better. Come along, I'll put you to bed.'

'But I don't . . . ' Bryony is too weak and weepy to argue properly, and she can already feel the medicine pillowing her bones and slowing down her thoughts.

'Come on, sweetheart.' Adele helps her up and leads her back to the dark bedroom. 'You'll feel so much better in the morning.'

19

Bryony is awoken by her mother's hand on her forehead. She blinks up at Adele with glazed, gummy eyes. The room is filled with pale grey light.

'Someone is definitely not going to school today, hey?' Adele says with a smile. 'Sit up, angel, let's get another spoon of good stuff into you, quick quick.' She supports Bryony's lolling head with one hand, and dishes in a sweet spoon of syrup with the other. 'Good girl, now lie back down again.' She helps her daughter back on to the pillow.

Bryony's eyes close almost at once.

'Dora is here to bring you anything you need this morning, OK? I'll be back just after twelve.'

'Why can't you be here?' Bryony mumbles.

'I've got an appointment, sweetie. It's my hair salon day, and after that I've got a big grocery shop to do. Don't worry, you'll be right as rain, and I'll probably be back before you even wake up.'

Bryony sinks back into oblivion.

'Gigi?'

Curled up beneath her own covers on the other side of the room, Gigi, who has not slept a wink all night and is no longer quite sure what is real and what isn't, hears Adele whisper her name. She holds her breath. Waits.

'Time to get up and get ready for school.'

Gigi's hands have been clenched into stiff,

aching fists for hours, but now she clenches them tighter. Little sparkles of pain dart up her wrists and shoot into her elbows. The air beneath the duvet is stuffy and hot and even through the bedding, she can smell the sugar-coated bitter stench of Bryony's medicine.

'Come on, Gigi,' Adele tries again, and Gigi can hear her stepping closer to her bed. She wouldn't dare, would she?

'It's enough of this now.' Adele's whisper is firm and furious, but quickly disintegrates into a sudden, unexpected sob. Gigi squeezes her eyes shut and waits. A minute ticks by. And then another. She hears Adele's feet on the carpet as she adjusts her stance and the very faint sound of Bryony's laboured breathing.

She forces herself not to move despite the fact that her muscles are screaming from lying in one position so long. Tears leak out from beneath her quivering eyelids. She bites her lip. *Don't move, don't move.*

'Hey, where is everyone?' Tyler's voice cuts into the silence. He's shouting from the landing at the top of the stairs by the sound of it. 'Mom? I'm going to be late for school.'

Gigi imagines Tyler missing a step, losing his grip on the banister, and falling. Bump bump, down and down till he smashes his head on the hard, shiny tiles of the entrance-hall floor. Then she imagines it again, only this time she makes his ankle catch in between the balustrades and snap against the force of his falling body as he plummets.

It gives her something to focus on in order to

maintain her now agonizing motionlessness.

'Shit,' Adele mutters and, at long last, moves away from Gigi's bed. Her footsteps grow fainter until Gigi can no longer make them out, but it is only when she hears the murmuring of Adele's voice talking to Tyler and Dora in the kitchen below that she allows her aching body to move. She's dying to stretch out into the cool corners of the bed and stick her head out for the relief of fresh air, but she only permits herself one position change, one shift of each muscle before she forces herself into stillness once more.

Strange dark flowers bloom on the inside of her eyelids.

★　★　★

Once Liam and Adele's cars have both left the garage below and the sound of their engines have faded and blended with the distant roar of morning traffic, Gigi removes the covers from over her head and sits up. Her muscles are stiff and quivery, and her hollow belly, which has now missed two meals, gives an echoey kind of growl. She glances over to Bryony's bed, but the patient does not stir; she sleeps with her mouth open and a heavy kind of limpness that indicates she would be very hard to rouse should anyone try.

The room smells of codeine, sugar and stale breath, and something acrid and animal-like, which Gigi finally realizes is herself. She gets off the bed and pulls yesterday's school tunic off over her head before unbuttoning the sweat-drenched shirt and peeling it away from her skin.

255

Glancing over to make sure that Bryony is still oblivious, she then takes off her underwear and pulls her mother's old dressing gown from the cupboard and wraps it around herself.

The bathroom seems very bright and cold after the bedding cave, and Gigi holds on to the side of the tub for support as she turns the hot tap on. The water gushing and swirling into the whiteness makes her head swim so she looks out of the window at the sullen, overcast sky. Then, as if suddenly instructed to get a move on, she straightens up sharply and strides over to the medicine cabinet and opens it without looking at her reflection in the mirror.

Rows of little pill bottles, rolls of bandage, half-squeezed tubes of mysterious ointments and two sets of tweezers stare back at her. There's also a box of plasters, a pair of very sharp-nosed nail scissors, and man's razor with some white residue around the handle from not being rinsed properly. Gigi shudders as she imagines Tyler running the blade over his almost hairless chin.

Behind her, the bath is almost full, and steam rises from the searing water to condense on the windowpanes.

* * *

Bryony wakes to the sound of rain and the indistinct hum of the vacuum cleaner somewhere downstairs. It hurts to open her eyes, and she has to keep rubbing them to get them to work properly. She sees that the lump has gone from the other bed, and after looking around the dim

256

room to make sure, she breathes out in relief to find herself alone. Gigi must have gotten up at last and gone to school like a normal person. Bryony remembers the demonic look on her cousin's face and the terrible screech of her voice as she forced them out of the room last night, and feels strange, icy goosebumps rise up all over her skin.

Bryony tries a tiny swallow to see how her throat is doing, and winces at the raw rasp at the back of her throat. Her skull feels dry and clogged and her mouth tastes awful. The water glass that Adele left beside her bed is empty. Very cautiously, she sits up, waits for her head to feel less woozy, and then slowly gets out of bed. As soon as she's upright, all the fluid in her body seems to collect in her bladder, and she speeds up her shuffle in the direction of the bathroom.

She pushes open the bathroom door and stumbles into the room, blinking her sore eyes against the steam.

And then she sees Gigi. She's sitting in the bath with her thin hair plastered to her skull and her eyes shocked, enormous, staring back. Neither girl moves.

Bryony is almost about to dart back out again, mortified, but then she sees the welling parallel lines of blood blooming up on her cousin's left upper arm and a pair of red-tipped nail scissors clutched in her shaking fingers. Her gaze slides back to lock on Gigi's, but out of the corner of her eye she can see slender trails of bright blood snake their way down Gigi's arm and billow out in soft pink clouds when they hit the bathwater.

For a very long moment, the girls remain frozen. The steam drifts and swims around them in the cool currents created by the open door. Waves of aching dizziness pound through Bryony's skull.

'What — ' she finally croaks, but Gigi cuts her off by suddenly rising out of the bathwater like a spare, otherworldly nymph with tiny, sharp-pointed breasts and prominent ribs.

'You don't look very well, Bryony,' she says, her voice quavering as it tries to hold on to its forced, motherly tone. 'Are you feeling all right?'

'No,' Bryony whispers, staring at Gigi. Her cousin's naked skin is very pink from the heat of the bathwater, and her bones almost seem to shine through it, making her look as if she could be made out of coloured, cloudy glass. The blood leaking out of her arm mingles with the water on her skin and forms diluted rivulets of red that pool on the end of her fingers.

'Come, let's get you back to bed, then,' Gigi says, stepping from the tub and wrapping herself in a waiting towel, immediately marking it with rusty smears. Blood courses down her arm, drips off her elbow and on to the bathmat. 'Where's your medicine?' Gigi marches to the medicine cabinet, swings it open, and starts rifling through the bottles.

'I don't . . . ' Bryony's voice wavers, and she sways on her sore feet. 'I just want a wee.'

'Of course.' Gigi turns round and gives her a strange sharp smile. Water drips from the ends of her hair and soaks into top of the towel, and the blood continues to flow from the gashes on her

258

upper arm. 'Go on, then. I'll wait outside.'

Once alone in the bathroom, Bryony pulls down her pyjama bottoms and sits down gingerly on a toilet seat that feels as if it is made of ice. She glances over at the pointed ends of the nail scissors resting beside some drips of blood on the white edge of the tub, and then looks away. She shuts her eyes so as not to see the pale pink bathwater or the blots of red on the bathmat and the smears on the edge of the medicine cabinet and begins to cry silently, her raw throat constricting in painful jerks as tears pour down her cheeks.

20

Lesedi sits on the colourful mat spread out on the mud floor of Ma Retabile's house and leans her back up against the unplastered, grey cinder-block wall. She takes a sip of hot, sweet rooibos from her enamelled tin mug and smiles, thinking back to how horrified she'd first been when she'd arrived at this place to do her apprenticeship, all those years ago. She'd been brought up in a nice house in northern Johannesburg, been sent to the best schools, and dropped out of varsity to end up on the floor of a glorified shack.

'You're remembering too,' Ma Retabile says with a wheezy chuckle.

'I felt like an alien when I first came.'

'I remember. You couldn't even speak Siswati properly!'

Lesedi grins.

'You were such a whitey.'

'It's not so easy to tell the difference any more,' says Lesedi with a grin. 'It's the new South Africa, remember.'

'Ayeye,' Ma Retabile says, 'I am a dying breed.' She crosses one leg over the other with a slight jingle of beads and shells, and Lesedi marvels at the state of the soles of the older woman's feet. Even the cracks have cracks.

'You could do with a pedicure, you know that, Ma?'

'*Haibo!*' Ma Retabile yelps, and waggles her crusty toes in Lesedi's direction. 'What do I need someone rubbing on my toes for, hey? My feet are that ticklish I would probably kick the poor girl in the head.' They both fall about laughing, and the creases around Ma Retabile's eyes deepen into ploughed furrows in the earth-coloured skin of her round face.

'It's good to be back, Ma.'

'Good, then maybe sometime you can tell me why you've left your nice husband and comfy comfy life to come and sit on my dirt floor, hey?'

'I will, Ma. Soon,' Lesedi says, and then suddenly freezes.

'What is it?' Ma Retabile asks, her own smile fading.

'Something . . . I don't know.' Lesedi shakes her head. Despite the warmth of the room, fresh goosebumps rise up down her arms and legs. 'I just had the bad feeling.'

'Uh-huh.' Ma Retabile nods in understanding. She waits for Lesedi to continue.

'Before I left Joburg, I saw a black dog.'

'*Haibo.*'

'A dog-cloud.'

'Not good. But it wasn't for you?'

'No,' Lesedi says, staring off into nothing for a moment. 'It wasn't for me.' For a moment, her blood seems to slow in her veins, and the hand holding the mug goes slack. A small dribble of sugary tea spills on to her jeans, shaking her from her reverie.

'Did you warn the one it was for?'

261

'I tried.'

'Whiteys, they won't listen, hey?' Ma Retabile says with a shake of her head.

'Tell me about it.'

21

'Come now, let's get you better,' Gigi croons as she spoons another sugary helping of medicine into Bryony's mouth. 'We've got to get your strength up for the journey.'

'Mom only gives me one,' Bryony mumbles as she sees Gigi tip the bottle for a third time.

'Nonsense. I stayed home especially to look after you, you know.'

'You did?' Bryony vaguely notes that Gigi is now dressed in jeans and a top and her red flip-flops. The cuts on her left arm are still leaking a little, but most of the blood has congealed into dark stripes.

'How are you feeling?' Gigi asks, placing a hand on Bryony's forehead as if to check her temperature. Through her medicated, fevered fog, Bryony realizes that this is the first time that Gigi has ever touched her.

'Cold.'

'Then let's warm you up.' Gigi bounds across the room to grab her oversized dressing gown. The strange, frantic energy that seems to have overtaken her since Bryony walked into the bathroom continues to build. 'It could rain again at any moment and we've got to get you to a nice safe place,' she says as she bundles Bryony into the gown and ties the cord tight around her waist.

'A nice safe place?'

'This house isn't safe. Anyone could come in here and do something to us.'

'Oh,' Bryony says, not sure that she understands what Gigi is on about. 'But Mom will be home soon.'

'Oh, mothers can't protect you, you know,' Gigi says, steering Bryony out of the bedroom and down the stairs. 'They're pretty useless themselves when it comes down to it.'

From the kitchen, Bryony can hear Dora's daily Zulu soap opera blaring out from the radio and the occasional clank of things being put into cupboards. She wants to call out to Dora, but can't seem to make her voice come out enough to do so. In any case, what would she say? Maybe Dora knows that Gigi has to take her to safety, maybe she's just finishing up and is going to join them wherever they're going? Bryony's head feels like it's stuffed full of glue and crumpled-up bath towels, and the thoughts don't seem to be able to get from one side of it to the other. Gigi's conviction that they need to get out of the house makes her feel as if she's missed some very important information that she's supposed to know about. She racks her brain trying to remember if Adele mentioned anything before leaving earlier this morning, but all she can recall are a cool hand and a few fragmented images from her dreams: a dog with its mouth open wide. Darkness.

She trips on the bottom of the too-long dressing gown and sinks down on to the hallway carpet. It is comfortable here. If she could just curl up here and sleep for a bit . . .

'No,' Gigi says through gritted teeth, hoisting Bryony to her feet again, 'you have to listen to me. I've got to get you out of here. They could be coming at any moment.' Gigi hustles Bryony out of the front door and then shuts it behind them with a quiet click. The rain has stopped, but the garden is dripping wet and smells of sap and soil.

'Who could be coming at any moment?'

'The black men.'

'What black men?' Bryony stops in the middle of the garden path. The grass is very wet and cold and her body beneath its enveloping folds of towelling is icy and shivery. She blinks at the overcast garden. It seems to be made up of very sharp edges and too much grey light. In the dark space beneath the leaves of the border shrubs, she's sure she can see the low, menacing shape of a crouching dog. When she blinks, it is gone. 'I want to go back to bed.'

Gigi turns and brings her face in very close to Bryony's so that their noses are almost touching. 'It's not safe,' she whispers. Her breath smells of unused stomach acid.

'Are you talking about the shadows?' Bryony asks.

'No.' Gigi shakes her head in frustration.

'There were some shadows behind the sofa cushions and over your bed and stuff. But I think they're all gone now that Lesedi has left.'

'I'm talking about the men.'

'Lesedi was a sangoma, you know. I think she tried to put a curse on me because I was spying on her. But I wasn't really spying, I just thought that she was nice and wanted her to be my friend and then I saw the mask and I didn't any more.'

'I have no idea what you're on about. I think the sickness is making you delirious.'

'Deliri-what?'

'You're losing your grip on reality,' Gigi explains, impatient now. 'Will you get a move on, please?' She tugs on Bryony's arm and almost pulls her over. 'See, you can barely stand up by yourself. You're a total sitting duck. They'll get you, easy.'

'But — '

'Shush. Come on.' Gigi's tone is urgent now, and her eyes have a peculiar, hot look to them. She forces Bryony to move, and marches her out of the garden gate, past the fever tree, and up the road. Bryony turns to look at the Matsunyanes' front drive, and is surprised to find herself disappointed that Lesedi is not standing there in her Levi's and bare feet with those long, strong braided ropes of hair hanging down over one shoulder.

'Come *on*,' Gigi urges. 'They're coming.'

22

Bryony wakes to find that she's lying on something hard that pushes into her aching hipbone and her shoulder. It's the floor. Why is she on the floor? Did she fall out of bed? No, wait a minute, this is a wooden floor and the floor of her bedroom is carpeted. *Where am I?*

'What's going on?' she mumbles, blinking her eyes to try and clear them.

'Shshsh!' Suddenly, Gigi is right up close to her face, pressing a skinny finger on Bryony's lips. 'You have to be quiet.'

'Where are we?' Bryony says in a whisper.

'Somewhere secret that nobody knows about. They won't find us here.'

Bryony runs her tongue around her biscuit-dry mouth, trying to work up some moisture. She feels strange and heavy and everything hurts. 'I want to go home. I want my mom.'

'Don't we all,' sneers Gigi, her face suddenly twisted and ugly. 'Now shut up and lie still or they'll find us.'

★　★　★

'Didn't you hear anything?' Adele asks Dora for the third time, panic rising in her voice.

'No, madam. They were quiet. The bathwater ran, I heard it in the pipes, but then for a long

267

time there was nothing. I thought they were both sleeping.'

'Shit.' Adele works her fingers over the crumples in her brow, and then touches the blunt ends of her new haircut. 'Where the hell did they go? Bryony has a serious case of tonsillitis, she could barely move when I left this morning, and Gigi . . . ' She trails off, uncertain.

She's been in and out of the girls' bedroom twice, called and called, been up and down the stairs and all around the garden, but nothing. Gigi and Bryony are nowhere to be found.

'They wouldn't just *go*, would they?' she mutters as she leaves the kitchen and heads up the stairs again for one more check.

'Go where?' Dora echoes, trotting at Adele's heels. Up the stairs they go. Into Bryony's bedroom.

'The dressing gown is gone.' Dora points to the empty hook behind the door. 'That big one that the girl is always wearing.'

'Yes,' Adele says. There's a dull thumping sensation in her temples, and her whole body feels light and peculiar, as if someone has pumped her veins full of air. 'And Bryony's medicine. I left it by the bed.'

They leave the room and cross the hallway to the bathroom. Adele had peered in briefly on one of her earlier rounds, but this time, she steps inside. The bath has a strange little trail of pink in the bottom of it. The medicine cabinet mirror is smeared with fluff as if someone has wiped it with a towel.

'Where's the bathmat?' Dora asks, pointing to

the blank spot on the floor by the bath. There are some faint, rusty smears on the tile. She marches over to the laundry bin, lifts the lid and gives a little scream. 'Madam!'

'What?'

'This.' Dora slowly lifts a blood-smeared towel out of the basket. And then another one with big, red blotches on it.

'What in the name of Christ — ' Adele's shocked whisper is cut off when Dora then lifts out a bloody bathmat.

'That's a lot of blood,' Dora says. The hand holding the bathmat begins to tremble.

'Oh my God.' Adele clutches the edge of the basin with icy, pale fingers. 'What happened in here? Whose blood is it?'

'You'd better call the master,' Dora breathes. Adele nods, and then rushes from the room.

★   ★   ★

Bryony's throat is in agony and the floor is very hard. 'Can we go home now?'

'Are you crazy? They could come any minute.'

'Who? Who could come?' There are tears in Bryony's voice now and she can feel big, heaving sobs waiting in her belly.

'I *told* you. The black men.'

Bryony tries to sit up, but the excess folds of the old dressing gown slip on the dusty floor, and she slides back down with a thump. 'Ow!'

'Shshsh.' Gigi's eyes are open very wide. 'It's like you *want* to die or something.'

'I don't want to die!' Bryony wails, and she

269

begins to cry in earnest.

'Shut up shut up shut up,' Gigi hisses through gritted teeth and clamps a hand over Bryony's mouth. Bryony's eyes bulge and she fights the hand away, gulping and gasping for breath. She howls.

Gigi leans back, tugs off her vest and jams the bunched fabric into Bryony's mouth. 'I told you, you have to be quiet.' Bryony gags and tries to pull the fabric from between her teeth, but Gigi presses her back down into the floor and holds the vest in place. 'Please,' she whimpers. 'Please be quiet, for God's sake.'

Bryony tries, but the crying won't stop, and the sound of her breath snorting through her nostrils is horribly loud. For long minutes, she lies on her back with tears and spit soaking into the crumpled vest, and Gigi in her 32A bra leans over her with one hand gripping Bryony's wrist and the other holding the gag in place. The fresh wounds on Gigi's arm have reopened in all the activity, and a trail of blood snakes down over her fingers and soaks into the vest

At long last, the intensity of Bryony's crying subsides, and the desperate snorts soften into sniffles. Slowly, with one hand, the other still on the gag, Gigi undoes the knot on the dressing gown cord and tugs it free from around Bryony's waist.

'You have to be quiet,' she whispers. 'I can't take any chances or we'll end up sliced to pieces.' She tenderly places the cord around the back of Bryony's sweat-damp head and ties it tight to hold the gag in place. 'That OK? You comfy?'

Bryony is not. Her jaw aches from being jammed open, and her nose is running, but she is no longer crying. She stares at her cousin with huge, frightened eyes and concentrates on breathing.

'You wanna know something?' Gigi asks. The skin of her face looks like pale cheese left out of the fridge too long with little beads of wetness slicking the too-smooth surface. There is almost no colour in it at all. 'I didn't come home to find my mother and Seb and Johan dead.' She bares her teeth in what is possibly supposed to be a smile. 'That's a secret I haven't told anybody.' She reaches over to test the knot in the dressing gown cord and Bryony flinches. Gigi doesn't notice; she is seeing something else entirely.

★ ★ ★

As Gigi made the long walk back from the dam with her rolled yoga mat, sticky with sweat, tucked beneath one arm, she was hoping that the lump of grey cloud hovering over the horizon would get it together to produce a storm. It was too hot and too still, and she longed for the furious relief of whipping winds and lashing rain.

Her stomach was rumbling, and she was dying for breakfast and a nice, cool shower, but when she reached the knot of stinkwood trees at the top of the drive, just before the clearing of the yard, she paused. She wiped the back of her arm across her face and huffed out a breath. If Johan was still sitting in the kitchen drinking his morning coffee, she would have to walk past him to get to her room, and that was just not an

271

option. She didn't want to see him or smell him or be anywhere near him, especially if her stupid mother was there too.

Two days ago she'd overheard the two of them by the fence near the gate: Johan, big, strong, lovely Johan, had been *begging* her mother to love him. Her mother. It was unthinkable. But what was even worse was the way he'd dismissed her own advances as if they were nothing but the mindless actions of a small child. *She's got a crush, that's all. Perhaps it's time she hung out with some kids her own age.*

And then last night. She can hardly bear to think of it. Last night she'd watched through her bedroom window as her mother crept out of the house and across the yard to Johan's cabin. Gigi had watched her knock on the door, had seen Johan open it and pull her inside. It was disgusting. The thought of either of them made her feel sick.

Scowling at the memory, she skirted the edge of the clearing, approaching the house like a spy on a secret mission as she darted between the animal hoks and the trunks of trees.

Gigi wrinkled her nose at the strange, burnt-bitter smell that hung over the yard and finally slipped on to the front stoep from the very far end, planning to peek through the window to check that her path was Johan-free before going through the kitchen door.

Then, a strange animal-howl sound stopped her in her tracks. It had come from inside the house. She pressed her body against the cool plaster of the wall and listened hard. Blood drained from her head when she heard the sound of her mother sobbing, a strange male voice barking out an order of some kind, and then the crash of something heavy falling to the floor. Gigi put down her yoga mat very carefully, and crept forward on suddenly trembly legs. When she reached the old veranda sofa that sat beneath one of the kitchen windows, she clutched at the faded fabric on the armrest for support before peering in.

Her mother was standing in the middle of the kitchen, rigid, her face red and distorted by gushing tears. It took Gigi a moment to register that she was being held from behind by someone else. Her mother's arms were trapped behind her back and one of the man's arms was locked across her chest like the coil of a constrictor, dark shiny brown against her faded T-shirt and pale neck.

'Mom,' Gigi gasped, and although it was just a breath, her mother seemed to hear her, for she turned her head a fraction and swivelled her eyes until they locked on to Gigi's. Even across the kitchen and through the grimy glass, Gigi could see how very blue her mother's irises looked.

Go, they begged. *Run*.

And once Gigi had crept back across the stoep and into the relative safety of the long grass, she did.

★　★　★

'I ran to Phineas and Lettie's place but they weren't there.' Gigi's voice is very sudden and

273

loud in the empty room and it makes Bryony jump. She had been very slowly moving her hands up towards the gag in her mouth, but now she freezes, staring at her cousin, who has been pacing up and down on the far side of the room in silence. Now that Gigi has spoken, Bryony battles to get a grip on the meaning of the words. She can now taste the metallic hint of Gigi's blood on the T-shirt fabric of her gag. She fights down a wave of panic, scared that she will cry again and make Gigi even madder.

'They were at church, of course. As soon as I got to their empty house I remembered.' Gigi turns to look at Bryony with fevered eyes. 'It was Sunday. What was I supposed to do?'

A response seems to be expected; Bryony makes a muffled humming sound and shrugs her shoulders, taking the opportunity to work her hands a little further towards her face.

'The Muckleneuks were the closest, I figured, but as soon as I started running I realized that they were miles away. It would take me hours to get to their farm on foot and by then, who knows what would've happened inside the kitchen. So I stopped. I stopped running and I turned back. My mind was going crazy trying to think what to do. There was never any cell reception out there, so no one had a cell phone. There was one phone in the whole place, but where do you think it was?'

Bryony gives another grunt. She has no idea what Gigi is talking about. Her cousin seems to be right in the middle of a conversation that she never started.

'Correct. In the kitchen.' Gigi marches back to Bryony and crouches down on the floor beside her. Her face is no longer cheese-pale; now it is a dark, angry pink. 'What was I supposed to do?' she pleads.

Bryony shakes her head as new tears leak out of the corners of her eyes.

'I went back, didn't I?' Gigi hisses, her breath hot and acid-smelling on Bryony's face. 'I went back to the window, hid behind the back of the old sofa, and I watched.'

★ ★ ★

I remember now. The feel of the man's arms, like hot iron bands, around my shoulders, holding me upright, holding me still; his old sweat and burnt smoke stink made bile lurch up the back of my throat. I remember the way the other two men used brown, shiny duct tape to bind the unconscious Seb and Johan's hands and feet and cover their mouths. I remember the way the veins in Johan's neck bulged beneath his skin when he came to and realized what was happening and he struggled to break free but couldn't.

I remember when the skinny man with the yellow eyes made the very first cut with his machete. The large, flat blade had looked dull, but it wasn't. Seb's T-shirt parted as if by magic and, for a moment, a smooth line of red could be seen in the gap as if someone had drawn a marker across the skin of his chest. And then the red line burst open and darkness gushed out.

I remember hearing this high-pitched horrible

screaming and a hand clamping over my mouth. I remember tasting soil and salt. I remember shutting my eyes and hearing the sound of metal hitting bone. I remember the way the man who held me had shuddered against my back.

He was laughing.

* * *

Gigi crouched down and slithered into the gap between the old sofa and the wall beneath the kitchen window. Very slowly, she pushed herself upwards on her haunches and looked through the smeared glass.

The man holding her mother must've pulled her backwards closer to the sink, because all Gigi could see of her now was the bright patterned fabric of the edge of her skirt. Yellow and pink flowers against blue. If the window had been open and Gigi had reached in as far as her arm could go, she would probably have been able to touch it.

After the brilliant outside daylight, it was harder to focus on the far end of the room, but gradually shapes began to emerge from the murk. The shapes were not human. There was a creature with bared, luminous teeth and a huge blade for an arm. There was a lump of red and ripped fabric on the floor that had dark curly hair just like Seb. There was a twisted monster with kicking feet . . .

There was Johan.

Gigi moved closer to the glass to make sure.

Johan was in nothing but his boxer shorts. His

ankles were taped together and his hands bound behind him. There was something stuck over his mouth. His hair was glued to his scalp with sweat and his eyes, wide open and frantic, were clearly fixated on her mother and her captor. When the blade swung down and sliced open his shin he made a muffled bellowing sound like a furious, wounded wildebeest.

Gigi opened her mouth but no scream came out. She could not turn her head away, couldn't even swivel her eyeballs; she was no longer in charge of the distant, heavy thing that her body had become.

The blade swung down again. And again. After what felt like hours, Johan had disappeared so deep behind a shroud of blood that Gigi did not know what bits of him were what any more. She had no idea when he stopped being alive.

★ ★ ★

'Finally, the blade-armed man stopped,' Gigi said. She is staring out of the window, keeping watch on the still garden below to make sure that no one is approaching. Behind her back, Bryony struggles with the knot in the dressing gown cord, her fingers digging into the towelling to try and loosen it.

'There was a piece of Johan's scalp, with the hair still on it, stuck to the kitchen wall.' Gigi squeezes her eyes shut, almost as if to lock the image more securely in place inside her head. She leans her hot forehead against the glass.

On the other side of the room, Bryony finally

manages to untie the dressing gown cord and pull it down beneath her chin. She wrenches the soggy T-shirt out of her mouth, gagging as the fabric scrapes over her palate and finally flops free. She rubs her aching jaw muscles, eyes riveted on Gigi's motionless, spine-knobbled back, and takes huge gulps of air. Her heart is thundering. Despite the fact that her head feels light and swimmy when she tries to lift it, she forces herself into a slumped sitting position. She waits. Gigi does not move. Bryony fights to free herself from the tangle of what feels like endless reams of stifling dressing-gown fabric, but every move she makes is slow and clumsy. Fresh tears of frustration spurt from her raw eyes.

'I'd never seen the inside of a scalp before. It was sort of orange and wet-looking. I thought I was going to vomit but I didn't,' Gigi whispers.

The dressing gown finally slips from Bryony's shoulders. Suddenly her arms are free. She glances at Gigi. Her cousin is still off in her own world, head turned towards the window.

Bryony suddenly launches herself in the direction of the doorway, feet and fingers scrabbling for purchase on fabric and floorboards. Beyond the doorframe, she sees the upstairs landing and the staircase banister going down and freezes. The familiarity of the view throws her. *I am in my own room! What's happened to the furniture and the carpets? Where's the picture of Granny on the landing wall? Where is everyone?*

'Mom! Dad!' she screams as she stumbles towards the staircase. 'Tyler!' It feels as if she is dragging her body through syrup. She is dreaming. It must be a nightmare. 'Wake up wake up wake up!' she howls, lurching for the banister.

But something grips her ankle, pulls her back and throws her to the ground once more. The sudden weight on her back knocks the wind out of her. Bony knees in her ribs. Stale breath hissing into her face: 'Are you insane?'

'Wake up!' Bryony screams, struggling against the sweaty hand that tries to clamp down over her lips. 'Wa — ' But the crumpled-up vest is jammed deep inside her mouth once more.

'You're going to get us both killed, don't you understand that?' Gigi grabs her arms to hold them still. Her strength is impossible. It feels as if Bryony's wrists are being gripped by something mechanical, all metal gears and ratchets. 'This is not a nightmare, Bryony,' Gigi whispers. 'The men are coming for us so you'd better wake up and get real.'

* * *

'They must've have left the complex.' Adele crosses her arms over her chest. Her fingers feel rubbery and strange when she clenches them. 'I just don't understand where they would have gone.'

'No girls came past the entrance gate,' the security guard repeats for the third time. He has been pulled off entrance duty and now stands against one wall of the poky Cortona Villas security office with Adele, Liam, a policewoman and the manager of Cortona Villas Security clustered around him. 'I would've definitely noticed.' His hat is on slightly skew. His eyes dart from one worried face to the next. 'I was watching all the time.

'But we've looked everywhere.' Adele's voice rises, and Liam places a hand on her shoulder. She frowns and hugs herself tighter. 'You don't understand; Bryony was really sick, she wouldn't have been able to walk very far.'

'I am sure they're all right,' the manager of Cortona Villas Security mutters, but Adele shoots him a furious scowl.

'Based on what, exactly?'

'Could they have left in a car, perhaps?' Liam says, and everyone turns to look at him.

'Don't be daft, where would they get a car?' Adele snaps.

'I don't mean they were *driving* it, Addy.'

'I didn't see any cars leave here with those two girls in it. The car would have to have stopped at the boom gate and I always look inside.' The security guard now removes his skew cap and rubs his hand over the fuzz of his hair.

'Unless they were in the boot?' the manager of Cortona Villas Security suggests.

For a moment there is silence as everyone contemplates the implications of this. Finally, Adele lets out a loud, broken wail.

'Jesus,' says Liam. His face has gone a pale green colour.

'Look, I've called in the K9 search-and-rescue unit. They will be here soon,' the policewoman says in a calm, measured voice.

'When the hell is soon?' Liam asks over his wife's sobbing head.

'There's a big situation out at Rivonia and all the dogs are there right now. I've requested that one unit be called off the search and brought here as soon as possible.'

'A big situation? How many people go missing on any given day, for heaven's sake?' Liam asks.

The policewoman's large dark eyes are steady, but something inside them flickers. She glances out of the small security office window at the grey sky.

'It's going to rain any minute,' she says.

*　　*　　*

Bryony tries kicking her feet, but they connect with nothing but the dusty floor.

'Stop it. You're making too much noise,' Gigi says and Bryony gives a muffled yelp as her arms are tugged up higher behind her back. 'Please. Please, Bryony. Be quiet.' Gigi's voice is tinged with tears of her own. 'Please. You don't know how horrible they are, the black men. If they find us we'll be sliced up like Seb and Johan were . . . like tinned tomatoes spewing red pulp and juice.'

Bryony goes still. Her whole body is vibrating and her breath snorts in and out of her nostrils.

'It's true. I saw them, Bryony. I watched through the window as they killed Johan. Seb was dead already, I think. At least, he wasn't moving.'

The weight of Gigi's knees pushes Bryony's ribs hard into the floor.

'I didn't want to watch, but after a while I

281

couldn't stop. I was too scared to move in case they spotted me and grabbed me and cut me up too.' Gigi's voice has gone very high and soft. Bryony has to quieten her frantic breathing in order to hear it. 'One of the men had yellow in his eyes where the whites should be. He was the one with the machete. The other man just used a piece of wood to hit and lots of kicking instead of a knife or anything. He kept kicking Johan long after he stopped moving. I remember thinking that it must've hurt, to keep on kicking like that.'

Bryony feels Gigi's grip on her arms loosen and she winces as blood flows back into her joints.

'There was another man, of course. But I couldn't see him most of the time because he was leaning against the sink to hold Mom up. I think she fainted because I could just see a piece of her hair hanging down as if her head was flopping forward.' Gigi remembers how impossibly fair that lock of hair had looked, like the dove feathers she'd once found and strung up from the curtain pelmet in her bedroom on a length of fishing twine to catch the light. She'd used a big blue glass bead to weigh down the end of the twine, and the feathers strung along it would turn and turn one way, and then stop for a moment and turn and turn the other, over and over again.

And then suddenly the hair flicked backwards out of sight and she could hear her mother trying to scream and the yellow-eyed man had spun around to look at her saying in English, *And now it's time for you, lady. Save the best for last.* The machete hung from his hand. There was no metal colour left on the blade. Just red.

'The man who was holding my mom pushed her forward towards the blade man and then I could see how little she looked crushed up against his chest. His arms were thicker than her neck. Dark and oily-looking, like river mud.'

Gigi releases her hold on Bryony's wrists and slides down off her back. Bryony's breath makes a whistling sound as she tries to suck as much air into her lungs as possible. She rests her forehead against the floor. She is shivering.

★ ★ ★

As soon as the man took his hand from my mouth, I retched. Nothing came out.

'Hush hush hush,' he whispered in my ear, just as one would soothe an ailing child.

'Why are you doing this? Why?' I begged.

The yellow-eyed man came towards me. He took my chin in his hand and squeezed. His fingers were slick with blood. I wrenched my head away. The men all laughed.

With my head turned towards the window, I suddenly saw that Gigi had returned. *No. She's meant to be hiding somewhere they'll never find her.* Her face was a pale half-circle sticking up over the bottom of the windowsill. Her eyes were enormous. *My baby girl, I told you to run.* I looked away. I couldn't bear to have the men follow my gaze and spot that fragile little half-woman face.

The man holding me suddenly released his

grip on my shoulders and I stumbled forwards, off-balance. Just a little kick from the yellow-eyed one sent me to the floor. I could see an ancient curled-up piece of old toast wedged down the side of the oven. I stared hard at it as I felt the man using the wet machete blade to lift my skirt and I remember thinking: *If I don't fight, if I can give them no reason to kill me I can survive this and see my daughter again.*

But I was wrong.

★   ★   ★

'I saw everything they did to her,' Gigi tells Bryony. She is lying beside her on the floor, face-to-face with her cousin. But for the bunched-up vest in Bryony's mouth, they look like two girls sharing secrets at a slumber party.

'I could see she was trying not to scream but she couldn't help it. They hurt her.' From somewhere outside number 22 Cortona Villas comes the distant sound of a barking dog.

'I don't remember seeing it happen, but suddenly there was this huge red slash across Mom's face and blood was pouring out of it. Into her eyes and everything. Just pouring. And then the man with the machete nodded to the river-mud man and he leant over my mom and put his huge, oily hands around her neck. I could see the muscles move beneath his black skin as he squeezed.'

The room is very quiet. The girls stare into each other's eyes. Outside, in what seems like a separate world, a dog barks again. Closer this

284

time. Bryony flinches at the sound.

'It was my fault, Bryony,' Gigi suddenly whispers. 'The men were there because of me.' She had been so angry with Johan, and had just hated and hated her mother for being the one he wanted. Gigi takes a big breath. 'I left the padlock open on purpose.'

Gigi remembers the way the solid lump of morning-cold metal had felt in her hand. Inside she'd been burning, furious. She kept remembering her mother going into Johan's cabin in the dead of night, his arm around her back. *How could he love my stupid mother and not me?* All she had needed to do was click the lock closed. Simple. But she didn't. She had left it hanging on the end of its thick chain like a useless ornament.

Bryony raises a shaking hand and brushes the tears from Gigi's cheek.

* * *

When I could no longer draw breath, I remember seeing shifting colours. Orange and pink and sunset yellow seemed to billow up out of nowhere and cover the face of the man who was strangling me. The colours brightened and swam together.

And then I was looking down on the kitchen from somewhere by the ceiling. I saw the men leave, carrying whatever useless things they'd decided it was worth it to steal from our little home. I watched Gigi run into the room after they'd gone. She slipped on my blood and fell to

285

the floor only to scramble and slither up again and crawl to my side.

She shook me and held me and shook me and then, finally, stopped moving altogether.

And then I was a thorn tree with long white points and almost no leaves. And then a rock on the beach being sucked on by mussels and pounded by salty Atlantic water. And then I was an eggshell-blue sky tickled by wisps of icy cloud. And then I was a vast plain of long, waving, brown-tipped grass with scurrying beetles going between.

And then I began to hear the stories.

★ ★ ★

The bark is throaty and deep. The dog must be a big one. Bryony, overwhelmed by Gigi's tale, and freshly feverish from the tonsillitis, decides that the black, darkness-vomiting shadow dog that has been following her for days has finally come for her. She can sense it out there, prowling, sniffing her out as it circles closer.

Gigi reads the panic on her cousin's face, and seems to wake from her reverie.

'The black men are coming, aren't they, Bry?'

Bryony's eyes widen. She nods. Black men with black dogs and blades. She is struggling for breath again, snorting and sucking against the vest in her mouth. She tries to pull it free but Gigi stops her with a touch.

'You'll make a noise; you'll give us away.'

Frantic, Bryony shakes her head. *I won't I won't.* But Gigi is already holding the dressing gown cord. Her hands tremble as she ties it around the back of Bryony's sweat-damp head and over the bulging gag. 'It's for the best. You really have to keep quiet, Bry.'

Bryony tries to pull the gag out at once, clawing at her face with desperate fingers. Her muffled voice seeps through the soggy fabric, and she can feel bile rising up the back of her throat.

'No. Hush. Stop it,' Gigi sobs. 'Please.' She grabs Bryony's hands and pulls them behind her back once more. 'I thought we'd finished with all this. It's for your own good, Bryony. I have to save you.' She takes the two ends of the dressing gown cord that hang from Bryony's gag and uses them to bind her cousin's small hands together behind her back. She ties the knot double, to be sure.

The dog barks once again. Closer.

'Come, quickly.' She wrenches Bryony to her feet and drags her towards the built-in cupboards that line one wall. They are exactly the same as the ones in Bryony's own bedroom back at home and she half expects to see all of her clothes and junk when Gigi flings one of the cupboard doors open, but there is nothing but a crooked, abandoned wire hanger on an empty rail.

'I'm going to lock us in the room as well, OK? There's a key in the door, which is why I chose this room. But even then they might break through, so we have to hide.' She manoeuvres Bryony into the wooden shell of the cupboard and arranges her so that no toes or bits of dressing gown stick out. It smells of chipboard and dust. 'You have to stay very still.'

Gigi closes the cupboard and runs over to the bedroom door to shut it and lock it from the inside. Then she hurtles back to the line of cupboards and opens another of the floor-to-ceiling doors.

'I'm right in the next one, OK, Bryony?' she whispers as she struggles, and then succeeds in closing the cupboard door behind her. It is unexpectedly dark in the cramped wooden space. She taps on the board that separates her from Bryony. 'I'm right here. It's OK; if we wait, they'll go away.'

23

The dog's name is Bella. She's a long-haired Alsatian with a bushy tan-and-cream tail, a slender black muzzle, and two orange eyebrow spots that give her an expression of permanent concern. She has been a tracker for the K9 unit for over two years and she has been responsible for finding lost children, missing children and murdered children, dead bodies in rubbish dumps, hikers on mountainsides, arms caches beneath floorboards, and wanted felons on the lam.

Now she stands on her hind legs beneath the kitchen window of number 22 Cortona Villas with her front paws up against the sill, and whines.

'There's a good girl. Good girl.' Her handler, Eric Masondo, ruffles the hair on the back of Bella's neck when he comes up beside her. Bella sniffs the rim of the small window and looks back at Eric with a pleading expression.

'We can't fit through there, now can we, Bells?' he says and she whines in response. Eric tries the window but it has been securely latched from the inside.

'We need a set of keys for this house,' he calls to the manager of Cortona Villas Security, who is puffing up the path alongside the policewoman and her partner, a tall slender man with coffee-coloured skin. 'Immediately.' Bella gives a loud emphatic bark of agreement.

'Jeez, I am not sure where those could be. I know that the owners gave it to the estate agent some time ago, but then the place was taken off the market ... ' He scratches his chin and shakes his head. 'Now where would the keys to twenty-two be?' Bella barks again. The manager of Cortona Villas Security radios through to the office.

'Look, we have no idea what the situation is inside this house, we can't bugger around waiting for keys that might or might not be here, OK?' Eric Masondo glances at the policewoman, who nods her head, once. 'We're breaking in.'

★   ★   ★

Once Gigi has shut herself inside the cupboard, the room is silent. I hover at its centre. The air in the empty bedroom hangs heavy and strange and, despite the fact that there is no sun outside the window to cast any, shadows seem to form and dissolve in every corner.

I peer through the cupboard door to look in on Gigi. She is curled up in her cramped wooden cell. Jewels of sweat glisten on her ashen forehead and her mouth moves but no words come out. Her eyes are wide and staring.

In the next partition I find Bryony trying to force the gag out of her mouth by working it with her teeth and tugging downwards on the dressing gown cord behind her back. Her face is puce and her nostrils flare in and out as she struggles for breath. Just then, the knotted cord

290

slips down from its spot over the gag, but instead of setting her free, it is now tugging tight around her throat, weighed down by her bound hands. Her eye pop open wide and she makes a gurgling sound. She tries to move her hands upwards behind her back to loosen the tension in the dressing gown cord, but she hasn't got the strength or the space to lift them much at all.

If she loses consciousness, the weight of her hands pulling on that cord will strangle her.

No!

And suddenly I am out of time, darting like a hummingbird between the girls who now seem frozen within their dark cubicles.

Gigi! I scream, but I am not even a breath of wind to move a mote of dust. *Help her, snap out of it!* Of course, Gigi cannot hear me. Just inches away from her choking cousin, she sits rigid, staring blindly at the tiny lines of light that seep around the edges of the cupboard door.

In a fragment of a moment, I am with the knot of people clustered at the front door of the empty house working on the lock. *Move!* With glacial slowness, one of the men prepares to kick open the lock.

Move! But I know that even if they could hear me, they are never going to find the girls and get into the bedroom in time. Only Gigi is close enough to help Bryony. How can I make her understand?

There must be a way I can stop this. There must be someone who can hear me.

Lesedi.

With the thought I am by her side.

Lesedi, freed from the bonds of urban Joburg life, is doing what thousands upon thousands of women all over Africa are doing in the bright-afternoon light: peeling, cutting, chopping, washing. With her hands immersed in an enamel tub full of sun-warm water, she rubs at a stubborn clump of soil that clings to a small knobbly sweet potato and glances across the sunlit yard to where Ma Retabile is snoring in the green shade of a twisted acacia tree.

For a moment, Lesedi pauses, thinking of Thabo and her lovely house and her Elizabeth Arden skin-care products all lined up in the bathroom cabinet; then she shakes her head and smiles. Since her arrival yesterday, she and Ma Retabile have discussed the best herbs to use for stomach cramps, a new way of preparing caju bark to make tea for colicky babies, and thrown the bones for a man who came walking towards the hut with a sorry expression on his face and a bundle of fresh peaches wrapped in a cloth.

Lesedi has not spoken a word of her Cortona Villas conundrum, but just being by Ma Retabile's side has sparked something inside her, and she has gained a surprising sense of clarity on how her two worlds might meet. She's realized that it is pointless to try and hide who she is from the people she lives alongside; and, equally, she knows that she cannot consult in a hut, because that is not who she is, either. But already, she can see how her new smart, consulting room in Johannesburg could look with its plaque on the door and elegant wooden furniture in the waiting room. No more hiding in back bedrooms at home and hoping that the neighbours don't cotton on; she will set up proper rooms, have business cards printed on thick, textured card stock, walk so tall that the word sangoma will become just another suburban norm. *Darling, I've got a sangoma appointment at three, could you fetch the kids from tennis? Please just make sure that Jayden doesn't leave his shoes in the locker room again.*

Lesedi grins, placing the washed potato on the plate on her left and picking up a new, soily one from the pile on her right. As she dunks it into the creamy brown water, her vision suddenly clouds, and her skin goes ice cold. She gasps as the bright yard vanishes behind a tracery of darting shadows. The toffee-coloured chicken pecking at the ground a little distance away pauses mid-peck, suspended in time.

Lesedi. At first, her name is whispering wind in dry grasses. Then it becomes a cry that seems to emanate from the surrounding hills: *Lesedi, help me! She's going to kill her.*

Ancestor?

Lesedi's body remains frozen in the act of falling backwards, her foot about to hook the rim of the enamel bowl, but she is no longer in the dusty yard with the green mountains peering down at her. She finds herself inside what seems to be a cupboard. She's overwhelmed by the sound of gasping. Her own breath suddenly chokes in her throat.

In an instant, Lesedi can feel little Bryony's peril; can sense how close the child has moved to the shadowed side. She can feel Bryony choking as the weight of her hands pulls the cord tighter around her neck. She remembers the black dog warning. She longs for breath.

You have to stop it. My plea echoes Lesedi's own, frantic heartbeat.

But the girls are hundreds of kilometres away. Lesedi's lungs are screaming, her blood pounds. *YOU will have to stop it, Ancestor.*

But I am nothing! The web of shadows erupts in a cloud of panicked, white moths that flutter into Lesedi's face and catch in her throat. *I cannot move or touch anything. Gigi cannot hear me.* Along with that of the helpless girl in the cupboard, Lesedi can feel her own life stuttering, flickering out. She needs to breathe.

ANCESTOR, TELL ME YOUR NAME. It takes all her remaining strength to command the shadows. It works. A thin stream of precious air rushes into her mouth.

Sally. The wordless reply. More air. Lesedi gulps it down. *No. Really it is Monkey.*

Monkey. Lesedi concentrates hard, head still swimming. *You may not think it, but you do have power. Look at what you've just done to me. You are an Ancestor now, a custodian of stories.*

I'm just a dead white woman. Lesedi feels a cord tighten around her neck again. *I know nothing of ancestors and such things.* White moths pour back out of the shadow clouds, swoop in sickening circles and then settle all around Lesedi and into the far distance, a menacing silver carpet of pulsing wing-beats.

You are Africa's daughter, you were born

in Her lap and you died in Her arms; She embraced you your whole life, and now you are a part of Her. Not the soil and scrub part, but the story part. As such, as an ancestor, you can reach Gigi.

But I am nothing but a memory to her. A wailing gale rises, whipping up the shadows around Lesedi into dark, coiling towers of smoke.

Then BE a memory, Lesedi commands.

The pale moths rise up around her in a whirl of wings. They gather and coalesce to form the tall figure of a woman. Streams of creatures make up a long flowing skirt, slender feet and strands of hair that fly back from a rustling, shifting face. The swarm figure rushes at Lesedi as if about to rip her apart with long fingers made of a thousand furred bodies. But when they reach her, the moths are soft against her face, caressing her, bringing her breath back with their wing-beats. The moths then begin to settle all over Lesedi, covering her from neck to toe in a delicate, shimmering mantle.

I was Sally, but now I am more.

Ants in my marrow, tadpoles in my throat, sun on my scalp, swallows swooping in the breath in my lungs. Stories singing at me.

I can be memory.

The front door of Cortona Villas bursts inwards as Eric's booted foot connects with the now weakened lock. Like a bolt from a bow, Bella darts past his legs and into the bare hallway. She pauses and looks back at her partner with worried eyebrows raised.

'Find the scent, girl.'

Bella's tail wags furiously. She wiffles her sensitive nose along the floorboards and starts up the stairwell with Eric close behind. Suddenly, she gives an anxious bark, and speeds into a run, her claws clicking on the wood.

* * *

My daughter sits in the dark. Her arms are wrapped around her knees. Her eyes, wet with tears, stare but do not see. Centimetres away, on the other side of the chipboard partition, Bryony's arms quiver as she battles to hold them high enough behind her back to release some of the tension around her throat. Her awareness is slipping, and she begins to float. Soon she will see me.

No.

Be a memory.

I see a thread I've not noticed before: like a story thread, but different. It is as fine as sewing cotton, and pale. It is accompanied by the lightest sound of bells. I follow it. It gets stronger; I grasp it and it thickens to string, and then rope beneath my non-hands. The bell sound grows louder.

And then I arrive, right inside Gigi's idea of me.

I am every moment she and I ever shared. I smell cinnamon cookies and turmeric tomato curry and library books and Savlon antiseptic and horsehair and wild cat and soil. Colours overlap and meld and swim, and the bell chime is lost amid the sound of my voice in a thousand moments.

Gigi, would you like another slice of Marmite toast?

Here we go round the mulberry bush . . .

Come on, Gigi, it's hot.

You want to call her Jemima? But she's not a puddle-duck, she's a serval, you silly sausage.

Ignoring the noise, I force myself to hunt for the brightest, clearest me.

I thought it would be the me on the kitchen floor with my hair full of blood and my skirt all torn and the dark hands around my neck. But it's not.

★ ★ ★

'Mom?' Gigi called, and I turned from the drying orange soil covering the jackal family's grave to watch her approach. Gigi at eight years old. The bunches that she insisted on doing herself were skew, one higher up on the side of her head than the other, and there was a small tuft of hair left out of both trailing down her back. She scrunched her eyes against the sun as she walked across the clearing to join me in the shade of the bottle-brush tree, and the scattering of freckles on her nose converged, making her look even more serious.

'Hey, love. How's it going?'

'Horrible. Simone's not talking to me.'

'I wouldn't worry about that, Gi, she's not talking to anybody today.'

'Is she still sad about the baby jackals?'

'*Ja.*'

'But why? She told me that nothing really dies,

297

Mom, that when we pass on we all kind of blend together into a big ball of light and then little bits break off the ball to become new lives in baby things.'

'My, you have been talking to Simone a lot, haven't you?'

'She *likes* to talk to me,' Gigi said with a look that could've been accusing had she put a bit more effort into it.

'Of course she does. We all do.'

'Simone especially.'

'Fair enough.' A light breeze lifted the damp hair from the back of my neck and I puffed out a breath along with it.

'So she shouldn't be sad about the jackals because of the ball of light.'

'That may well be the case, Sweetpea, but Simone doesn't really know what happens afterwards, no one does.' I dropped down to my haunches and poked a finger through the crust of the soil. It felt warm and moist beneath the surface. Alive. 'Whatever the case may be, it's OK to be sad about things going away, Gi. It's better to let yourself get sad if you want to.'

'But Simone — '

'Gi, I know Simone's the smart one who knows all the flower remedies and asanas and the Buddha quotes and that, but are you open to a word or two of wisdom from your funny old mom?'

'Uh-huh,' she said, hunkering down beside me. I could feel the humming life in her small, taut body through the sharp point of her elbow that pressed against my leg.

298

'If you don't let yourself be sad about things, then that feeling can build up and turn really nasty.'

'Nasty?' She poked one of her own fingers through the topsoil alongside mine.

'*Ja*, all festering and horrible.'

'I don't understand.'

'Think of the way *vrot* veggies go all slimy and stinky at the bottom of the fridge.'

'Oh. *Sis*.'

'Exactly.'

'But being sad sucks.'

'I know, hon,' I said, and placed an arm around her shoulders.

I remember how we sat like that for a long time, listening to the chattering of the birds as the afternoon slowly softened around us; but now, I do not let it get to that. I draw on the power of all the story noise that has been screaming at me without cease for all the time since I passed on. I channel the vibrant surge into something I can wield. I take charge of the memory. I change it.

Gigi, look at me.

I can speak! As I say the words, the fleshless me and the memory me are suddenly one. When Gigi turns to us, her eyes are no longer sky-coloured; they shimmer shining black with blue lights like a glossy starling wing.

'Mom?' The breeze turns into a wind. My hair whips against my face. The bottle-brush seeds rattle above my head and I can smell the dust and chipboard smell of the cupboard inside 22 Cortona Villas.

Your cousin.

'What?'

Bryony. She needs you. The cord has slipped around her neck and she is choking. You must go to her. NOW.

★ ★ ★

Somewhere between that time and this time and all times, a dog barks.

★ ★ ★

Lesedi falls backwards on to the compacted earth of the yard. Her foot hooks the edge of the enamel tub of potato-washing water and sends it flying. The chicken squawks and skitters off in a rustle of feathers and Ma Retabile wakes with a snort.

The washing water foams out in a wave and then soaks into the dry ground.

★ ★ ★

Gigi hears footsteps on the stairs. The men. They're here. But it doesn't matter any more. She takes a breath, steeling herself, and then kicks open the cupboard. The room is so bright after the gloom that for a moment she is blind, stumbling. She grabs the knob on the adjoining cupboard door and wrenches it open.

'Bryony!'

Her cousin is purple-faced. The vest is no longer in her mouth, and her bluish lips are still. Her eyes are huge and bulging. The dirty-white

300

dressing gown cord coils around her neck like a rigid, towelling snake.

'Oh God, oh no.' Gigi pulls Bryony from the cupboard and they both fall backwards on to the floor. Gigi scrabbles to get behind Bryony and pulls her arms upwards behind her back, immediately loosening the noose. 'Breathe, breathe, please breathe,' she intones in a frantic whisper. Then, using her knees to hold Bryony's wrists up to keep the cord slack, she begins to work on the knots.

Bryony makes a tiny sound, a whimper of pain at the ripping feeling in her shoulder joints.

And then the knot comes free.

'Bryony?' Gigi sobs.

For a moment there is silence, and then the girl takes a strange, choking little breath. And then another. Her face turns from purple to white to brilliant red and she curls up on her side, coughing and gasping.

'Oh thank you thank you thank you,' Gigi cries and throws her arms around her cousin, cradling her like an oversized doll. All the frantic activity has reopened the slashes on her upper arm, and fresh trickles of blood roll down her blue-white skin and soak into the towelling dressing gown.

Beyond the door, the girls can hear the click of animal claws and an excited whine followed by heavy footsteps. Someone tries the door handle. The key wobbles in the lock.

'Mommy,' Gigi says. She shuts her eyes.

* * *

'Gigi? Bryony? Are you girls all right?' No answer. 'Move away from the door!' Eric Masondo tests the strength of the lock by pressing his shoulder against it, and then steps back and lunges forward. The lock pops open easily beneath his body weight and he steps into the bare bedroom.

The first thing he sees (and Bella sniffs) is blood. He takes a cautious step towards the huddled children. The one with her back to him has no shirt on, and the knobs of her spine almost seem to pierce through her pearl-white skin and the thin, grubby elastic of her bra strap. She does not turn to look at him, but the blonde girl in her lap peers around her ribs and stares at Eric with huge, terrified eyes.

'The black men are here,' she mouths.

'It's all right, I'm not going to hurt you.' Eric's voice comes out thinner than he expects it to. Usually, he would rush over and crouch beside two frightened kids like this and tell them that they're safe, but for some reason he holds back.

He notes that the blood seems to be coming from the older girl's arm, but the wound looks fairly superficial from where he is standing.

'They're in here,' he says softly to the policewoman as she comes up behind him, and, as he does so, the pale girl whimpers and curls her body protectively over the younger child huddled in her lap.

★ ★ ★

Lesedi switches on her BlackBerry and notes the one little bar on the screen that indicates at least some chance of getting reception. She walks away from the yard with the toffee-coloured chicken and the pile of sweet potatoes and the dark patch of spilled water on the orange earth, and heads to higher ground, stepping between tufts of long, juicy grass stems and over stones as she makes for the top of the small hill that borders Ma Retabile's homestead.

The sun is a milky white disc behind a soft fuzz of drifting cloud in the western sky and a light breeze cools the film of sweat still coating her skin.

Lesedi wishes she could phone Adele Wilding from next door and ask her if her daughter is all right, but in the ten months that the Matsunyanes have been living in Cortona Villas, the two have barely exchanged greetings, let alone phone numbers.

She glances at the screen. Three bars. She keeps on walking, determined now to reach the top of the low rise. The breeze drops and the air feels hot and close. A large, khaki-coloured locust springs from a grass stalk and clings to her shirt for a moment before launching itself off in another direction. Four bars.

Finally, she stops. She presses a few buttons on her phone and holds it to her ear. It's ringing.

'Sedi!' She smiles at the sound of Thabo's voice.

'Thabo.' She shuts her eyes against the encircling peeks of the vivid green mountains with their aloe-print skirts. 'Have you sold the house yet?'

'No.'

'Good,' she says. 'Don't.'

303

'OK.' She can hear the grin in his voice. 'No problem, babe.'

'But please tell the estate agent that I'm going to be looking for office premises to rent. Northern suburbs, high end.'

'Sounds interesting.'

'And I think I'm going to need to visit my mom when I get back. Have a little chat . . . '

Lesedi opens her eyes. The mountains are still there, looking down at her. *Go*. They sing. *Go home.*

24

I am a rutted, dirt road that winds through the bush. I am a dense clump of fragrant grass tipped with little brown seeds. I am a tick, clinging to a stalk and waiting for a duiker to pass by. I am a low cloud with a thunder rumble deep in my grey, churning belly. I am the first drop of rain that plummets down and slams into the waiting, thirsty earth.

I hear all the whispers and the calls and the sighs and the stories — all but one. It is silent, my story noise. It no longer screams at me.

I listen hard for it, expecting it to start at any moment, to build to its all-encompassing crescendo and force me back to the Wilding house, but it is gone.

The wide sky beckons, but I hesitate, and although there is now nothing making me do it, I listen for the familiar cadence of my daughter's sleeping breath and follow it. My sister is there too, awake. Once more, I am at her side.

* * *

Adele, who is exhausted and can no longer summon the energy to stare at the two sleeping girls attached to their respective drips in their hospital beds in adjoining rooms for one more minute, steps into the corridor and leans her head back against the wall. She hears the squeak of shoe rubber, and glances up to see Liam returning from his trip to the cafeteria with a paper cup of coffee in each hand. Hospital lighting and a day full of worry are doing him no favours: his skin looks green and pitted. He hands Adele her coffee.

'Thanks.' The cardboard is hot beneath her fingers.

'The girls still cased out?'

'*Ja*. Neither one of them has so much as stirred.'

Liam glances through the doorway and into the first room. Gigi has a block of white gauze plastered over her left upper arm and a drip needle in the opposite wrist. She is asleep. The drip is for dehydration and sustenance, apparently. The doctors, with a searching look at himself and his wife, proclaimed her to have been in dire need of both.

Bryony looks very small in her own, white bed in the next room. Her face is less flushed than it was, probably because the drugs have helped her fever to come down a little. He follows the transparent worm of the drip cable all the way down to where it stabs into the flesh above her small, sore wrist. The bruise there is more prominent now, an ugly bangle of dark grey and purple. Liam notes that the mark around her neck is still an angry crimson. He quickly turns away.

'What the hell happened, Addy?'

'I wish I could answer that.' Adele takes a sip of her coffee and walks over to the row of chairs in the corridor. 'Neither of them has said a sensible word since we found them.' She slides

306

down on to the worn chair cushion. 'Gigi, of course, has not made a single peep, and Bryony was whispering about how Gigi tried to save her from a dog or some such nonsense.'

'But Bryony's bruises? I don't . . . ' He shakes his head, squeezing his eyes shut for a moment. 'The cops are sure there was no one else there?'

'You know they are, Liam: they told us both. They searched and sniffer-dogged and finger-printed our house and number twenty-two. Nothing.'

'I know, it's just . . . ' Liam comes over and sits down beside her. 'Did the girls get into a fight? I mean, who cut up Gigi's arm?'

'I don't know.'

'Surely not Bryony?'

'Liam, I don't know.'

'And all Bryony's bruises and her damaged windpipe — she was almost strangled. To death.'

'I know.'

'Gigi?' Liam asks, and he and Adele exchange a look. After a long moment, Adele sighs and turns her head.

'It had to be. No one else was there.'

'Christ, I knew she was screwed up but this is . . . well, this is dangerous stuff.' There is another long silence. 'She can't stay.'

'Liam — '

'What?' Liam remembers the way Gigi rose from her bed yesterday evening, screaming at him, demonic. 'She's a bloody psychopath.'

'So what do we do with her, Liam? Chuck her out on the street? We're her legal guardians, for God's sake.'

'We could send her away for a bit, to a special

307

boarding school or something. There must be places for kids like these.'

'What, like Girls and Boys Town? Isn't that for juvenile delinquents?'

'Well, how would you describe this recent crazy behaviour?' Liam says. He remembers Gigi taking him by the hand and showing him around the farm every single time he drove up to Limpopo to visit Sally. Even on the brink of fourteen she had been wide open and generous with her smiles and eager to teach. *The honey badger eats snakes — did you know that, Uncle Liam? The name makes it sound all cute and fluffy and stuff, but one of these little guys can rip the head off a cobra, no problem.*

'Or maybe just a boarding school where the teachers can keep an eye on her,' Liam mutters. 'Christ.' He pinches the bridge of his nose and squeezes hard.

'I suppose,' Adele says. 'I can make a few calls, see what our options are; but before we decide anything, we need to know from Bryony exactly what happened.'

Liam takes another sip of his coffee. 'Your hair. You had it cut. It looks nice, by the way,' he says, and Adele bursts into tears.

★ ★ ★

Consciousness returns to Gigi as a series of bright blobs of light that tease her flickering eyelids to open. When at last they do, she spends long minutes just staring at the strips of aluminium that hold the ceiling boards together, until gradually the rest of the room makes its presence felt. *I'm back in a hospital.* She listens to the sound of voices and footsteps and life in the corridor outside, and then lifts her arm to stare at the place where the drip needle goes in.

Finally, she looks over to the adjoining bed. It is empty. Carefully, she extracts herself from beneath the covers and slides her feet on to the cool floor. Clutching the drip stand in one hand and the back of her gaping hospital gown in the other, Gigi edges her way out of the room and into the corridor. A nurse in a dark blue uniform zooms past carrying a folder of paper. 'Where's my cousin?' Gigi want to ask, but her mouth is too slow.

She peers around the doorframe of the next room, and sees Bryony, asleep in her bed. She blinks at the bright mark around Bryony's neck and the ring of bruises around each of her wrists. For a moment, she is unsure about how the wounds came to bloom on her cousin's tender, pale skin; was it the black men? Did they come as she knew they would?

No. It was me.

She shuts her eyes again, the better to absorb this sudden knowing. She probes her inner world cautiously, feeling out for that guilty swirling place, that mottled and sick-feeling centre seeping acid that had become such a familiar retreat inside her.

But it is gone.

She opens her eyes with a start, and scours the strange room as if the answer to the mysterious disappearance of her darkness is hiding behind the window blinds or lurking under Bryony's bed. After a moment, she realizes that Bryony is awake and staring at her with huge blue eyes rimmed with sore pink-looking flesh.

'I'm sorry,' Gigi whispers. The words feel wonderful. They taste like hot, buttery popcorn. For a moment, it looks as if Bryony is going to say something back; her mouth moves and a soft hiss comes out of her damaged throat before she closes her eyes and lets her head fall back against her pillow.

'I really thought they were coming for us, Bry, and I know it sounds dumb and you probably don't believe me, but I didn't know I was hurting you,' Gigi says. 'I didn't know much of anything.'

Silence.

Gigi watches Bryony's chest as it rises and falls with each silent breath.

25

Adele replaces the phone receiver with great care, as if it might suddenly explode in her grip and send chunks of her flesh flying off in all directions. She stares down at the notepad where she just wrote down the number that Gigi's psychiatrist, Dr Rowe, has given her. Her script is round and even. Top marks for neatness, Adele.

The number is for a school in Kwazulu-Natal that she has never heard of, a private holding pen for the druggie kids and difficult teens from well-off families that no one knows how to handle. Adele imagines plonking Gigi in her car and driving there through the brown flat fields of the Free State and then along Van Reenen's Pass with its winding ribbon of road and those lovely green hills: the route of countless family holidays from her childhood.

From the back seat of her own parents' car, she and Sally had giggled and bickered and played licence-plate word games and I-Spy and eaten hard-boiled eggs and cheese-and-tomato sandwiches out of crumpled foil, counting the slow hours until they'd be close enough to spot the first impossibly delicious blue patch of sea.

One year, they had fought bitterly over a little plastic bucket and spade that was the exact colour of a Granny Smith apple; neither of them had been the slightest bit interested in the yellow one with the red handle. Adele remembers running down the beach clutching the apple-green bucket to her wet swimming costume in triumph, but has no recollection of how it came to be hers.

She remembers her sister many years on from the beach holidays at Umhlanga: Sally pregnant with Gigi. She can see Sally's pale arms curving over her protruding stomach and the little knob of belly button pushing through the fabric of her T-shirt like the knot of a balloon.

★   ★   ★

Lesedi manoeuvres her car slowly through the afternoon quiet of the Cortona Villa streets, and marvels at just how far she has come in the past six hours: there are no cinder-block cubes with corrugated-iron roofs and straggly vegetable patches here, no funny little igloo-shaped outhouses surrounded by fleshy, spike-leafed aloes. Every red-bricked street is swept and litter-free, edged with blank-faced garage doors (well oiled, of course) and tidy little garden gates.

Lesedi smiles at the clipped edges of the immaculate front lawns until she passes number 22. The patch of grass outside the empty unit is criss-crossed with drying tracks of mud as if troops of people have trudged in and out of the property in the rain. Lesedi slows down even further, and notes the round little divots of soggy earth pushed up by what can only have been a running animal. A dog.

She tightens her grip on the steering wheel

and gives her head a brief shake. She can't help but glance across to the passenger seat, and then into the rear-view mirror to check the back, half expecting to see the pale monkey-woman coming along for the ride. The car is empty.

Round the corner and past the next two blocks, she finally sees the remaining brave little arms of the storm-damaged fever tree beckoning her home. Beside it, the Wildings' garage door stands open and Lesedi peers in, just managing to catch a glimpse of Bryony's retreating back as her father leads her from the car and out of the garage towards the house. The child's fair hair is all mussed up at the back, as if she's been lying on it, and although she sits behind a sheet of glass, Lesedi's nostrils are suddenly filled with the astringent smell of disinfectant.

'Hospital,' she whispers.

Just then, one of the back doors of Liam's white Mercedes swings open and the skinny cousin-girl climbs out. She stands with her palms pressed against the smooth metal for a moment, head bowed. There's a patch of white gauze on her left upper arm.

'Come on, Gigi.' Adele pokes her head into the garage. Her hair is shorter than before, her face pale and pinched-looking, and her voice weary. 'It's time to come inside.' The girl nods; Adele retreats. The girl slowly raises her head and looks towards the street. Her eyes meet Lesedi's and, for a second, Lesedi sees something black flutter within the blue. A robin calls from the fever tree, one high, clear note, and then the small, ragged patch of dark is gone.

Tyler turns his pillow over so that he can lie on the cool side, and tries, once again, to get comfortable on the TV-room couch. The house is humming with silence, and has been ever since the girls arrived home from hospital that afternoon. Tyler is surprised at just how much space his little sister's voice used to fill, and its absence is like a rip in the suburban normality of the household that he has spent so much energy resenting.

'Are you OK, Bry?' he'd said, shocked by her dark ugly bruises, and even more horrified when she'd tried to answer him, but couldn't.

'She's doing much better.' Liam had spoken for her, ruffling Bryony's grubby-looking hair. 'The doctors say the tonsillitis is winding down and she should be right as rain in a day or two.'

Right as rain? Tyler had wanted to yell. *She's had the bloody sound strangled right out of her.*

And now the strangler herself is in *his* room, surrounded by all of his stuff, including the iPod which he now wishes he'd remembered to grab when he'd gathered his pyjamas together for a night on the couch. 'Just for a night or two,' his mother had assured him. 'She can't share Bryony's room. Not after . . . ' Her voice had trailed off, and she'd left the room. Not after *what?*

Tyler thinks of the blood on the bathmat and the welt on Bryony's neck, and the way that the policeman had described finding them: *Curled up in each other's arms, terrified, as if they were*

314

hiding from something.

Tyler squirms as a strange little worm of revulsion wiggles up the back of his throat, remembering Gigi's thin, ice-cold fingers right inside his mouth.

★ ★ ★

Gigi lies and stares at the blank ceiling of Tyler's bedroom and finds that she misses the chemical greeny glow of the luminous stars that are glued to Bryony's. She glances around at the posters, but it's too dark to see any detail, and then looks over towards the door, which has been locked from the outside.

'It's just for tonight, Gigi,' Liam had said in a strange, cracked voice as he'd stood in the doorway, turning the key over and over between his fingers. 'I'll open it in the morning, first thing. Do you need one more trip to the loo?'

Gigi shuts her eyes.

★ ★ ★

In the adjacent bedroom, Bryony dreams. She's walking towards Dommie's house. The light is golden green and filled with small fluttering insects with translucent wings. Suddenly, a large Alsatian with a dark muzzle, a shaggy flame of a tail and worried ginger eyebrows steps out into the road in front of her. Bryony stops. The insects drift around them both, caught in currents on the breeze. The dog gives its tail a cautious wag. Bryony takes a step closer. She

315

holds out her hand.

The dog trots over to her, tail now wagging furiously. It drops to its haunches before her and then rolls over to expose a belly the colour of cream. Bryony bends down and buries her hand in the warm fur.

26

I wait.

I wait for Liam to remember me.

He does so while brushing his teeth, eyes locked on to their own reflections in the bathroom mirror. Perhaps it is the smell of mint from the toothpaste that makes him think of me. We once shared a choc-mint ice cream that we bought from the man with the icebox on his bicycle who used to wait outside campus to ambush exhausted students with sweet, childish treats. I remember watching Liam's tongue as he licked the pale green frost, and then, when he handed the ice cream to me, casually placing my own into the depression his lick had left behind.

He is not thinking of me with the ice cream, though. He is remembering the rusty padlock on the farm gate in Limpopo, and the last time he saw me alive.

Just as I did with Gigi as she crouched inside that cupboard, I follow the slender story thread back, and slip into the memory along with him.

*   *   *

'Care to escort me to the front gate?' Liam grinned up at me through the open car window and gestured to the passenger seat. 'Get in.'

'I've got muddy boots on, Liam.'

'Doesn't matter.'

317

I walked around the car and climbed into the dark grey, leather-scented interior. I placed my feet very carefully on the carpet, but I still saw a mustard-coloured streak on the pristine pile. I hoped it wasn't something's poo.

Liam began to move the car slowly along the rutted track of the driveway. I watched the back of his hand on the gear stick: knuckles covered with tanned skin and little golden strands of hair. The vibration from the engine seemed to throb right through my boots and the soles of my feet, up through my legs and into my lap. We arrived at the front gate too quickly. I tried to ignore the heat in my groin as I climbed out of the car and made for the gate.

'I can't believe you still think that silly thing is enough protection out here,' Liam said as he watched me unlock the padlock. There was a clank of metal as the chain swung down and slapped the side of the gate.

'You say that every time.' I said.

'I mean it every time.'

It's easier this time, to change the memory. The sudden sweet mint stench of toothpaste is overwhelming. I take charge of the memory now, and I know Liam will hear me when I speak:

You were right, Liam. Every time.

Liam's skin goes pale. A gust of warm wind sighs in my ears.

Don't abandon her.

'Sally?' His lips are bloodless now. He does not blink.

Please, Liam, don't send my daughter away.

318

* * *

Liam chokes on mint foam and spit. The electric toothbrush drops from his hand, bounces on the edge of the basin and goes flying across the floor where it hums against the tile grout, still vibrating. He grips the edge of the basin and coughs and coughs until at last he manages to steal a breath. His face, when he looks back up at the mirror, is crimson.

* * *

Gigi stands in the middle of Tyler's bedroom. She picks at the edge of the white bandage on her left upper arm and then touches her fingertip to the sticky patch that the peeled-up corner leaves behind on her skin.

'What am I supposed to do now?' she asks the silence. She stares at the closed door. The sound of the bedroom key turning in the lock had woken her earlier, but no one had said anything or poked their head into the room. Is she allowed to leave?

Gigi knows that she must be in very big trouble. The bruises on Bryony's neck and wrists are like great big black marks against her name and there will be consequences, she knows that. 'Big trouble,' she whispers. The skater boys and bikini girls in the posters on Tyler's walls stare back down at her, not disagreeing.

For a moment, her face twists and a sob lurches up her throat, but then she forces it back down.

She takes a big breath and glances to where her school uniform is draped over the chair by Tyler's messy desk. She'd grabbed it last night before bed when Adele had told her she wouldn't be sharing with Bryony. Gigi reaches out and touches the heavy fabric of the tunic. Below the chair, her new school shoes stand like two giant shiny-shelled beetles.

'I forgot the socks,' she says. Again, the sob threatens. Again, she swallows it down. She marches over to Tyler's cupboard and wrenches it open. He must have a pair of white socks in here somewhere.

★ ★ ★

And now, Adele.

I don't have to wait long for my sister to think of me. She is awake in her bed, lying on her side and staring at the bright block of yellow light created by the early sun streaming through the blind on the east-facing window. She is remembering.

★ ★ ★

'Monkey, let's make them go to the beach.' Adele smoothed out the woollen braids of her rag doll as she placed it beside mine on the rug between us. 'Hey? What do you think?'

Adele had just turned seven. She was wearing the dress with the sailing ship printed on the front and little puffed sleeves that used to be mine. I remember being glad when I grew out of

320

it because the armpits made me itchy, but Adele
loved it. She pulled the skirt down over her knees
and then reached out and patted her doll's soft
belly.

'Jasmine could do with a break, you know. She
told me earlier. We can get them all ready for
their holiday and then take them outside to the
pool, hey?'

I watched Adele as she began to rifle through
the pile of doll's clothes that had been tipped out
on the rug earlier, searching for suitable outfits
for a beach holiday. I slid my fingers into the
gaps between all my toes and pushed hard, liking
the feeling of stretching skin.

'Come on, Monkey.' She glanced at me,
sensing my disinterest. 'Don't you think Jasmine
and Jennifer need a holiday?' She picked up my
rag doll, held her up to my face and gave her a
little waggle. Jennifer's cloth arms and legs flapped
around in a mad dance, making me smile.

'Ja. I guess so.' I took the doll from my sister,
ending the dance, but then put her right back down
on the rug again and slid my fingers back between
my toes.

'Do you want them to go somewhere else?'
Adele asks.

'Not really.'

'Then what's the matter?'

'I don't know. I guess I just don't really feel
like playing dolls right now.'

'You say that a lot lately,' Adele said, covering
her doll's face as if to stop her from hearing me.
'Don't you like them any more?'

'No, it's not that, it's just . . . ' I stared down

321

at Jennifer's blank stitched face. It was impossible to tell my sister that Jennifer had just somehow stopped being alive for me, and that our usual games now made me feel silly and self-conscious and bored.

'It's OK,' she said quickly, suddenly not wanting to know my reasons. 'You don't have to do anything. I'll look after Jennifer and find her something to wear.' She picked up my doll and held her against her chest, stroking the back of her woollen head to comfort her. 'She'll be well taken care of, don't you worry, Monkey.'

Now.

* * *

Adele, I say, hijacking her memory.

For a long moment, she does not look at me, but continues to cuddle the doll to her neck.

Please. The child me's voice has a deeper harmonic to it. My sister shakes her head, not wanting to hear it. She closes her eyes. Her hands gripping Jennifer have gone bone white. *Please look after my Gigi.*

Adele jolts upright in bed and rubs her fingers over her damp face. She listens to the comforting, everyday buzz of Liam's electric shaver coming from the bathroom, and waits for her heartbeat to slow back down to normal.

* * *

Gigi, dressed in her school uniform and a pair of Tyler's socks, opens the bedroom door and steps

322

out on to the landing. At the distant sound of a toilet flush coming from Adele and Liam's en-suite, a sudden stab of panic grips her guts, squeezes hard, and then almost immediately lets go. Whatever happens, whatever they decide to do with her, she will deal with it. The men did not come and Bryony is safe and that is all that matters.

Bryony's bedroom door is closed. Gigi lightly touches the white-painted wood before continuing past it to get to the stairs.

The clock on the kitchen wall ticks like the throb of blood in a vein. Gigi counts the seconds as she makes herself toast with peanut butter and a mug of rooibos tea. She chews mechanically, listening to the clock and the hum of the fridge. She has to take a sip of tea for each swallow because without it her mouth is too dry for anything to go down. When she is finished, she sits at the table with her hands on her lap and counts her breaths. Every time her thoughts try and slip off somewhere else, she brings them back, gently, as if training an exuberant puppy, just as Simone once taught her to do: breath in, breath out, up to seven and then start again from one.

Adele appears in the kitchen doorway and freezes when she sees Gigi all dressed and ready for school. 'Oh,' she says.

They hear the sound of rushing water in the pipes; someone upstairs is taking a shower.

'You're all ready for school.' Adele rubs the crumples of confusion on her forehead with nervous fingers. The second her eyes meet Gigi's they slide away.

Beneath the tabletop, Gigi's own fingers clench till the tips go numb. 'Yes,' she answers. Her voice is almost a whisper.

'Right, then,' Adele says, launching herself into the kitchen and heading towards the coffee machine. Her vision blurs. In her head, the girl sitting at the table with her hair in a neat ponytail and her oversized, wrinkled school uniform looms enormous for a moment and then shrinks down to the size of a teacup. Adele clutches the edge of the sink for support as she turns on the kitchen tap.

She suddenly remembers exactly how Sally's little rag doll had felt when she'd pressed it against her neck all those years ago. Its stuffed cloth body had been soft and defenceless, like a sea creature that had lost its shell.

27

Bryony sits up in her bed and stares around the room, trying to place the hour. It feels as if she's been asleep for days. What day is it? What time? She gets up on legs that no longer wobble beneath her and walks over to the window. She pulls the curtain open and looks out. The sunlight has lost that peachy early-morning look, moved on past lemon yellow, and now burns bright and clear. It must be well after school starting time.

She pushes the window open wider and sticks her head through the gap, breathing in the green smell of just-cut grass. She can hear the muted roar of a lawnmower somewhere close by and, on top of that, the light buzzy zipping sound of bees in the lavender pots by the front door below her window.

Without really thinking about it, she touches the tender welt on her neck, running her fingers along the slight bump in her skin. Her finger comes to rest in the hollow of her throat, and it is still there when she hears her parents' footsteps on the landing outside the room.

'Look who's up,' Liam says in a jolly tone as he pushes her door wider to step into the room. His smile looks not very well glued on.

'Feeling better, my girl?' Adele asks, coming in behind him.

Bryony blinks at them both. She can't

remember when her parents last came into her bedroom at the same time like this. Her birthday? No. Maybe the one before last. It looks like they're stepping on to a stage, about to launch into a song-and-dance routine.

'You must be hungry. I've brought a treat.' Instead of sashaying into a number, Adele walks across the room and places a bowl on Bryony's bedside table. 'Jelly and custard, just the thing for a girly-pie with a sore throat. Come and have some, darling.'

'For breakfast?' Bryony asks in astonishment. 'You guys are acting seriously weird.'

She trots over to the bed, climbs back on to it, and picks up the bowl. A slithery spoonful of jewel red wobbliness covered in sweet yellow goo slips down her throat. She takes another. It is only after her third spoonful that she realizes that her parents are staring at her as if she is an alien from another planet.

'Your voice,' Adele says at last, her own oddly croaky all of a sudden. 'It's back.'

'Oh,' Bryony says. 'Ja, I guess it is.' She watches her parents exchange a look. 'Why aren't you at work, Dad? What day is it?'

'It's Friday, love. But I just popped home to see how my girl was getting on.'

'I'm feeling better. Tonsillitis gone, I think,' Bryony says through another mouthful of pudding.

'Oh good.'

Two more spoonfuls go down. Adele and Liam share another look. Liam clears his throat.

'Now that you're talking again, Bry, your mom

326

and I would really like to ask you a few questions about . . . the other day.'

Bryony dips her spoon into the bowl and very carefully sheers off a thin slice of jelly. A corner of it slips off her spoon: a delicate flap of transparent pink that catches the light before she puts it to her tongue.

'Darling' — Adele sits down on the duvet beside her — 'we need to know what happened on Wednesday when you stayed home from school. How did you and Gigi end up at that abandoned house?'

'I was really sick and I had some medicine,' Bryony says. 'Gigi was scared and we needed to find somewhere safe.'

'That makes no sense — ' Liam starts, but Adele cuts him off with a look.

'What was Gigi scared of?' Adele asks in a gentle voice.

Bryony glances up at her parents and then back down again. 'Just . . . stuff.' She shrugs. 'She was remembering things, from the day Aunty Sally died. She just freaked out a bit.'

'Freaked out?'

'Liam, for heaven's sake, keep your voice down.'

'But all that blood in the bathroom? How did . . . did you and Gigi have a fight?' Liam steps closer to the bed and drops down to his haunches. Bryony can see the shape of his knees pressing against the dark stripes of his suit trousers. She remembers the shiny points of the nail scissors poking into her cousin's flesh.

'Is Gigi's arm OK?' she whispers. 'Where is she?'

327

'She's at school.'

'And her arm?' she repeats, insistent.

'The doctors stitched it up nicely when you two were in hospital.'

Bryony concentrates on drawing lines in her custard with her spoon. The jelly is almost finished. 'I'm actually feeling quite tired again, now,' she says.

'I know, darling, but it's very important that you tell us how you got that mark on your neck and on your wrists. Were you tied up? Did Gigi do that to you?'

Bryony is quiet for a long time.

'It's OK to tell us, darling, we understand that it must've been really scary and you probably don't feel like talking about it, but we need to know what happened.'

'It wasn't scary,' Bryony says in a different voice. She scrapes the last of the custard into her spoon and lifts it to her mouth. 'It was just a game.'

'What was a game? Gigi tying you up? Strangling you? That was a *game*?' Liam forces himself to pause, take a breath. 'Don't be silly, my girl.'

'It was a *stupid* game, that's for sure,' Bryony says and places the bowl on her bedside table. 'But I asked Gigi to tie me up like that. I wanted to try it. She said it was dumb but she did it anyway. Because I asked her to.'

'Why in God's name did you ask her to do that?'

'To see what it was like. Aunty Sally was strangled. So I wanted . . . to know.'

Liam and Adele seem to have stopped

breathing. Outside, in one of the neat green gardens of Cortona Villas, the lawn-mower growls and whines.

'How did you know she was str — We never mentioned that to any of you . . . ' Adele trails off.

'It all turned out OK.' Bryony climbs back beneath the covers and turns over to face the wall. 'Gigi realized that I was being an idiot and got really worried about me and she untied the dressing gown cord and I was fine, so I don't know what the big deal is about.' She squeezes her eyes shut and waits.

Finally, after what feels like forever, the mattress shifts as her mother stands up. Then she hears her parents leave the room and softly close the door behind them.

★   ★   ★

Bryony has chicken-noodle soup for lunch, drinks a glass of apple juice with Dora watching her like a hawk to make sure she finishes it, and then, still in her pyjamas, walks outside into the garden, down the path and through the wooden gate, only stopping when she gets to the fever tree beside the Matsunyanes' driveway. She places her palm on the lime-coloured bark, sliding it up until it rests on the torn place.

For the hundredth time today, Bryony thinks about Gigi's story: the men, the blade, the blood, and Aunty Sally dying on the kitchen floor. She touches her throat, once again, and wonders how long it will be before her mother comes back from fetching Tyler and Gigi from school. She imagines the car pulling up and Gigi getting out and what will happen next. What will Gigi say, if she says anything at all?

What will I say?

Bryony presses her fingers against the welt on her neck, hard and sudden. She swallows, and then releases the pressure.

'Hey.'

She spins around at the sound of the voice, kicking the warm, dusty pebbles. It is Lesedi. She's in Converse tackies, dark blue jeans, and a soft grey T-shirt that has the outline of a butterfly on it. She leans her head against the wooden post of her garden gate and gives Bryony a cautious smile.

'How are you doing, Bryony?'

'OK,' Bryony says, and then clears her throat. 'You went away.'

'I did. Now I'm back.'

Bryony looks down at her feet. She pokes a pebble with her smile-toe and it rolls over with a click.

Lesedi notes the child's bruises and remembers the dark cupboard and the feeling of a band across her own throat. 'I'm very glad to see you up and about.'

'How did you know I was sick?'

'You're at home on a school day. In your pyjamas . . . and anyway, word gets around. You know what this place is like, hey? Everyone seems to know everyone else's business.'

Bryony does not look up. A car drives past.

'I'm sorry I told on you.'

330

'Oh, don't worry about that. You were right. Absolutely right. And so was the Body Corporate. This is no place to run a real business, now is it?'

Bryony removes her hand from the fever-tree trunk and runs her palm over her pyjama shorts.

'I am looking for a proper spot to rent to run my sangoma practice, by the way, a real professional consulting room,' Lesedi says. 'Thabo and I have found a few options; I'm still deciding which one will work best, though. Hey, I might need some help in choosing furniture for the waiting room, if you're interested?'

The top of Bryony's white-blonde head moves in what could be a nod.

'I'm going to have fancy business cards and everything. What do you think of that?'

Bryony nods again. Stronger this time.

'You know, there are many ways of being a sangoma, just like there are many ways of being anything else in this life. Everyone has a choice to do things with light, or to work in the dark. Just in case you're still wondering, I am partial to the light, myself.'

'It's not always a choice,' Bryony mutters.

'No?'

'You were right.' Bryony looks up at Lesedi. Her eyes are blue with threads of grey in them. 'About the shadows in my house.'

'Ah.'

'But the darkness wasn't Gigi's. She didn't choose it.' *It was hijacking her*, thinks Bryony. *It got in when she saw the things those men did. They brought it with them and some of it slipped off and got inside Gigi when they killed Aunty Sally.*

'But then she still made a choice, didn't she?' Lesedi asks.

Bryony presses her heel into one warm pebble and thinks of her cousin's trembling fingers pulling the cord from her throat and the way her chest had exploded with darts of fire when she'd taken that first free breath. 'She did.'

A slight breeze ripples down the Cortona Villas street, shaking the branches of the fever tree.

'Well, I am going in now,' Lesedi says after a long pause. 'Good to see you up and about, Bryony.'

The girl nods. She touches the trunk of the tree with both hands and looks up to watch the leaves dance against the sky.

*　*　*

When Adele's white Mercedes pulls up outside the school gates, the hissing snake inside Gigi's belly stops writhing (it is a dark snake with bands of white around its throat, just like the rinkhals that Johan once caught under Simone's bed). Adele is no more than ten minutes late, but Gigi has spent every second of them imagining herself waiting and waiting until nightfall, and then finally crawling into the corridor with the abandoned desks piled up inside it to spend the night.

She is careful not to run towards the car. When she reaches it, Tyler climbs out of the passenger seat and slides into the back. He does not look at her.

'You sit up front,' he mutters in a gruff voice. 'Ma wants to talk to you.'

'OK,' Gigi says and her stomach snake is alert once more. She gulps back a little acidic burp and gets into the passenger seat, bumping her shins on her school bag as she jams it in by her legs.

'How was school?' Adele asks. She doesn't look at Gigi; her eyes are on the line of cars.

'Um, all right,' Gigi says. She'd spent the whole day with the worry snake growing in her guts. *Where are they going to send me? Am I going to be taken to juvenile court and tried for kidnapping and attempted murder? Am I too young to go to jail?* She'd sat inside a cubicle in the bathroom throughout both breaks, but hadn't stabbed or sliced herself. She hadn't even wanted to. She'd just practised watching her breath. It was the only way she could get the snake to lie still.

'Bryony's got her voice back,' Adele announces.

Gigi grips the webbing strap of her school bag with both hands.

'She told us what happened.' Adele pulls out into the traffic. The car behind them gives a loud hoot. Gigi closes her eyes, squeezing the lids together as hard as she can. 'It was really very irresponsible of you to tie Bryony up just because she asked you to. I know you're going through all sorts of difficult stuff since your mom died, but that's no excuse for letting her put her life in danger like that.'

Gigi opens her eyes. Blood thumps in her ears. The snake goes very still.

333

'It was a very stupid game for you girls to be playing, and you're old enough to know better, Gigi.'

'A game?' Tyler pipes up from the back seat. 'What kind of retarded game involves strangling someone half to death?'

'Aunty Sally was strangled,' Adele says, her voice catching on the words. 'Your dad and I didn't mention it before, so I'm not sure if you knew, Tyler.'

'No. Still, what does that have to do with Bryony?'

'Well,' Adele says, glancing at her son in the rear-view mirror, 'Gigi told her all about how Aunty Sally died.' She addresses Gigi once more: 'That was also very irresponsible, by the way. She's just a little girl, for goodness' sake.'

'I know. I shouldn't have. It just came . . . out.'

'So you strangled Bryony?' Tyler barks from the back seat.

'No, I . . . I didn't. It was . . . ' Gigi trails off, unsure of how to explain any of the blind panic and frantic flickering darkness of that afternoon.

'Bryony told me, Gigi. She told me that she *asked* you to tie her up. She called it a game, but you, as a much older girl, should've known better.'

'Bloody hell,' mutters Tyler.

'She was taking her own medicine, which means that she was probably took way too much and was most likely high as a kite, the poor child. Personally, I find it quite shocking that you saw the state she was in, and still let her goad you into playing such a dangerous game.'

334

'I'm . . . sorry.' Gigi's voice is so soft that Adele barely hears it over the hum of the engine. Gigi feels a strange pressure beating against the inside of her ears. *A game. Bryony said it was a game? She asked me to tie her up?* Gigi presses the button to roll down the window and takes a gulp of rushing air. *Why?*

'Needless to say, there will be absolutely no games of that sort played anywhere, anytime, ever again. Do I make myself clear?' Adele says in an icy voice.

'Yes,' Gigi says through dry lips.

'Tyler?' Adele demands.

'What are you asking me for? I never even — '

'Tyler?' Her voice rises to a shout.

'OK, *ja*, all right. Yes. No strangling games or anything of the sort.'

Adele nods. They drive along in silence for a minute.

Finally, Adele speaks again: 'And as for you, Gigi, I want you to promise me that you will start acting like the young woman you are, and make sure that Bryony doesn't do anything daft like this again. Can you promise me that? Will you watch out for her?'

'Yes,' Gigi says, and then again, with more emphasis, 'I promise.'

'Good.'

The snake vanishes with a wriggle, just as the rinkhals did when Johan let it out of the pillowcase and set it free in the grass by the dam. One twitch of the tail and it was gone.

28

Adele does not drive Gigi straight home right away, instead she takes her to Dr Rowe's consulting room, hands her a tub of shop-made lentil and butternut salad to eat while she waits for her appointment, and zooms off to drop Tyler at the house. When she returns to collect her an hour and a half later, Gigi emerges from Dr Rowe's office pink-eyed and wrung-out from talking. She climbs into the front seat once again and sits like a statue, only really breathing easily when the car pulls into the Wildings' garage at Cortona Villas.

By the time she finally climbs the stairs, it is early evening, and she opens Bryony's bedroom door to find the room flooded with thick, buttery light from the lowering sun.

'Hey,' says Bryony. She has changed out of her pyjamas and is sitting on top of her bed reading a book. She shuts it now, and places her palms flat against the cherry duvet.

'Hey.' Gigi steps into the room and closes the door behind her. She lets her school bag drop to the floor. For a long moment, the two girls are silent. Gigi can hear the muted sound of the TV and someone's feet on the stairs.

'You — ' Gigi is cut off by a knock on the door followed by Tyler's voice.

'Mom wants you girls to come help with supper.'

'OK,' Bryony calls back. She listens to the scuff of Tyler's feet on the carpet outside the door as he moves away, and then she slips off the bed and puts on her slippers. Gigi has not moved. 'We'd better go down.'

'You lied for me. You . . . Why?' Gigi asks. Bryony halts, but she does not turn. 'Why are you protecting me after what I did to you?'

Bryony rubs her purple wrists. Her eyes meet Gigi's and then dart away again. 'Because . . . ' she says. She licks her lips. 'Because then they would've gotten you too.'

'Who?'

'The black men.'

At those three words, Gigi thumps backwards, hitting her shoulder blades on the wall and sliding down it until she is sitting on the carpet. 'What do you mean, they would've gotten me?'

'Ended your life, just like they did to your mom, only without actually killing you.' Bryony drops down to her haunches in front of Gigi. Her cousin's pale skin is tinted gold from the light of the setting sun; her freckles look like flakes of copper. 'I could tell that Mom and Dad were really freaked out about you, and I figured that if they sent you to some horrible place, or took you to the police and put you in jail and stuff, your life would be . . . I don't know . . . totally messed up. It seemed wrong. Not fair. So I lied.'

'Oh,' Gigi breathes. Her eyes are locked on Bryony's now.

'You see, I know that what you did to me,' Bryony whispers, touching the welt around her throat, 'was really them, not you.' She leans closer, her eyes searching Gigi's. 'But now they're gone.'

'How do you know?' Gigi can feel tears welling up and spilling down her cheeks.

'Because the shadows have gone, and so has the black dog.'

Gigi nods her head, not understanding about the black dog, but not really needing to. She knows about shadows. Tears plop down on to her school tunic.

'I didn't say anything about you actually being there that day and seeing what happened to your mom and everything, though; I figure you'll know when's the right time to tell people that.'

Gigi nods again, and wipes her damp cheeks with the back of her hands.

'Now we'd better go down and get that salad started or Mom will have a wettie.' Bryony stands up and opens the door. The sound of the TV from downstairs mixes up with the thud of Tyler's iPod and floods into the room along with the smell of something savoury that Dora prepared earlier warming in the kitchen.

Gigi gets to her feet. She tries to move her mouth to speak, but nothing comes. Instead, she reaches out and touches a lock of Bryony's hair. It is the exact same colour as her mother's was. It feels like feathers beneath her fingertips.

'Come on then,' Bryony says, grinning. 'Now that you're a Wilding, you'd better get used to the slave labour in this house. I bet you Mom's going to make you chop the tomatoes again.'

29

Adele carries her empty tea mug into the kitchen just as Liam switches on the dishwasher. 'Sorry,' she says, handing it over to him with a small smile. 'I always seem to get the timing wrong.'

'No problem.' He presses a button to pause the cycle, opens the dishwasher and pops her mug into it before shutting it again. 'I always leave a spot for one more mug.' The kitchen fills with the swishing sound of water as the machine starts up again and Liam and Adele both stare at its blank white surface as if waiting for a TV show to start.

'Going to empty the bin,' he says after a long pause. Liam lifts the full bag out of the kitchen bin, ties up the top, and heads out of the back door into the night.

After a moment, Adele follows. Moths spin around the light fixture above the door. She can hear the thump that their soft bodies make as they bang into the glass.

'Hey, one of these boards is broken.' Liam's disembodied voice floats out from the darkness.

'What?'

'On the dustbin-cover thingy. Looks like one of the kids has been buggering around out here.'

Although the night is warm, Adele tugs her cardigan across her chest before jogging around the side of the house to join her husband at the dustbin housing.

'See here? One of the slats has been snapped.' He steps aside to show her the broken piece of wood. She can just make it out in the gloom, and reaches out to touch one of the splintered ends.

'Oh.'

'I'd better get a replacement piece of wood for that tomorrow. I'll go to Timber City, see if they've got.'

'*Ja.*'

Adele looks up. There is no moon tonight, and the sky is inky black with little pinprick stars.

'She's different, don't you think?' she says after a while.

'Who?'

'Gigi. I spoke to Dr Rowe after her appointment today. He said they had a bit of a breakthrough.'

'Meaning?'

'Meaning she actually talked.'

'I guess that's a good start.' Liam leans his back against the wood and stares out towards the end of the garden where the remaining green limbs of the fever tree, illuminated by a Cortona Villas street light, stick up above the front wall. 'She did seem a little less . . . weird at dinner. A lot more like the Gigi I used to know.' Liam catches his breath as if to suck the words back in.

Adele does not move. Somewhere close by, a cricket starts its shrill, incessant song.

'Tell me what she was like,' Adele whispers. Liam glances over at his wife, but cannot make out her features.

'She was . . . well, she was sweet, I guess,' he begins, and then stops, waiting. Adele says nothing. 'Man, but she loved all those animals they used to look after at Simone's place,' he continues. 'She was so capable with them, and always eager to tell me every little detail. She was pretty clued up, actually. Really bright.'

'Uh-huh.'

'She used to collect things' — Liam's voice strengthens as he slips back into the past — 'like feathers and bones that she'd found, and arrange them all on her windowsill.' He laughs. 'Every time I came to visit she would have to show me her latest treasures. Some of that stuff was pretty macabre.'

'I see.' Adele tries and fails to keep the hurt out of her voice.

'Sorry. I'm going on a bit. I . . . Sorry.'

'No. I asked.'

For a while they stand in silence, staring into the dark.

'How often did you visit Sally and Gigi out there at the farm?'

'Once or twice a year. Sometimes more.'

'Every year?'

'Every year.'

The cricket stops chirping.

'Why?'

'Why?'

'Yes. Why did you visit them? Why did you keep making trips behind my back to the other side of the country?'

'I figured I had no choice *but* to do it behind your back, doll. You wouldn't even let me mention Monkey's name.'

'OK. But still, why go at all?'

'At first I was really worried about her,' Liam says. 'You knew Monkey, she was never as . . . I don't know . . . *together* as you, and when you kicked her out of your life she kind of fell apart. I wanted to see if she and Gigi were going to be OK.' Liam takes a breath. Alongside the clean, soily night-air smell is a slight undertone of garbage from the bins at his back. 'And after that, well, I just . . . wanted to see her, check in, you know? Monkey was my friend. I know that sounds lame but she was. She always made me feel, I don't know, like I was this really great person.'

'But haven't I — '

'It was different. She didn't expect anything of me, doll; she just liked who I was. I know it makes me sound selfish, but I just didn't want to lose that.'

Adele is about to make a snide comment about how it sounds as if Sally was his fix, but she stops herself. She clears her throat. 'I know what you mean,' she says instead. 'She *was* my sister, after all.' The summer night seems suddenly too cool. Adele pulls her cardigan tighter, and wraps her arms across her chest. 'That's just how she was.'

'*Ja*,' Liam whispers. 'Poor old Monkey.' A large moth flutters past his face, so close he can feel the movement of its wings along his cheek.

'Liam, I . . . I understand how it feels', Adele says at last, 'to want Sally in your life.' Liam puts his arm around his wife's shoulder and draws her rigid body close. 'And as mad as this sounds, coming from me, I kind of admire you for doing something about it, for not letting her go. I couldn't, not after the things I said to her that day, I was so . . . I wish . . . '

'Don't, doll, don't beat yourself up about it. Sally wouldn't want you to. You know that.'

'I guess . . . '

'She wouldn't, Addy.'

Adele lets her body relax against her husband's chest. The tears that come, this time, taste only of salt.

30

Adele wakes in the empty dark hour before dawn. Liam is fast asleep, and she counts off his soft snores like the tick of a clock. Finally, after counting five snore-minutes, she slips out of bed and leaves the bedroom.

The landing carpet is warm beneath her bare feet. She takes one small step, and then another, and then stops at Tyler's bedroom door, tracing her finger over the letters of the 'Keep Out' sign before pushing it open to peer in.

Her son lies on his belly, just as he did when he was a baby, arms tucked up against his sides and fingers curled into loose fists. The blond fringe he insists on wearing in a greasy curtain over half of his face is tucked back now, and his bare forehead looks vulnerable. Adele finds herself smiling in the dark. Once those pimples clear up he'll look just like Liam.

Then Adele checks in on the girls. They're both lying on their sides, facing each other across the untidy room like sleeping bookends. Bryony's bruises are invisible in the gloom, but the white bandage on Gigi's upper arm glows like a beacon. Adele takes a step further in, but stops when she almost trips over one of Bryony's roller blades.

It's a large enough room for two, but with all Bryony's mess, it seems overcrowded. During supper, when Adele had suggested that the

344

family clear out Liam's home office and turn it into a bedroom for Gigi, the girls had looked at one another for a long moment before both shaking their heads in unison: 'No.'

Adele leaves the sleeping girls and pauses on the landing before heading to the stairs and trotting down them, across the hallway and into the lounge.

She switches on the light and goes to the bookshelf, selects a thick, brown-covered photo album from the pile and tucks it beneath her arm. She stops for a moment, considering, and then heads to the small, antique desk in the corner where she keeps her stationery. In the top drawer, beneath a pile of old birthday cards, some writing paper and a host of almost-out-of-ink pens, she finds what she is looking for: a small, pewter picture frame, still in its shop wrapping.

She drops to her haunches on the carpet and places the frame on the floor in front of her, and then the photo album beside it. She holds her breath and opens the cover. The first page is full of baby pictures, some in faded colour and some in black and white. There's Adele as a toddler with two rick-rack ribbons in her hair, and Sally as a baby in the garden with a gummy smile and a trail of soil and spit spilling down her chin.

Adele turns the pages until she finds the picture she is looking for: herself and Sally smiling in the sun on the 'last family holiday', their blonde heads touching and their eyes bright.

With great care, she peels back the plastic

covering and removes the picture from the page, holding it in one hand while she removes the cellophane from the pewter frame and prises the back off it with the other. Finally, she places the photograph inside the frame, smooths down the corners, and then slots the back into place.

She closes her eyes and sits with the framed picture folded in her arms and pressed against her chest until the birds begin to sing the morning in.

NOW

I hear a new call above the crooning of the wood pigeons and zither of cicadas. It is nothing like the story noise that hounded me before; this one is the opposite of sound, the promise of peace and something indefinable that is so much more than peace. It whispers and hums and beckons me to follow it up and out and away from here.

As I listen to its song, I begin to feel myself dissolving, blurring at the edges. I can go.

Wait.

I root my feet back down into the red soil, feeling the earthworms wriggling at my soles, and search for the story thread that tied me here.

I find Tyler's thread almost at once: it is ammonia sharp and all tangled with hormones and confusion. Then there is Bryony's: purple with new things that cannot be unknown, but still sweet-scented, like a bowl of plums left standing in the sun. Adele's is ivory, lace-delicate in patches, swollen dark with barbs in others. It flows alongside the threads of her children, and knots in with Liam's, whose own story thread is no longer navy blue and salty as it was the day I first discovered it. It is mown-grass green.

I reach out to touch the green thread, but then stop, realizing that I no longer want to wrap it around me. I move back and watch as it flows out, unencumbered, beside the others, towards a place that I cannot see.

My own thread has gone.

However, I find that I am holding loosely on to another. It is red, lightening towards autumn orange as it spools out alongside the others, sometimes weaving in along with them, sometimes loose and alone. Gigi's story thread. I do not let it go.

Cool, like the breath before a storm, the silence that is more than silence beckons me again.

But Gigi's thread is warm in my hand.

For a moment I am stretched tight between them like an over-tuned guitar string, and then, quite suddenly, I know that I do not have to choose. This knowledge comes with the rattle of mussel shell against rock and the faint echo of Lesedi's laughter, joyous on the dry air: *I am not just one thing*. I am made up of myriad pieces: both a story that has already been told, and a journey waiting to begin.

ACKNOWLEDGEMENTS

I am so grateful to Oli Munson for his support and brilliance, and to Laura Palmer for her astonishing faith in me, her patience, and her invaluable editorial insight. Huge thanks, also, to the wonderful team at Head of Zeus.

Many thanks to Peter Caldwell, who took time out of his busy schedule ministering to Africa's threatened wildlife to share a much-needed fragment of his vast veterinary knowledge with me.

A special 'cheerleader' thank you goes out to my loving friends and family who've been unfailing in their support for so many years (with Joe Vaz, pop-poms a-waving, leading the charge).

Finally, I owe a lifetime's debt of gratitude to Grant for his huge heart, his endless reserves of encouragement and pragmatic wisdom, and for being the gentlest first reader ever. Without him at my side on this journey, I might never have found the courage to begin.

We do hope that you have enjoyed reading this large print book.

Did you know that all of our titles are available for purchase?

We publish a wide range of high quality large print books including:
Romances, Mysteries, Classics
General Fiction
Non Fiction and Westerns

Special interest titles available in large print are:
The Little Oxford Dictionary
Music Book
Song Book
Hymn Book
Service Book

Also available from us courtesy of Oxford University Press:
Young Readers' Dictionary
(large print edition)
Young Readers' Thesaurus
(large print edition)

For further information or a free brochure, please contact us at:
Ulverscroft Large Print Books Ltd.,
The Green, Bradgate Road, Anstey,
Leicester, LE7 7FU, England.
Tel: (00 44) 0116 236 4325
Fax: (00 44) 0116 234 0205

Other titles published by Ulverscroft:

THE GOOD ITALIAN

Stephen Burke

1935: Enzo Secchi, harbourmaster of Massawa, Eritrea's main port, is a loyal Italian colonial servant. But he is lonely, and when his friend suggests he find an Eritrean housekeeper to cook, clean — and maybe share his bed, Enzo takes the plunge and advertises. He surprises himself by choosing Aatifa, a sharp-tongued woman in her early 30s with a complicated family life. What neither of them counts on is falling in love. But when Italian forces bent on invading neighbouring Ethiopia begin arriving at the port, they bring with them new laws — including one forbidding 'Relationships of a Conjugal Nature' with Eritrean women. While Enzo and Aatifa strive to keep their relationship hidden, the bitter campaign lays bare all the brutality of Italian colonial ambition, and the consequences will change their lives forever . . .

THE HAREM MIDWIFE

Roberta Rich

1579: Hannah Levi, a Venetian exile, has set up a new life for herself as the best midwife in all of Constantinople, tending to the thousand women of the Sultan's lively and infamous harem. One night, when Hannah is unexpectedly summoned to the palace, she's confronted with Leah, a poor Jewish peasant girl who has been abducted and sold into the harem. The Sultan wants her to produce his heir, but the girl just wants to return to her home and the only life she has ever known. Will Hannah risk her life and livelihood to protect her?